FLAWLESS

MANHATTAN KNIGHTS 1

EVA HAINING

COPYRIGHT

DEDICATION

To Brandon Redgrave:
You inspired me to write.

PROLOGUE

LILY

I met my soulmate on an average Monday, on my way to the library at Columbia University. If there's one thing I've learned, it's that life can change in the blink of an eye, when you least expect it…

I grew up on a ranch in Texas, spending most of my childhood riding horses with my sisters and following my dad around as he worked the ranch. He and I were thick as molasses, inseparable, the best of friends. He was my hero, but unfortunately, he wasn't invincible. Two weeks after my fifteenth birthday, he died, and my life imploded. Everything I knew—gone. My dad came to pick me up from the movies, and never made it home. I will never forget that night as long as I live. Even if I tried… my nightmares wouldn't let me.

A year later, my mom sold the ranch and moved us to New York to be closer to her family. That move altered my path in so many ways. I thought my life was ending, but it was just the beginning of the journey that would lead me to *him*.

I'm not really a morning person, but when the aroma of coffee and fresh baking fills my room in the mornings, Addi, my roommate, manages to convince me of life before noon! I pad barefoot down the hallway of our New York apartment, trying to tame my bed-hair into a messy bun, which is almost impossible. Her voice sings out in the morning silence, full of excitement.

"Of course, we'll be there, we wouldn't miss it... can't wait... see you Friday."

As I round the corner, I'm happy to see her alone, throwing her phone onto the couch. I ask a question I know I'll regret. "Who's *we*, and what wouldn't *we* miss?"

"Morning, grumpy, that was Jason. Remember him... opening his own restaurant, devastatingly gorgeous, loves men more than I do?" Okay, so she's going for snide this morning.

"Hilarious. What's going on?"

"I was just checking. You seem to have your nose so deep in the books lately that I thought there might not be any space left in that brain of yours to remember life in the outside world." She starts jumping up and down when she remembers she has news. "Well... you know the restaurant will be opening officially next week. Everything is fitted out and Jason is throwing a party on Friday night for some friends and the NY elite! He wants us to come. Maybe I'll find myself a dashing CEO to party with this weekend!"

Typical Addi. When it comes to guys, she has a one-track mind. $$$$$$. Maybe a two-track mind—she also has a tendency to think with 'little Addi' a lot of the time, too.

"I told him we would totally be there, Friday at eight."

"Thanks for asking, I've got no plans, and I'd love to go."

"Wow you're moody today, what crawled up your ass last night?"

"Sorry, you know I'm a mean girl before coffee. Prep for finals is getting to me, and I'm still trying to get this damn thesis finished. Of course, we'll go. I wouldn't miss it. Anyway... what's cooking? Smells amazing."

"Your favorite. Banana nut muffins. There's a fresh pot of coffee waiting for you, too. Don't say I'm not good to you." I grab a muffin, still warm from the oven, a giant mug of coffee, and head back to my room.

I team my favorite skinny jeans, grey needle cord, with my faded tight Superman t-shirt. I'm ready for a day locked in the campus library with William. I'm sure today will be the day I get my thesis finished—Sexuality in Shakespeare. I've been working on it all year, becoming an almost permanent resident in the library.

Addi is running around like a headless chicken, zigzagging from room to room. "Hey, Lil, wait up! I'll tag along. I've got some stuff to do on campus."

"Professors won't flirt with themselves!" I shout down the hallway.

"Very funny, just sit your skinny ass down and wait two minutes." Ten minutes and a makeover later, we're out the door.

The sun is splitting the skies as we enjoy an unusually pleasant and leisurely walk to campus, stopping for coffee-to-go at our favorite café, before heading our separate ways for the day with a plan to hook up for dinner. It's Addi's way of making sure I leave the library and interact with the outside world. She's a firm believer in the saying *all work and no play makes Lil a buzzkill.*

Addi Warner has been my best friend since sophomore year in high school, when I moved to New York with my family. We sat next to each other in first period English, and have been inseparable ever since, coaching each other through it all—first kisses, dates, and broken hearts. The woman is ridiculous. She's tall with model proportions, black sleek hair that hangs down her back like a waterfall, and the deepest blue eyes. Not enough of a winning hand to be dealt, she's also intelligent, funny, and caring. If not for the fact that she's hands down the best person I've ever met, I'd hate her guts! She's the only reason I had any kind of social life at high school, and why I remotely registered on the cool crowd's radar.

Me on the other hand... how would I describe myself? I'm tall, but not in a model kind of way, more of an 'I feel like a lumberjack' way. My mom would always say I have a classic hourglass figure, however, standing in front of the mirror in my underwear, I would say my butt and hips are disproportional to my waist. My chest is... ample, and my legs are long but kind of gangly. I don't paint a great picture, do I? When I'm dressed up for a night out, I can work what I have, so I'm fine with it. My hair is long, blonde, and wild, but a styling wand can make it killer! My forest green eyes are my best feature—something I've always been complimented on.

Anyway, back to the reason you're reading...

CHAPTER 1

LILY

THE DOORS OF BUTLER LIBRARY ARE IN SIGHT. JUGGLING MY BOOKS, bag, and coffee, I'm lost in thought. As usual, I'm so caught up in my own head, oblivious to my surroundings. I don't even know what hits me. The concrete beneath my feet disappears, the world turning upside down as my vision blurs, and the sky is all I see. Coffee soaks into my pants, a burning sensation spreading down my leg. As I watch in slow motion, bracing myself for impact, my papers flutter down around me like butterflies in spring... but the pain of my body smacking to the ground doesn't come. It takes a moment to register the man looming over me, holding me just shy of the ground with one arm, the other hitting the harsh sidewalk. I stare in disbelief as a trickle of red runs from beneath his palm, dripping onto the vast expanse of gray.

"Oh shit! Are you okay?"

I must have hit my head, because the voice speaking to me right now is smooth like silk, almost angelic with a rich breathy tone of sin itself. I struggle to focus as I'm lifted and set down on my feet. He holds me firm against his chest until I'm steady enough to hold my own. Luckily, he didn't let go. When my eyes glance from a firm chest... up to his face, my knees buckle at the sight before me. Six inches away from my lips is the most attractive face I've *ever* seen, and I'm not talking in 'real life,' I mean *ever*.

Chiseled cheekbones, a perfect nose, full lips that look capable of wicked, wonderful things... and his eyes—I feel like I've been punched in the chest with the force of feeling his eyes stir inside me. They are the lightest blue, almost sparkling silver, made even more spectacular by gorgeous dark hair, with a slight curl to it. My fingers itch to touch it, but I'm returned from my blatant daydreaming by his voice—sultry yet commanding.

"Are you okay? Are you hurt? I'm so sorry, I wasn't paying attention... stupid phone never stops ringing." Oh. My. God. My brain is broken. I can't speak. I just stand here looking like an idiot, begging my mouth to comply with my mind. I want to say that I'm fine and it was my fault for being completely oblivious, but what comes out, is something else entirely.

"You're perfect." Shit! Did I just say that? Please, tell me I did *not* just say that. What the *actual* fuck?

He begins to chuckle, and it's the sweetest sound to ever grace my ears, it makes me tingle in ways that I couldn't describe even if I wanted to. Then I realize he's laughing at my ridiculous outburst. I tear my gaze from him and drop to my knees to grab my stuff.

"Let me help you with that, Miss...?"

"Lily... my name is Lily Tate." My cheeks are on fire. He drops down next to me and starts gathering my thesis. "You don't have to help, I'm fine." Lifting the loose pages, he scans the text, before stopping dead.

"Sexuality in Shakespeare. You don't strike me as the type..."

I'm not the type to what? Be interested in sexuality? I know I'm a walking disaster, and he's way out of my league, but where does he get off saying something like that to a stranger? "Well, as you know nothing about me, and we'll never see each other again, I guess it doesn't matter worth a damn what I strike you as." I grab my papers from his hand and run toward my building.

I can hear his footsteps behind me, trying to catch up without running. I'm sure he wouldn't want to ruin his perfect hair and expensive suit by running after the likes of me. He's probably never had to run after a woman in his life. Not with that face. I refuse to look back. I've endured enough embarrassment for one day.

"Miss Tate, please stop for a moment." He grabs my shoulder, sending a jolt of electricity straight through my body.

"Don't touch me."

I disappear through the double doors and into a sea of students, hidden from the stranger doing unfamiliar things to my insides. I can still hear his voice shouting for me to come back, but I can't let myself turn around, so I just keep walking, relieved to be away from his intense stare and judgment.

CHAPTER 2

LILY

My day is a complete washout. I won't get my thesis finished. I can't concentrate enough to study, and every time I try to get my head together, I'm assaulted by visions of sparkling ice-blue eyes.

No matter how hard I try to focus, he is all I can think about—the tingling sensation that coursed through my body at his innocent touch. I have never experienced such intense attraction before, such raw lust towards anyone in my life. It's a foreign and unwanted development. I liked my high school sweetheart. He was my first love, but we never took that last step together. It's not that I wasn't interested in sex, I guess I just wasn't ready when we were dating. Then I left for college, and we went our separate ways amicably. I've been on dates in college, but no one has ever made me really *feel* anything sexual in the core of my being. In all honesty, I'm in love with literature, and have been striving to do the best I can here at Columbia, and there hasn't been anyone who I felt warranted being a distraction. How pathetic am I?

I decide to call Addi and meet up earlier than we'd arranged. I'm clearly not going to make any progress in the library. When I rummage around in my bag, I realize my phone is missing. I know I had it when I left the apartment this morning, and then it hits me—I must have dropped it outside in South Field when I knocked into Mr. Opinionated. I grab all my crap and head out to see if I can find my lifeline! I spend a good thirty minutes checking the grounds, but with no luck. Of course! Why do I think this day will cut me some slack? I know where Addi will be at this time of day, so I'll just go to the student bar in search of her. It doesn't take me long to track her down.

"Oh my God! It's the first sign of the apocalypse. Lil is out in daylight. Has the library burned to the ground?"

"Very funny. Just what I need. Your smart-ass remarks. Like my day hasn't sucked enough already." I sit down next to her and the latest victim of her charms. I honestly don't know where she keeps finding new guys to crush on. I don't think I've ever seen her with the same guy twice.

"Aww, poor baby. Tell me what's up and I'll turn that frown upside down, even if I have to get Jeff here to hold you up by your ankles!" That gets a hint of a smile on my face. I know she'll give me no end of grief about my morning mishap, but I need to tell someone, just to get it off my chest and maybe stop myself from obsessing about him.

"Okay, okay, here goes nothing" I relay the whole story, from my lack of awareness to the painfully embarrassing outburst of "you're perfect," ending with me running away like a twelve-year-old after shouting at him for making an observation. Her face contorts trying to stifle the inevitable laughter… until I describe the way his touch affected me. Her face drops, her jaw slack, all hint of amusement gone.

"Oh my God, Lil. It really *is* the end of the freaking world! Not only are you out during the day interacting with other humans, but you met a guy who makes your panties tingle." She snorts, clearly proud of her snide remarks. Why am I friends with this girl? "What's this guy's name?"

"Did you *not* hear the story? I didn't wait around to find out." I'm subjected to a ten-minute lecture on how moronic I am for not getting a tattoo of his name and number, and something about thinking less with my giant brain, and more with 'little Lil.'

She does a shitty job of taking my mind off the beautiful stranger who has taken residence in my head, teasing and berating me all afternoon, and throughout dinner at our local diner. Little did I know, he would infiltrate my dreams that night, and every night since: Stunning, ice-blue eyes staring down at me, lush dark hair and lips made for sin, tending to my every desire.

I wake with a start, tangled in my sheets, a warm tingling sensation all over my body. I'm damp between my thighs, my cheeks flushing with the realization that I've just had a sex dream about a total stranger. A run in Central Park is the only answer right now. I pull on my yoga pants an old top, grab my sneakers and I'm off.

The park really is the most beautiful place. You move from the crazy hustle and bustle of Manhattan, straight into an idyllic oasis where you can lose yourself for hours, and just slow your mind. It's a slice of heaven, and it does the trick for me today.

As I wander back to the apartment, drinking in the city as I walk off my run, I relax. I'm ready to tackle some Shakespeare. But that contented feeling doesn't last long as the doors to the elevator open onto our floor. I notice a box sitting outside our apartment. It has 'Miss Lily Tate' written in elegant script on an envelope attached to the box. Before I read it, I sneak a peek inside, and I can't believe my eyes. It's my cell phone. I'm stunned that someone has gone to the trouble to return it to me. It's such a thoughtful and kind thing to do. I was so sure I'd never see it again.

I scroll through the apps quickly to find everything intact, which is awesome. I then turn my attention to the envelope, anxious to find out the identity of my Good Samaritan. There's a letter inside, and as I begin to read, all color drains from my face:

Dear Miss Tate,

I hope you haven't been too lost without your phone. Again, I would like to apologize for causing this inconvenience when I walked into you yesterday in South Field. One thing I'm not sorry for, is getting a chance to meet you.

I found you quite... enchanting. I can't tell you how many times I have replayed our encounter in my head. It is not the first time I have been called "perfect," but it was by far my favorite.

With regard to my observation, I never meant to cause offense. I was merely taken aback that a woman so angelic would be studying a topic intended to entice sin.

You intrigue me, Miss Tate, and that doesn't happen very often. I took the liberty of entering my number into your contacts and expect to hear from you in the next twenty-four hours.

Until then,

Mr. P

Oh. Holy. Mother. Of. Pearl.

~

I COULD HAVE IMAGINED A HUNDRED REALISTIC SCENARIOS AFTER MY brief encounter with this guy, but this was not one of them. The only conceivable explanation is that he's a cruel bastard who wants to make fun of me—as if I can't make an ass of myself *without* help. And where does he get off making demands, '*I expect to hear from you in the next twenty-four hours*,' who says stuff like that? Not only is he a demanding egomaniac, he's been snooping around my phone to save his number. Just to check if he's telling the truth, I grab my phone and scroll through the contacts list.

Sure enough, under *Mr. Perfect* there's a phone number. He hasn't given me his real name. Why would I contact a stranger who won't even tell me his name? He could be a crazy person for all I know. He might be planning to tie me up and torture me. Why do I feel turned on at the thought of him tying me up? There is something seriously wrong with me! I think Addi is right—I really need to get laid already.

I quickly text Addi to let her know I'm back in the land of communication before I shower and head back to the library.

I'M NOT ONE TO BLOW MY OWN TRUMPET, BUT I KICKED ASS TODAY. I finished my thesis! It wasn't as easy as it would have been a week ago. My brain kept wandering off on me every five minutes, going to a place where a sexy as hell voice tells me the naughty things he's going to teach me about sexuality that I could never learn from a book. I think it took me about three times as long to get finished and I had to press my thighs together more than a few times to get rid of the ache beginning to stir inside me, thinking about a man I'll never see again. When you get worked up over *A Midsummer Night's Dream* and *Measure for Measure*, you know you're getting a bit lonely. I need to go on a date, and quickly, to distract myself from dreaming of an unattainable dark haired, blue-eyed man. I console myself with the assurance that he's an asshat, so a dream is way better than reality!

I go about the rest of my day and don't give another thought to contacting Mr. P. That's not to say I don't think a lot of other things about him, but contacting him… No!

WEDNESDAY NIGHT, AND ADDI'S GETTING RESTLESS. SHE SUGGESTS going for a few drinks with friends from Columbia, and for once, I think it's a great idea. A bit of time off for good behavior is exactly what I need. We head out to an awesome little bar/club called Retro. I love this place. It's retro, and dancing the night away to seventies music is one of my favorite pastimes.

We've been strutting our stuff for at least an hour when we decide on some well-deserved cocktails. Our poison of choice, the French Martini! While Addi is ordering drinks at the bar, I grab a space for us with our friends. Then I do what we all do when we sit down for a millisecond—check my phone. A violent churning erupts in my pit of my stomach, and that's when I almost blow chunks on our friend Melissa. There are four missed calls and one new message from Mr. Perfect.

> Mr. P: Miss Tate, you should know something about me. I'm not a patient man. I was hoping to hear from you by now. Stop ignoring me. Call me.

What the hell is wrong with him? No 'how are you,' or 'do you remember me?' Having already had some liquid courage tonight, I decide text him back.

> Me: I wasn't ignoring you. I'm out with friends and I wasn't certain I would contact you. Thank you for returning my phone. I appreciate it more than you know.

Almost immediately my phone buzzes.

> Mr. P: Why wouldn't you want to contact me? I apologized for what I said the other day.

> Me: I know that, but there is no reason for us to be in contact with each other.

> Mr. P: I beg to differ, sweetheart, I think there is EVERY reason for us to be in close contact.

> Me: And that is?

> Mr. P: Don't be so coy, Miss Tate. I know you felt it when I held you in my arms.

> Me: Wow, you really are full of yourself, aren't you?

Mr. P: I am when I know what I'm talking about. I know what I want, and I always get what I want.

Me: And what is that?

Mr. P: YOU

I drop my phone on the floor as if it's on fire, and quickly drop to my hands and knees under the table looking for it... when I notice someone standing in front of me. I take in the visibly expensive shoes and tailored pants. My eyes travel higher and higher until I see Mr. P standing right here in front of me.

The grin he flashes me can only be described as a perfect, text-book, panty-dropping smile. Fuck! He. Is. Gorgeous. I quickly avert my eyes and search the floor for my phone. The moment the shock-proof case brushes against my fingers, I clutch it to my chest, preparing myself to steal another glance at *him*. He really is... wow! He leans down to my ear, a look of pure sin dancing across his flaw-less features.

"You look good on your knees at my feet, Miss Tate." He holds out his hand and helps me up, my body vibrating at his touch. "Sadly, I have to go just now, but we'll see each other again." He gives me one last scorching look, before turning on his heels and heading for the exit.

Before I can even blink, Addi is in my face.

"Who the hell was that?"

"The guy I was telling you about from the other day!"

"Holy shit, Lil. Your description did *not* do that fine specimen of a man justice. I think I just came a little! How weird that you bumped into him here." I show her the texts I received right before he arrived. She's giddy. "You have to call him back! He is smoking hot, and he totally wants you. Time to give up the goodies, my friend. I can say, without a doubt, you will never find a man as fine as him. He is perfect for your introduction to the dark side."

I'm dumbstruck. Her encouragement ignites a fire I've been trying to quash since I laid eyes on him.

"You can't be serious, Addi. He could be a stalker, or mentally unstable. How did he even know where I was tonight, and how did he know where to send my phone?"

"WHO CARES? I'm not saying marry the guy, I'm saying you deserve to have some fun, and he could definitely provide that. Wink, wink."

"We're not talking about this. I don't feel like dancing now. I'm just going to go home. You stay and have fun." She tries to argue, but in the end, I convince her to stay with our friends.

If I was using the intelligence I was born with, I'd have waited a few minutes before leaving, but alas, my brain didn't engage, and I walk outside to hail a cab. Within seconds, a black SUV pulls up. I have the good sense to step back, but I freeze when one of the tinted windows rolls down and a familiar voice tells me to get in. My brain is screaming at me to walk away, but my hand is reaching for the door handle.

I open the door and the most amazing scent ensnares me. It's a mixture of clean laundry, cologne, and something I can't quite place. I'm just going to call it his unique man smell. Whatever it is, it's amazing, and it makes me feel... safe. I might faint on the sidewalk just breathing him in. There are no words—well there are plenty of words, but apparently, I've lost the power of speech and cognitive thought.

"Nice to see you again, Miss Tate. I wasn't expecting it so soon."

"I wasn't in the mood to dance."

"Would you like a ride back to your apartment?"

"Sure." I have so many questions but get the distinct impression that anything to come out of my mouth right now would be incredibly bitchy. Silence is golden... as they say—whoever 'they' are.

"David, take us to Miss Tate's apartment, please."

"Right away, sir." I know he has my address. He sent my phone to the apartment. But I'm surprised by how nonchalant he is about invading my privacy.

"How did you find out where I live?"

"I have my sources, Miss Tate. I had to get your phone back to you."

"Well, quit it. It makes you look creepy and stalkerish." He throws his head back and laughs, a proper belly laugh. The sound is divine but annoys me at the same time. "What's so funny? I'm a young woman in a car with a stranger who knows where I live. Not smart on my part. I don't even know your name."

"All in good time, Miss Tate." This guy is infuriating. Just tell me your damn name! And what's with the 'Miss' all the time?

"Where do you get off calling me 'Miss?' It's the twenty-first century. It's polite to say 'Ms.,' and for all you know I'm married." He gives me a knowing smile.

"Now, now, *Miss* Tate. Do you think I would go to the trouble of finding out your address and *not* do my due diligence on your relationship status? Besides, I like the way it sounds and feels, caressing my tongue. I imagine *you* will feel just as good on my tongue... *Miss* Tate."

Holy Shit. I want to jump a complete stranger. Silence is safer for the remainder of this short journey.

When we pull up to my building, I reach for the door, but I'm stopped by a firm hand on my arm. "When will I see you again?" His voice is softer, almost nervous. But that can't be it—this guy has more confidence than anyone I've ever met.

"How about never, Mr. I-won't-tell-you-my-name." Again, with the laughing, really! He urges me to stay put while he jumps out of the car to open my door.

I barely have room to step out of the car, and when I do, I'm pressed tight against his chest. He's definitely built under his dress shirt—lean and toned and mouthwatering. Staring at me, his brow furrows, his full lips set in a firm line. "Why won't you give me a chance, Lily?"

"What's your name?" My voice barely a whisper.

He leans in, his breath on my face, minty with a hint of alcohol. "It's Xander. Alexander Rhodes."

Oh God. Even his name is sexy. I am so royally screwed.

"Why won't you give me a chance?"

"A chance for what?" My breath betrays me. I can't get it under control—my voice soft and vulnerable.

"To make you mine." My lungs constrict, leaving me gasping for air.

"Breathe, Lily. I won't do anything you don't want me to. But you *will* want me to." Holy. Shit.

He takes my hand in his, leading me to the door of my building. My heart hammers in my chest, my hand shaking. His is large, warm, rough, and so perfect entangled with mine. When we reach the door, he hesitates for a moment before letting go, and the lack of contact is palpable in the air that surrounds us. There are a million dancing butterflies going all kinds of crazy in my stomach. I don't move as he leans in. I can't. The scruff on his jaw brushes my cheek. A ghost of a kiss and a whisper in my ear, "Until tomorrow," and he's gone.

I can't process his words. I'm glued to the spot, studying him as he walks back to his car. His movement is almost fluid, and sexy as hell. I've gone from believing he's an asshat, to a nauseating disappointment that he's leaving. I am beyond confused. I stand in a daze, infiltrated only by a sultry voice calling from the idling car at the curb.

"Go inside. I'm not leaving until I know you're safe." Stifling a goofy grin, I make my way inside, the scent of him lingering on my cheek.

CHAPTER 3

LILY

I AWAKE TO THE SOUND OF VOICES. ADDI'S TALKING TO THE DOORMAN, signing for what I assume is a delivery for her. I never order anything. I pad down the hallway to get some coffee when she closes the door, holding the most beautiful bouquet. Long stem red roses. My favorite —dozens of them. She holds them at arm's length.

"For you."

What? There's been a mistake. Addi is the one who has guys chasing after her all the time. The shock on my face must be comedic. Wow, they're heavy, already in a stunning glass vase with intricate pearls weaving throughout the foliage. There's a card nestled in the middle of the bouquet.

Dear Miss Tate,
When I contact you today, please reply.
You'll make my day.

Xander

ALEXANDER RHODES

Okay. Maybe he's not quite the asshat I thought he was. Why is he getting under my skin? I know nothing about him. It would be rude to ignore him again if he contacts me though, right? I mean it's just common courtesy after he returned my phone, gave me a ride home last night, and sent me exquisite flowers today. My stomach coils with the anticipation of hearing from him again. Addi practically knocks me down trying to read over my shoulder.

"Wow. This guy has it bad, Lil."

"I'm just a challenge. You saw him, he can have anyone he wants, why would he want me?"

"WTF? I am the most awesome person you know, right? And therefore, it's only reasonable that my best friend in the whole world would be equally awesome! You're also *knockout* gorgeous with a killer rack and an ass I would sink my teeth into, if I was that way inclined! So don't give me any shit about this guy being out of your league. He would be damn lucky to date you." She's out of her mind crazy, but I love her even more for it.

We sit and have coffee and pancakes, while admiring my flowers. I fill her in on my conversation with Xander last night, and she tells me to give him a chance. I'm inclined to agree, so I send him a quick text.

> Me: Thank you for the flowers. I've never seen anything so beautiful. You picked my favorite flower. Lily

I don't expect to hear from him right away. He seems like one of those important businessmen, but two minutes later my phone beeps.

> Mr. P: I'm glad you liked them. I can think of something more beautiful than your flowers :) I have to go into a meeting right now, but I'll be in touch later today. Xander x

The butterflies that have taken up a permanent residence in my stomach spring to life. He keeps his word, texting to ask if I want to meet him on Friday.

> Mr. P: Hi. How was your day? I was thinking late drinks tomorrow night.

> Me: Hi. It started off so well, I had a smile on my face all day. I have plans with my roommate Addi tomorrow night. Maybe Saturday?

> Mr. P: If I can't see you tomorrow, I insist you spend the day with me on Saturday. Sound good?

> Me: Sounds perfect.

> Mr. P: I'll pick you up at ten. Until then x

> Me: Until then x

I wish I wasn't going out with Addi tomorrow night.

WE DECIDE TO GO GLAMOROUS FOR JASON'S PARTY. I HAVE TO SAY, WE'RE looking foxy with our smoky eyes, sultry dresses, and killer heels.

I'm excited to see the restaurant for the first time. It's Italian food. Not classic Italian, more modern and from what he's told me, it will be catering to the financially blessed in Manhattan. The cab pulls up on the Upper East Side, and I'm filled with a rush of pride for Jason as I stare at the façade of his new restaurant, La Cattedrale. That's *The Cathedral* to you and me. It looks spectacular from the outside, and I can't wait to see the interior.

The place is already packed, and the atmosphere is electric.

Addi and I weave through the crowd, grabbing some tasty looking cocktails along the way. I don't want to overdo it on the drinks tonight. I need to be presentable by 10 a.m. and not look like ass… but wow, this cocktail is good!

When we find Jason, he's surrounded—everyone eager to congratulate him. He deserves it, this place looks phenomenal. We manage to catch his eye.

"I'm so glad you guys made it. You girls look hot tonight!"

"Congratulations. We're *so* proud of you."

"Thank you. There are a few people I want to introduce you to. Investors who helped me turn this idea into a reality. Follow me." Addi has a massive grin on her face. I know what she's thinking— investors equal money. My girl is on the prowl tonight.

We follow Jason toward the bar where there are a few guys chatting and laughing, with their backs to us. He gives the tallest of the men a friendly nudge. The butterflies are back, alerting me to the familiar dark hair and lean body I was *not* expecting to see tonight.

Seconds later, my eyes are fixed on the ice blue that has been haunting my dreams all week. He breaks my gaze, heat rising in my body as I watch his eyes devour me, lingering for a long moment on my legs. When his eyes finally meet mine, I'm practically panting. The sound of Jason's voice distracts me.

"This is my friend and investor, Alexander Rhodes. You've probably heard of Rhodes Industries? That's this charmer. These are a couple of his partners in crime, Carter de Rossi, and Logan Fitzgerald. Logan and I go way back."

It's like an Adonis Anonymous meeting in here. These guys are completely stunning, and all in different ways. I'm probably biased, but Xander is definitely King Adonis. While checking out the handsome buffet in front of me, I don't even register Jason telling me what they all do for a living. When I look back to Xander, his fists are clenched at his sides and the look in his eyes is glacial.

"Miss Tate, how nice to see you again," his tone cold.

At this point it becomes obvious to the entire group that we know each other. I anticipate having to explain my embarrassing moment earlier in the week, but he wraps his arm around my waist and asks to speak to me privately for a moment. As we walk down a hallway toward the kitchen he tightens his hold, stopping only when we're far from the crowds. He presses me up against the wall. Every nerve ending in my body burns with his proximity.

"Did you like what you saw back there?"

"What do you mean?" I whisper, confused.

"My friends, Miss Tate. I saw the way you were looking at them. Do you want me to put in a good word for you?" His voice is cold and unforgiving.

"I don't know what you're talking about."

"I don't appreciate lying… and I don't share." That riles me—I am *not* a liar.

"If you must know, *Mr. Rhodes*, I did notice that your friends are good looking, because I'm not dead. And if you didn't have such a huge ego, I would tell you that I was *also* thinking none of them even come close to how handsome you are. More importantly, I am *not* your possession to share or keep to yourself." I pause for a moment to catch my breath. He doesn't respond. "What's wrong, Mr. Rhodes, cat got your tongue?"

He's staring at me, the beginnings of a smirk lifting the corners of his delicious looking lips. "Far from it. I'm just thinking about your naughty little tongue, and how nice it's going to taste, and the things you're going to do with it."

He's so incredibly close, everything inside me is screaming, begging for him to kiss me. The smell of him invades my senses, the look in his eyes making me weak at the knees. He reads my mind.

"I know what you're thinking, Miss Tate, but not here. The first time I kiss you is not going to be in a room full of people." He laces his fingers with mine and pulls me back into the restaurant.

When we return to our friends, they clearly notice us holding hands, but no one mentions it. Xander is obviously not a man to be messed with. Addi is busy flirting outrageously with his friends but stops long enough to give me a sly wink and a smile. She approves. I'm not sure if that's good or bad!

The rest of the evening is spent chatting and laughing. Xander and I don't talk much, but he ensures I'm by his side, in constant contact. Every now and then he leans in, so only I can hear, and compliments me.

"That dress should be illegal."

"Your legs are killing me right now."

"I can't wait to run my hands through your gorgeous hair while I kiss those sumptuous lips of yours."

Every word he whispers has a direct line to 'little Lil.' My body hums, a delicious ache building in my stomach and between my thighs, in anticipation of our first kiss.

By the end of the night, Addi is cozy with Xander's friend Carter. He's hanging on her every word and she's just being herself—gorgeous, sexy, and irresistible. Xander offers to drive them home, but Carter says he'll make sure she gets home safely. I take her aside and give her my usual safe-sex lecture, but she just kisses my cheek and tells me not to wait up.

After thanking Jason for inviting us, and saying our goodbyes, Xander places his hand on the small of my back, leading me out to a waiting town car. I recognize his driver David from the other night, giving him a small smile as he opens the door for me.

"So nice to see you again, Miss Tate."

"Thank you, David."

I slide into the plush backseat, making sure not to show more than I should in this short dress. Once I'm settled, Xander climbs in next to me, leaving no space between us, his thigh brushing against mine, sending jolts of pleasure pulsing through me. Oh my God, if I ever actually kiss this man, I might explode with sensory overload. He cuts short my daydream, asking how I know Jason.

"We go way back, I've known him since school. Addi's known him her whole life. I moved to New York when I was sixteen and she took me under her wing. Her friends became my friends, and the rest is history."

"Why did you move to New York?"

"My dad died when I was fifteen. We lived on a ranch and my mom couldn't manage it without him, so she sold up and we moved to be closer to my grandparents." He interlaces our fingers once again.

"I'm sorry to hear that, Lily. I don't know what it's like to lose a parent. Even at the age I am now, I know I'd be devastated. It must have been awful for you. What happened?" Tears well in my eyes, and I'm powerless to stop them.

"I can't... I..."

He pulls me onto his lap, wrapping his arms around me.

"It's okay, Lily. You don't have to tell me. When you're ready, I'll be here if you want to talk." The last time I felt content in someone's arms, it was my father's, and the realization scares me. I never really recovered from his loss, and the thought of letting another man give me love and a sense of security is something I avoid. I don't think I would survive that kind of loss twice in one lifetime.

I try to pull away, to put some distance between us, but he won't let me. He just holds me close, understanding my need for quiet. I know I have to stop whatever this is between us before I get hurt, but for tonight, I just want to enjoy the bubble we're in, where nothing else matters.

When we pull up outside my apartment, our bubble is burst. I crawl out of his lap and grasp the door handle.

"Allow me."

He walks round to my door to help me, so graceful and at ease with his own body. He's ripped in all the right places. Noticing every delicious inch of him isn't exactly helping with the 'distance myself plan.'

He insists on accompanying me to the entrance of my building and when we reach the vast glass doors, he reminds me he'll be picking me up at ten for our date. I'm surprised.

"I didn't think you'd want to go out tomorrow because we saw each other tonight, especially after my tears in the car. Not the best impression to make on a guy."

He lifts my hand to his lips, gives me the lightest kiss. My heart just skipped a beat. His lips feel amazing on my skin, so soft but firm.

"Of course, I want to see you, can't you see how captivated I am by you?"

He's so intense, and it's hot as hell, but we've only known each other for a few days, and have only been in each other's company for a matter of hours. I don't understand what this GQ model, businessman wants from me. He can have anyone he wants.

"You already agreed to spend the day with me, Miss Tate, and I'm holding you to it. I'll be here at ten."

He kisses my hand one last time, lingering for a moment, as if he's breathing me in before he leaves. I feel lonely all of a sudden. How can you miss the presence of someone you hardly know? I feel like part of me just left the building with him, and a chilling unease settles in the pit of my stomach. Having strong feelings for someone as unobtainable as Xander Rhodes, will only end badly for me.

I resolve to tell him after our date tomorrow that it would be wise if we don't spend any more time together. It's for the best, but as I drift into a fitful sleep, I dream of ice-blue eyes, warm embraces, and a contentment beyond compare.

CHAPTER 4

LILY

I NEED TO GET READY FOR MY DATE WITH XANDER AND I HAVE NO IDEA where he's planning to take me, so I send him a quick text.

> **Me:** Dress code for today? Where are we going?

> **Mr. P:** Anything you wear will be perfect. Casual is fine. I'm not telling, it's a surprise. Xander x

I can do casual. My hair still looks good from last night. I just need a quick shower, minimal makeup, and some jeans that make my ass look good.

I'm chewing over the various conversations from last night when I remember Jason assuming that I'd heard of Rhodes Industries. I guess the company Xander works for must be a family business. So, like every self-respecting woman my age, I decide to do a quick Google search on my date for the day.

Holy. Frigging. Shit.

Xander doesn't work for Rhodes Industries—he *owns* it. I am way out of my league here. As I read on, it becomes apparent that he's a savant with more money than God. Rhodes Industries owns what seems like half the commercial real estate in Manhattan. Not only does he make a fortune leasing premises, but he also invests in several companies, helping transform them into something bigger than they ever would have been on their own.

It's a staggering achievement for anyone, especially someone so young. I'm not sure how old he is, but I would guess late twenties. Thoroughly intimidated by his business achievements, I slam my laptop shut, afraid to look any further.

The phone rings and I glance at my watch. It's 10 a.m. to the second. The doorman informs me that Xander has arrived. I tell him to send him up and unlock the front door before grabbing my jacket from the closet and heading back to the living room.

My breath just evaporates.

He's standing in the doorway of my apartment, leaning his broad shoulders against the wall, with his toned arms crossed over his chest. I drink him in.

He's wearing a white t-shirt that highlights his muscular arms and abs to perfection. There's not a morsel of fat on him. He has an open tailored black shirt over his t-shirt, the sleeves rolled up to reveal strong, sinewy forearms. I don't know how he does it, but even arms are sexy. The way he's leaning against the door makes his t-shirt lift ever so slightly, revealing a hint of those mouthwatering V muscles heading down into the low waistband of his jeans. Oh. Fuck. That's hot. He has on black fitted jeans and charcoal grey biker style boots with the laces loose. This is not the businessman I met this week. He's more reminiscent of a bad boy model, giving me a panty-melting smile.

"You look beautiful today. Are you ready to go, or are you going to stand there with a sexy as hell look on your face that says you're going to rip my clothes off any second?" I can't answer. I'm gob-smacked by how amazing he looks, and as soon as he says those words, I'm picturing stripping him and seeing every... last... inch.

"Miss Tate, I will not be responsible for my actions if you keep looking at me like that. I'm trying to be a gentleman here, so please, get your sweet ass over here and let's go before I lose the small amount of control I am currently exercising."

I grab my keys, my cheeks flushed with a little embarrassment and a lot of arousal. As I brush past him, he gently takes my hand and leads me to the elevator. His large, warm hand fits perfectly with mine.

When we step outside into the bright New York sunshine, I spy a familiar face walking toward us.

"Addison Warner. Doing the walk of shame."

She gives me the biggest grin and bites her bottom lip. "Who said I'm ashamed? I had a fabulous night. Tell Carter I said 'Hi' when you see him."

Xander smirks. "I will pass along your regards." His voice lowers. "Thanks again for helping me out yesterday."

She smiles. "No problem, Casanova." Raising her eyebrows, she stares him down. "Just remember you owe me, *and* remember what I told you about my girl here."

With a massive hug, she tells me to have a great time and cut loose for a change, then disappears into our building.

As I turn my attention back to Xander, I notice the most expensive looking car I've ever seen double-parked right outside the doors to my building. Of course, he doesn't abide by the rules the rest of us do! "Really… a sports car. Could you be anymore cliché?" Shit, shit, shit. I can't believe I just said that out loud.

He lets out a belly laugh. "Don't hold back. Say what you really think." Shit. "You are right, though. This is a Ferrari 458 Italia. The word cliché was invented for this car. I fucking love it. I wanted a Ferrari when I was two years old. It's the first thing I bought when I made my first big deal. Just wait until you take a drive with me, you'll understand when you feel the engine purring beneath you."

How can a car make me horny? There is most definitely something wrong with me. He opens the passenger door and the moment I sink into the leather seat, I have a bit of a crush myself. He slides into the car with the elegance of a dancer. It's a joy to watch.

He starts the engine and I swear it sends a jolt straight to my lady bits. He has a massive grin on his face, like a little boy at Christmas.

"See, I told you."

I can't help but laugh. "Touché."

I sit back, enjoy the ride, the company, and the sense of ease I feel when with him. I ask a few times where we're going, but he isn't going to give it up that easily. I'm surprised by how natural it feels to be alone with him. I'm usually nervous on first dates, but something about Xander and the way he seems genuinely interested in everything I have to say makes him so easy to talk to.

I realize while we're talking that we're dressed in similar outfits. Black jeans and a white t-shirt. We match. When I point it out, he moves his hand from the steering wheel onto my thigh.

"I like it. Everyone will know we're together."

I can't think straight when he's touching me, and he makes no attempt to move his hand back to the wheel. We drive for a while in silence, make a snack stop, (I'm surprised he lets me eat in this car) and start chatting back and forth again until we arrive in the Hamptons.

"Do you have a house here? Is that your devious plan, to lock me away in your beach house?"

He gives me a wonderfully wicked grin.

"As tempting as that sounds, I have other plans for you today. I know I'm a walking cliché, so you'll be surprised to find out I do not, in fact, own a property here. My friend Carter who you met last night has a beachfront property and kindly gave me the keys for the weekend." Weekend? What the Hell?

"I thought we were only here for the day?" My heart threatens to burst straight out of my chest, it's beating so fast.

"We are. Don't worry. I said he gave me the keys for the weekend, not that we had to stay for the weekend. Although... I could be persuaded if you ask nicely." He has a sinfully sexy, cocky grin. Oh. My. God. I am not equipped for this. I'm a virgin for crying out loud. Starting to panic slightly, I divert my attention to our surroundings and try to clear my head.

Not long after, we pull up in front of a gorgeous house, right on the beach, with a wrap-around porch and windows everywhere to take advantage of the view.

It's a picture-perfect dream house.

Xander switches off the engine and jumps out of the car to come and open my door, taking my hand to help me out. He laces his fingers with mine and leads me past the house, down to the beach. I'm speechless when I see what's waiting for us.

There's a beautiful white tent, like a mini marquee on the sand, and a table set for two with the same arrangement of roses he sent me. It's stunning. There's a waiter ready with a bottle of champagne on ice, waiting to serve us lunch.

"Xander, this is… oh my God… I'm lost for words."

He pulls me toward the table and holds out my chair. I hear him asking the waiter if everything has been arranged as requested, and he's assured everything will be to his liking. I figure he's talking about lunch and don't give it a second thought.

The food is delicious—seafood chowder with freshly baked bread and a wonderful, fruity champagne. The view is beyond amazing, and the conversation flows easily. Dessert is my favorite, vanilla cheese-cake, washed down with another glass of champagne. The bubbles are starting to go to my head. I make a mental note to keep the drinking under control. I need to keep my wits about me.

"How did you know that vanilla cheesecake is my favorite?"

"I have my ways." He raises his eyebrows, a wicked grin touching the corners of his mouth.

"What else do you know about me?"

"Definitely not enough, I want to know everything." Wow.

"You don't want to unleash the crazy, mister. There's no putting it back in!" The sexy look he's giving me right now is *really* turning me on.

"Trust me when I say this, Lily, I will take *anything* you want to unleash on me. I welcome it." I'm nervous and excited as butterflies take flight in my stomach.

How can he make anything sound dirty, and hot?

"Would you like to take a walk along the beach with me? We can stretch our legs and walk off lunch"

"I'd like that." I can't take my eyes off him.

He stands from the table, holding out his hand. As I take it, the now familiar buzzing returns and I relish the touch of his skin against mine. We walk along the waterfront, taking in the view, listening to the waves. Xander tells me some funny stories about his antics with Carter when they've spent time here together. It's lovely to hear him talking about his friends, he doesn't seem so intimidating—not so much the business mogul—just a beautiful man, young, and fun to be around.

We walk to a secluded cove and it's breathtaking. I stand letting the waves splash my feet, close my eyes, and soak up the sun. It is so peaceful. I feel truly content, holding his hand. I don't feel the need to fill the silence with conversation. It's like being back in our own little bubble.

"This place is stunning. Thank you for bringing me here. The view is…"

"Truly exquisite." He leans in, searching my eyes for permission. His breath is warm on my lips. He takes my silence as a sign of consent, closing the remaining distance between us.

When his lips touch mine it's indescribable. I feel like my soul is fighting to break free from my chest, and soar above the clouds. His kiss is gentle but firm, his lips soft and full. He slowly glides his tongue over my bottom lip, seeking entry, and as I part my lips, he darts his tongue in to meet mine.

There's an explosion of sensation coursing through my entire body. The butterflies are back, and swarming in my stomach, an ache developing lower, forcing me to clench my muscles to curb the desire that threatens to take over. His tongue tangles with mine, stroking it, exploring my mouth with his expert touch. His hands move into my hair, holding my head in place as he deepens the kiss, sending shivers down my spine.

The taut muscles on his back flex under my fingertips as I pull him closer, my breasts pressed tight to his chest. He hardens against me, his kiss becoming more urgent. He tastes so sweet, and I want more. No matter how close he is, it isn't enough.

As our tongues dance together, my hands start to roam down his back, but when I feel his firm, sculpted ass in my hands, he breaks the kiss.

"Sweetheart, you need to keep those little hands of yours in check. I'm sure you can feel that I'm already struggling to stay in control." He says pressing his hard-on against me. "If you keep touching me like that, I'm going to take you right here in this cove and I won't be able to stop myself once I've started."

My breath is labored, like I've just run a marathon. My lips are swollen from the passion of our kiss, and my cheeks are flushed with arousal.

"You're right. We should get back." I remove his hands from my face and turn to walk back to the house.

I feel strange. I'm embarrassed that he stopped kissing me, and because I grabbed his ass. Why did I do that? The first time we kiss, and I grab his ass. I don't realize while I'm mentally berating myself that I've picked up pace and am almost running back in the direction we came. A strong hand wraps around my arm, spinning me round, stopping me in my tracks.

"What's wrong? Why are you running away from me? What did I do wrong?" I can't even look at him.

"I'm so sorry." I whisper, my embarrassment choking me from the inside. "I shouldn't have grabbed your ass like that. It was just a kiss. I'm such an idiot."

He puts a finger under my chin, lifting my head until I'm staring into his ice-blue eyes filled with warmth and tenderness.

"Don't ever apologize for grabbing my ass, and if that was just a kiss, I don't think we experienced the same thing back there. That was *not* just a kiss, not for me. Didn't you feel it? Tell me you felt it, too?" His eyes are searching mine, he looks... worried?

"I felt it, Xander. I feel it every time you touch me. Every time you're near me." He gives me the sweetest kiss and pulls me into his arms.

"No more running away. Promise me." I nod. "Say the words."

"I promise. No more running away." My voice is barely a whisper.

We make our way back to the beach house, our fingers intertwined.

When we arrive back at the tent I saw earlier, the front drapes are swept back to reveal the most romantic setting. There are two daybeds side by side, a table covered with books, a selection of sunglasses, and as I look around, I see a rail of swimwear and sundresses in the corner.

"I thought you might like to relax and read for a while, or we can lie out in the sun. I took the liberty of arranging some swimwear and outfits for you to choose from in case you wanted a dip in the sea, or the house has a pool if you prefer. Obviously, you don't need to change if you don't want to. You look fantastic."

"This is amazing. Thank you for being so thoughtful. I'd love to go for a swim."

I pick out a bikini and sundress, before Xander takes me inside to change. The house is spectacular—so open and airy. He shows me to the master bathroom and leaves me to get changed. This room is awesome. There's a sunken tub big enough for at least four adults, and a walk-in shower that's like a room in itself. I'm definitely trying it out before we go home.

I quickly change into a simple white bikini, and it doesn't leave much to the imagination. I'm self-conscious as I take in the sight of myself in the mirror. It's a perfect fit... of course. How does he do that? I just wish there was more of it! I cover up with a white lace sundress, and head outside.

When I enter the tent, Xander is nowhere to be seen, but I can hear him shouting my name and turn to see him swimming in the sea. I give him a small wave as he makes his way back to shore. When he stands up in the water, I think my brain goes into meltdown at the sight of him. If this were a movie, everything would be in slow motion right now!

His hair is dripping wet, water running down his toned body, wearing nothing but low-slung blue board shorts, showing that phenomenal V and a delicious happy trail disappearing below his waistband. Perfection.

"You look gorgeous." His ice-blue eyes, rake up and down the length of my body, drinking me in, my flesh heating under his gaze. There's a look of wonder on his face as he stares at me, and I visibly see him shake it off to compose himself before he continues. "Do you want to come for a swim, or would you like to read for a while?"

"A swim sounds like fun." I walk into the tent and remove my dress, leaving it on the daybed.

"Wow. You have an amazing body, just… flawless." I quickly make my way into the water splashing him as I go, eager to move away from any further conversation about my body.

We have a great time, laughing, playing, swimming, and just goofing around in the water. After that, we spend the rest of the afternoon chilling, switching between reading in the tent, and lying out on the sand chatting. It's so relaxing, and a lot of fun. This is by far the best first date ever.

As I sit reading Jane Austen's *Persuasion*, Xander tips my book down to tell me he's going to make dinner for us. I offer to help, but he insists I enjoy reading just a little longer.

I stay outside for a while before heading into the house to get cleaned up for dinner. I choose a cute purple dress, tie my hair up, leaving some loose tendrils, and apply a small amount of makeup, taking one last glance in the mirror before I go in search of my date.

CHAPTER 5

LILY

I FOLLOW THE ENCHANTING AROMAS DOWN THE HALLWAY TO THE kitchen. This house is gorgeous, with a large open-plan living area and a full wall of windows showcasing the view to perfection. Xander's standing in the kitchen area with his back to me. I take the opportunity to study him.

He's changed into a crisp white shirt, sleeves rolled up, classic blue jeans hugging his firm ass. I could stand here for hours just looking at him.

"Like what you see?" I didn't think he knew I was here. Damn.

"Yes, actually, this kitchen is awesome, I was just admiring it." He turns to face me, a smirk pulling at the corners of his lips.

There are a few buttons open at the top of his shirt, showing just a hint of chest hair. Oh Lord, help me. That's hot. He stalks toward me, his bare feet making no sound on the hardwood floors. Circling his arms around my waist, he nuzzles at my neck, nipping and biting me softly.

"You look edible in this dress. I'm starving. What about you?" Everything has a double meaning with this man.

"Yes, I'm starving." My breath falters as he continues his sensual assault on my neck, up toward my ear, and I start to panic. He's obviously experienced and I don't want to be a disappointment. "What are you cooking for me, Mr. Rhodes?"

He stops kissing me and takes a moment to just breathe in my scent—Chanel. I'm sure he can sense my discomfort because he pulls away and goes back to cooking the dinner.

"I'm making tagliatelle carbonara. Is that okay?"

"Sounds delicious, and it smells amazing. Can I help with anything?"

"I've got the table set up over there by the windows. If you could grab a bottle of Prosecco from the fridge, I'll plate this up and be with you in a minute. Thanks."

The table is lovely, with floating candles in a crystal dish in the center. As I look outside, I notice there are glass lanterns set up all over the porch creating the most romantic setting. Xander appears with dinner and pours us each a glass of Prosecco.

"You didn't have to go to so much trouble. This is stunning. The meal, the setting, the company. I feel really spoiled."

"I haven't even begun to spoil you yet, sweets. Now eat up."

We eat, drink, and talk. He's a great cook, and we're onto our second bottle of Prosecco in no time.

"How are we getting home if you're drinking?" I'm a bit tipsy at this point.

"David will come and pick us up later, unless I advise him otherwise."

"And why would you advise him otherwise?" I'm getting giggly now. "Are you trying to keep me here and take advantage of me?" I need to shut up now.

"I would never take advantage. I told you, I will only do what you want me to. I've been getting mixed signals today. You're a mystery wrapped in an enigma. One that I would very much like to solve. When I think I know what you want, you pull away. Tell me, Lily, what do you like?"

"I don't know what you mean."

"Don't be coy. I'm serious. I'm not trying to embarrass you. I want to know what you like in a lover. What can I do for you that will drive you wild?"

I shouldn't have had so much to drink. My brain to mouth filter has completely shut off, and before I know it, I'm saying it out loud.

"I'm not being coy. I really don't know. I've never been wild... or had a lover."

His face is frozen, a look of shock spreading across his flawless features. Then the look in his eye changes. He seems pained. He drops his head into his hands and starts muttering under his breath.

"I'm a fucking idiot. I thought you were just a little shy."

"Xander, its fine. I understand. It wouldn't be enjoyable for you sleeping with a virgin. I wouldn't know how to please you. I'd be a disappointment. Don't worry about it. We'll just head back when David gets here and leave it at that."

It's my turn to be frozen to the spot. He looks angry.

"Is that what you really think of me? I'm pissed at myself for how I acted earlier in the cove. Saying I was going to take you right there if you kept touching me, pushing my cock against you like a horny teenager. I'm so sorry. I should never have done that. I wouldn't have even suggested staying here for the weekend if I'd known." He gets up from the table and kneels in front of me.

"Trust me. Making love to you would never be a disappointment. Please look at me, Lily." I lift my gaze to see only reverence in his eyes. "You are the most beautiful woman I've ever seen. I want to kiss every inch of your delectable body. I want to give you pleasure like you've never felt before. I want to ruin you for other men... but... I would never take this from you. I know you deserve better than me."

As he sits before me, I stare into his eyes, sparkling with tenderness and affection.

"Touch me, Xander." I don't know where this sudden surge of confidence is coming from.

"Don't ask that of me, Lily. I know if I touch you, if I taste you, I'll want more."

I part my legs slightly, inviting him to move closer. I take his hand, guiding it slowly up my thigh.

"Touch me, Xander." My voice is a whisper.

He lets out a strangled moan. "Stay here with me tonight. Let me show you what it could be like between us." I hesitate. I'm scared to let this man too close, but my body is screaming at me to give in. "I'm not going to have sex with you tonight. You've been drinking, and I want you to make this decision when you're ready, and when you're sober. I *do* want you to stay here and let me pleasure you in other ways. Please, say yes."

"Yes, Xa…"

His lips crash down on mine before I finish saying his name. This is a different kind of kiss—desperate and needy—like he wants me more than his next breath. His hands fist into my hair. This isn't gentle, and I love it. There's a dominance in Xander that calls to me, and I'm more than willing to submit.

"God, Lily, you taste so sweet. I want to taste every inch of you." He takes my hand and leads me down the hallway, his eyes never leaving mine. The bedroom is magnificent, soft green walls, decadent French style furnishings, and the biggest four-poster bed I've ever seen in my life. It's draped with organza, crisp white linens, and gorgeous, plump pillows. "I'll give you one chance to change your mind, to stop before it begins, because once we do this, there's no going back. You'll be mine." He takes my silence as his answer, walking me over to the bed. "You. Are. So. Beautiful." He kisses me softly between each word. My body is alive with anticipation, my skin burning under every touch, and every kiss.

He slowly pushes my dress down, revealing a white lace bra. Trailing kisses across my shoulders and down my chest, his skilled fingers flick the catch, and he gently removes it, all the while, holding my gaze. When my bra drops to the bedroom floor, he claims my mouth, teasing me, stroking my tongue with his. I want to feel him.

I unbutton his shirt, sliding my hand underneath to feel his taut skin. As soon as I touch his chest, he tugs his shirt off dropping it next to my bra. His lips never lose contact with mine, and when I press my breasts against him, I'm rewarded with a seductive groan.

"Fuck. You feel amazing." He pulls my hair, exposing my neck to his gaze. "So fucking pretty." He kisses behind my ear sending a shiver straight down my spine.

He continues leisurely kissing down my neck. His hands move to cup my breasts, rolling my nipples between his thumb and forefinger until they harden under his touch. I moan. It feels incredible.

"You fit my hands perfectly."

He moves his lips down to my right breast, taking the nipple into his mouth, flicking his tongue around and over the tip, his groans of pleasure sending delicious vibrations through my nipple and straight to my sex. His hand continues to knead my other breast while his free hand pushes my dress down over my hips to the floor.

"Lie on the bed, sweets." I do as he asks, very aware that I'm naked apart from my white lace thong. "Christ, you're gorgeous."

He climbs onto the bed, parting my legs with his knees so he can move closer, kissing me with such passion that my lips begin to swell, but I don't care. Every touch is magnificent, and I want more. There's an ache building inside me that I know only he can satisfy.

"I need to taste you. I can't wait any longer." He moves down my body, kissing and nipping at my flesh, his hands caressing my sides, sliding down to my hips.

"I hope these aren't your favorite panties." Before I know what's happening, he rips the lace, exposing me to his burning gaze. "Your pussy is so pretty. Fucking perfect." He runs his finger down my slick folds. I can't watch anymore. I close my eyes, fisting my hands in the sheets, letting the sensations wash over me.

"You're so wet. So responsive. Look at me while I pleasure you, Lily." As I open my eyes, he lifts his hand to his lips and sucks the evidence of my arousal from his fingers. "You taste amazing. But I'm afraid a taste just isn't going to be enough for me, I want to feast on you."

His head dips between my legs, his tongue licking me from my entrance slowly up to my clit. An explosion detonates in my body, every nerve ending singing with delight at the sensation his tongue creates.

"Oh my God, Xander. Oh my God…" I spread my legs as wide as

they'll go, welcoming anything he wants to give me, arching my back off the bed with pleasure. He's teasing me, alternating between licking my pussy and kissing my inner thigh, right next to where I need him. The ache between my legs builds slowly, becoming almost unbearable. He moves his fingers to my slick entrance, gently pushing one finger inside me.

"You're so fucking tight." He works his finger slowly in and out of me, and it feels phenomenal, but I can't watch. Suddenly there are two fingers pushing into me.

"Fuck!"

His lips kiss, while his fingers work inside me. His warm wet tongue flicking over my clit, placing open-mouthed kisses down my folds. When I can't take it anymore, I try to move, but his hand is splayed on my stomach, holding me in place.

"It's okay, sweets, I've got you." His tongue is relentless, moving together with his fingers inside me, creating a perfect rhythm...

"Oh God, don't stop, please don't stop... oh my God... Xander... Yes... Yes... Fuck!" My orgasm rips through me, detonating in a perfect wave of sensation, spreading throughout my entire body, radiating from my core to my toes and out to my fingertips. He gently kisses and nuzzles my sex as I ride the aftershocks, bringing be back down slowly.

He moves from between my legs and comes up to lie next to me, leaning on his side, his head propped up on his arm.

"You are exquisite when you come. I've never seen anything more beautiful in my life."

He brushes my hair from my face and places a soft kiss on my lips. I can taste myself on him, and as I suck his tongue into my mouth, he groans in appreciation. I lie back down on the bed trying to catch my breath, before realizing I'm completely naked. I move to get under the covers, but he stops me.

"Let me look at you. Don't be shy. Your body is perfect... fucking flawless." He holds his arms out, and as I cuddle into him, I feel unsure of what should happen next, but I know I want to please him.

"What about you?" He's stroking his fingers up and down my back.

"What about me?"

"I want to give you an… I don't know what you want, though." He kisses my forehead, squeezing me tight against his side.

"Sweets, it's an orgasm. You can say it out loud. Besides, you just gave me the most immense pleasure. I'm fucking ecstatic right now. Tonight is about you. I don't expect anything." He kisses my head. "Are you too tired or would you like a bath in that great big tub?"

"A bath sounds amazing."

"Okay, then. You relax while I get it running." I crawl under the covers as he disappears into the bathroom. I figure it will take a while to fill up the tub. It's enormous.

I must have drifted off, because what seems like seconds later, I'm woken up with him stroking my face. "Come on, gorgeous, your bath awaits." He lifts me from the bed, cradled in his arms, I wrap myself around his neck, his chest hair tickling my face.

As we enter the bathroom I gasp, taking in the sight before me. He's dimmed the lights, filled the bath with sweet smelling bubbles, and candles surround the edge of the tub. It's so beautiful, I have a lump in my throat.

He gently sets me down on my feet and holds my hand as I descend into the sunken tub. The water feels fantastic. I look up at him, his eyes watching my every move. Holding my gaze, he unbuttons his jeans and pushes them down, his hard length springing free as his boxer shorts drop to the floor. Holy… shit. He is huge. I'm pretty sure he will never fit inside me. God, he is beautiful. Masculine, muscled yet lean, and every glorious inch of his body is made for sex. My stomach is doing somersaults at the sight of him standing naked before me.

He holds my gaze as he lowers himself into the water, the look in his eyes fierce with an emotion I can't quite place. Before I can say anything, he lifts me, and positions himself at my back before pulling me in between his legs. I lay my head back against his chest and just enjoy the warmth of his arms wrapped around me. Placing small kisses on my shoulder, he enjoys my little moans of pleasure, and it makes me feel cherished.

"Mmm… Lily. A beautiful name for a stunning woman. Is that your mom's favorite flower?" He continues to kiss my shoulders and up my neck.

"No. Actually, she named me after her favorite poem by Ted Hughes *To Paint a Water Lily*. It's inspired by Monet's series of water lilies oil paintings. The poet is talking about the artist depicting the beauty of the lily above the surface of the water, but he delves deeper to explore what lies beneath the surface. He describes the creatures and plant life that no one thinks about because they're not pretty. I've always thought it was quite fitting for me. I'm rambling, aren't I?"

"What do you mean?"

"Just that people see what they want to see, and generally don't look at what's under the surface. Once you see the crazy, there's no putting it back in the box."

His grip tightens around me. "There is *nothing* bad about you, Lily. Inside or out."

"You don't know me."

"I might not know everything about you, but I *know* you. There is nothing you could tell me about yourself that would make me look at you differently." His tone becomes almost defensive.

I turn to face him. "Let's just agree to disagree and leave it at that."

I don't give him the chance to answer me, instead kissing him with everything I have, pouring all my insecurities into this one kiss, savoring every touch of this wonderful man's mouth. I flick my tongue across his lips, taking his sharp intake of breath as an invitation, dipping my tongue into his mouth, gently stroking and exploring him, twisting and tangling together in a perfect dance.

"I could kiss you forever." My heart soars at his words, relishing the effect of my touch as he hardens beneath me. I slide my hand down into the water between our bodies, wrapping it around his hard length.

"Fuck, baby. Calm down or I'll embarrass myself. You don't have to do this."

"I want to please you. Let me."

Xander's large hand grips mine around his base. "Are you sure? Don't touch me unless you're certain you won't regret it tomorrow."

My voice betrays my nerves. "I'm sure."

He slowly guides my hand up and down the length of him. "God, that feels so good. Keep doing that." He removes his hand and stretches both arms out over the edge of the tub. I watch as he succumbs, his head falling back to rest on the tiles, eyes closed, his breathing shallow, his cock hard as steel in the palm of my hand.

"That's it… faster." I do as he asks. The arousal that swells within me just from watching him makes me ache for my own release. I quicken my movements, sweeping my thumb over the head of his cock, eliciting a sexy as hell growl from his chest.

"Fuck, me. That feels amazing, I'm going to come." I'm pumping his cock hard and fast with my hand, mesmerized by the look on his face, and suddenly he's shouting my name.

"Fuck, Lily… Yes... Fucking Hell!" I feel his orgasm rip through him, pulsing down his impressive length. I have never been so turned on in my life. He grabs my face in his hands and ravishes my mouth with his tongue. "You. Are. So. Fucking. Sexy." He kisses me after each word. "You'll be the death of me."

His hands move from my hair down onto my breasts, one hand continuing a seductive trail to where I have a growing ache, expertly working me with his fingers until he brings me to a quick and intense orgasm.

"Your body was made for me. You're mine. Say it. Say you're mine."

"I'm yours, Xander." I know in this moment that it's the truth.

I'm so exhausted after our exertions in the tub that he has to lift me out, and wrapping me in a towel, he carries me through to the bed, laying me down gently.

"I'll be back in a minute, sweets." He quickly dries off and pulls on his jeans. He disappears from the room, and I hear the front door open. Within five minutes he's back in the bedroom with two bags. I recognize one of them.

"Okay, don't get mad at me. I wasn't assuming anything would happen between us, but I like to be prepared, so I called Addi on

Thursday and asked if she would make an overnight bag for you just in case you wanted to stay here... with me."

I know I probably should be mad that he went behind my back, and maybe even for hoping I would spend the night on our first date, but I just can't be annoyed at him. I believe he just wanted to take care of me.

"It's fine. I'm not mad. Let's see what she's packed for me." I grab the bag and head into the bathroom.

Of course, she didn't pack anything comfortable! The bag is filled with sexy lingerie, and a less than practical outfit for tomorrow. Thanks a lot, Addi. I put on a pair of silk panties from the bag, brush my teeth and open the door. I grab Xander's white shirt off the floor and quickly slip it on.

"Damn, woman. My shirt has never looked so good. Get your fine ass over here."

"Do you mind if I wear it? Addi didn't pack anything comfortable or practical."

"It's yours."

He's changed out of his jeans into a pair of PJ bottoms, low slung on his hips, showcasing the hallowed V in all its glory! Turning down the covers he looks up, giving me the sweetest smile.

"I won't bite, sweets. Not unless you ask."

I quickly jump into bed, nervous about spending the night with this man. I doubt I'll I get any sleep. I might have to stay awake just to savor the moment. As soon as he gets into the massive bed, he closes the distance between us, pulling me close. He positions me so my back is to his front and snakes his arm around my waist, kissing my hair.

"Get some rest." It feels like the most natural thing in the word to be cocooned in Xander's arms.

"Goodnight." I cuddle in and drift off into the most peaceful sleep I've had since I was fifteen years old.

CHAPTER 6

LILY

I WAKE UP IN THE SAME POSITION I FELL ASLEEP, WRAPPED IN THE WARM embrace of an incredible man. The only difference is that Xander has slung a leg over mine in his sleep, so even if I wanted to escape, I'm pinned to the bed. Of course, I don't want to move a muscle. I lie listening to the soft sounds of his even breathing for what seems like hours, enjoying the warmth and connection.

"Good morning, Miss Tate." He presses his body against mine and nuzzles at my neck. "I could get used to this. Did you sleep well?"

"I did. I haven't slept that well in years. You?" I look at him expectantly.

"I had a great sleep." He continues to kiss my neck, his cock pressing against my ass, hardening with each kiss.

"What would you like to do today? I thought maybe we could grab some breakfast here, take a shower and then do whatever you want for the rest of the day."

His voice is rough and sexy. I would literally do anything with him today.

"I really don't mind. I'm just happy to spend the day with you." I'm interrupted by his phone ringing.

"Shit, I have to take this," he says, frowning at the screen.

"Go ahead, I'll rustle up some breakfast and give you some privacy."

When everything's ready I go in search of Xander and as I walk down the hall, I can't help but overhear his conversation.

"What the fuck is she playing at? Find out what she wants David… I get that… I don't care… fuck… just ask her what it will take to get rid of her and make it happen. I'll be back tonight. We'll talk then."

I don't want him to know I overheard his conversation, so I creep back toward the kitchen and shout that breakfast is ready. He comes striding out, his hair tousled from running his hands through it. There's a storm in his eyes, frustration, fear even, and I wonder what's gotten him so riled. Maybe I don't want to know.

"Everything okay?" That gets his attention, and his face softens as he drinks me in.

"Yes. Just some work stuff to sort out, nothing that can't wait till Monday. This smells delicious. Is there no end to your talents?"

We eat our breakfast with an uninterrupted view of the sea, watching the waves lap at the shore. With the decision made to visit the marina and grab some lunch, I begin to clear the dishes. He comes up behind me, snaking his arms around my waist. His breath soft on my ear.

"Will you shower with me, Lily?" I turn in his arms, utterly beguiled by his ice-blue gaze.

He lifts me up and across to the kitchen island and places me on top, parting my legs with his body. He gently caresses my skin with his lips, planting soft kisses every few seconds, his tongue running down the length of my neck and back up to my ear. My breath is shallow and erratic as his lips connect with mine. I can't stop the groan his taste elicits. His hand grasps the back of my head as he deepens the kiss, moaning his appreciation into my mouth. He pulls away panting and grabs my waist, throwing me over his shoulder, making his way back to the bedroom. I can't stop laughing, yelling at him to put me down, but he just smacks my ass.

"No can do, baby. We're going for a shower. I can't take no for an answer." He doesn't put me down while he switches on the water and grabs some towels.

What I'm not expecting is for him to lift me right into the shower, still wearing his shirt. I squeal when he finally puts me down.

"Oh. Sweets. You're soaking wet, I better get you out of this shirt." With a cheeky grin on his face, he unbuttons the shirt, pushing it down my arms, letting it slap down onto the tile floor, then he removes my panties. He quickly removes his pants and kicks our clothes to the corner. We stand still, taking in the sight of each other. He looks glorious standing naked before me, the hot water raining down his body. I want to lick every inch of him.

"You're perfect," I whisper.

"You said that the day I met you. I can't believe it's not even been a week. Somehow, you're already a part of me I didn't realize I needed." His eyes roam up and down my body.

"God, you're gorgeous." Moving closer, he presses his wet body against mine, his impressive length hardening between us. His hands begin to roam all over my body, leaving behind a trail of fire and desire.

"I. Want. You. So. Badly." Kissing me between each word.

"Can you feel how it would be for us? Tell me you do." He drops to his knees in front of me, kissing my stomach, nipping and biting from hip to hip, his hands cupping my ass. He grabs my leg and places it on his shoulder, opening me up to his gaze. Running his fingers over my sex. "This is mine. Do you understand?" I'm mesmerized by him, letting myself bask in the sensation of his touch, together with the water beating down on me from above. "Answer me, Miss Tate. Do you understand?"

"Yes, Xander… God… Yes." His mouth is on me, ravaging me, sucking on my clit. Fucking hell, that feels good. My hips grind into his face, forcing him to take more of me, to work me harder with his tongue. He kisses my clit down through my throbbing folds and with a decisive thrust, his tongue is inside me, thrusting back and forth, circling my entrance. I grab his hair in my hands, holding his mouth to my pussy, grinding harder against him, faster and faster.

"Oh God… that feels unbelievable." The delicious build-up in my core heralds an explosive release.

He stills his head, letting me set the pace as he sucks on my clit. I can't hold back anymore. Lights flash behind my eyes, electricity shooting through my body, causing my legs to shake.

"Fuck… Xander." His name is a litany on my lips. He holds me up as my legs give way, pressing me against the wall taking my mouth with the same passion he showed my sex.

"Mine." The word repeating as he kisses me senseless.

When I come down from cloud nine, Xander is smiling at me.

"Let's get you washed."

He squeezes my favorite shower gel into his palms, tenderly washing every inch of me, worshipping my body with his hands. When he's finished, he reaches for the shampoo and starts massaging it into my scalp. I could go to sleep it's so relaxing.

"Rinse."

I let the water cascade over my body, washing my insecurities away as I see myself through his eyes. He's hungry for me, arousal evident in the sparkle of his eyes… and the hard-on between his legs.

I have a surge of confidence and take control, pressing him against the wall with my hand, letting him know my intentions. I grip his growing length while I lower to my knees, my eyes never leaving his.

"Lily. Are you sure about this?"

My tongue darts out to flick the head of his cock. "Yes." flick "I want you in my mouth."

I have never seen the attraction with giving a guy head before. It just seemed kind of gross to me. But looking at Xander and his beautiful cock, I'm desperate to taste him, to feel him on my tongue, to hear him groan in ecstasy. I kiss the tip before running my tongue down the length of his shaft to the base, gently cupping his balls in my hand, and as I run my tongue back up to the tip, I hear him hiss through clenched teeth.

"Fuck, baby… that is… fu-ck." I swirl my tongue around the tip before taking him fully into my mouth. Moving my head slowly back and forth, his hands fist in my hair, guiding my pace, holding me where he needs me.

"God, that's so good, just like that." I gradually increase my speed circling his thick shaft with my tongue, sucking him harder.

"Fuck... I'm close! You need to stop now before I come in your mouth."

He tries to pull free, but I don't stop. I take him deeper until he hits the back of my throat. He thrusts frantically, losing control, and it's such a turn on seeing him come apart for me. With one last thrust of his hips, he explodes in my mouth, his hot salty come shooting down my throat.

"Holy shit, Lily... Fucking Hell!"

Sucking every last drop, I let him rub out the aftershocks of his orgasm. He grabs me into his arms and holds me tight against his chest.

"Sweets, can I just say, you look even better on your knees than I imagined.

"Not bad for my first time, I guess." A chuckle escapes my chest.

"That was your first blowjob?"

"I've never wanted to before." I'm suddenly shy.

"You didn't have to do it. I wanted to go down on you, doesn't mean you had to reciprocate."

"I wanted to. You... feel amazing in my mouth." I can't even look at him.

"How did I get so lucky? A sweet innocent virgin with a naughty streak. You're every man's wet dream." That makes me laugh. We take a few minutes to rinse off and finally make it out of the shower. We need to get dressed otherwise we'll never leave this beach house. A tempting thought.

On second inspection, Addi hasn't messed up my overnight bag completely. There's a sexy black halter-neck top and a cute pair of black dress shorts. She's also included my favorite wedge sandals. Okay, Addi, you kind of rock! I get dressed and apply just enough makeup to show I've made an effort. I wouldn't have chosen this outfit for today, but it's working for me.

I make my way into the lounge when I see Xander gazing out the window, hot as hell in dark blue jeans, a black and white baseball t-shirt, and a black pair of Cons. Sexy. Sexy. Sexy.

"Hey, handsome. You ready to hit the marina?" Clasping my arms around his waist, I lean my head against his back.

"Sure thing. I'll just grab my keys." Something is troubling him. I can hear it in his voice.

"You okay?" He gives me a tight smile and nods, extricating himself from my embrace.

I'm not going to push him. He obviously doesn't want to talk to me about whatever is bothering him. I get the feeling it has something to do with the phone call earlier, but there's no point in pressing it. I'm just going to enjoy the time I have left with him and push reality, and the fact that I know next to nothing about this man, far from my mind. I knew coming into this weekend that this can't go any further, so I need to make sure I don't let myself get too attached to him. I'm already screwed. We jump in the car and head out to the East Hampton Marina.

The weather is perfect, as we stroll hand in hand looking in local shops, watching the boats in the marina and generally just soaking up the atmosphere. Xander stops in front of a particularly nice-looking seafood place.

"What do you think? Do you want to eat here?" This is the first he's really spoken since we left the house.

"Sure. Looks lovely, you want to sit inside or out?"

"Outside is perfect. Pick a table and I'll be back in a minute." He ducks into the restaurant while I sit down at a beautiful little table with a perfect panoramic view of the marina.

I feel his breath on my neck before he speaks. "I've been remiss, Miss Tate. I neglected to tell you how spectacular you look today." Slipping his hand under the fabric of my top, he cups my breast with his warm strong hand. "Mmm, I love this top, sweets, and your legs go on forever in these little shorts." A blush creeps over my cheeks at his words.

He pulls a seat round next to mine and slings his arm around my shoulder. "I've ordered the seafood platter and a nice bottle of wine. I hope that's okay." I nod, happy to acquiesce to his choices.

We have a lovely meal, chatting and laughing as his good mood returns, circling his fingers on my thigh as we eat. When we're done, he won't let me pay, and I don't feel like an argument, so I let him settle the bill and spend the rest of the afternoon enjoying his company.

As I pack my overnight bag, a sadness creeps in, settling in my stomach. This weekend has been perfect and being around Xander just feels so... right. I'm going to miss him when we go our separate ways.

He takes the bags out to the car, and we're ready to leave. I take a moment to memorize this beautiful place where Xander awakened a sexuality in me I didn't know was there.

It's quiet on the way home, and I notice he isn't driving as fast as he did yesterday. Maybe he isn't so keen to get back to reality either.

I decide to break the silence. "Thank you for this weekend. I had such a wonderful time."

"You're welcome, Miss Tate. I had a great time, too, but if you had such a nice time, why do you look so sad?"

"I guess... it's just a shame to leave our little bubble and return to reality. You'll go back to your life, and I'll go back to mine."

He squeezes my thigh. "You don't think you're getting rid of me that easily, do you? I want you to be a part of my life, Lily." As much as I want to believe him, I can't shake the feeling that he's keeping something from me,

"You don't have to pretend. I don't expect anything when we get home. You run your own company. You're super successful. I Googled you. I'm just a college student with no prospects." My heart sinks as the words leave my mouth, the realization hitting me—it bothers me much more than I want it to. "Besides, I don't think I could deal with the fall out when you're done with me if I let this go on any longer." I turn my head to stare out the window, trying to hide the tears forming in my eyes. I do *not* want his lasting memory of me to be a pathetic crying mess in his car.

"Look at me."

"I can't."

"Goddammit, Lily. Look at me. Now."

I turn to face him. His hands gripping the steering wheel so hard his knuckles are white. When I finally make eye contact, I'm frozen. I couldn't look away even if I tried. His eyes are no longer icy blue, they're dark and menacing.

"Firstly, why the hell would you Google me? Secondly, why didn't you mention any of this before putting my cock in your mouth? And thirdly, is that really what you think of me? That I would use you like that?"

A flash of pain mars his flawless features before anger returns.

"Am I missing something here? Did we *not* have the same fucking weekend? What am I saying? Of course, we didn't." I hate seeing him like this, annoyed with himself because of me.

"I was dumb enough to think it meant something. I'm such a fucking idiot. You would think I'd learn from experience. I love how my past can still fuck with my life, even now."

Oh my God. I'm pretty sure he didn't mean to tell me all of that, but I need to take the opportunity. "Your past?"

"I don't like talking about this stuff." I can't speak, a crushing dread pressing down on my chest. "Do you think it's easy for me to date? It's not. Sure, I can get girls who want a quick fuck and some nice gifts, but they don't want me for me. I thought you were different, but the goddamn Google search says otherwise. Lily, this weekend meant something to me, and I hoped it did to you, too."

"Oh God. It *did*... It..."

"Don't. Just... don't."

The drive is endless, the silence deafening. But no matter how hard I tried, I couldn't find the words to make it better. I'm not ready to leave him and return to my apartment alone. I already miss him and I'm still in the car. It's around eight o'clock when we pull up outside my apartment. He jumps out of the car to grab my bag and places it down next to me.

Without a word, his hands travel up my body to clasp the back of my head, lifting my face to his. He closes the gap between us, lowering his lips to mine, kissing me with a soul-melting intensity. I part my lips to allow his tongue to tangle with mine, stroking, flicking, exploring. It's the best kiss of my life. When he breaks the connection, he leans his forehead against mine, calming his breath, allowing me to do the same.

"God, I'm going to miss you."

I run my hands up and down his back. "Me too. Xander, I'm sorry…"

"Goodbye, Miss Tate."

With those final words, he jumps in the car, and I watch as he runs his hands continuously through his hair. I take one last chance to soak him in before heading up to my apartment. How could I have fucked up so badly?

CHAPTER 7

XANDER

I CAN'T BELIEVE I THOUGHT THIS GIRL WAS DIFFERENT. I WATCH AS SHE disappears into the building, taking my misplaced hopes with her.

From the moment I met Lily, I haven't been able to stop thinking about her. I'm not usually this aggressive in pursuing women, and if I'd known she was the type to Google me, I would never have done the things I did with her this weekend. I knew from the moment I first looked in her big green eyes, she had the power to hurt me. But I thought it was worth the risk.

As I throw the car into gear and peel away from the curb, my heart is pounding. I'm breaking every traffic law there is, but I'm so fucking angry with myself. The radio is blaring in my ears when I hear the faint ringing of my phone, and I hate that I want it to be her, telling me she's different, and that this weekend meant something to her. It's Carter. Against my better judgment I answer.

"Hey, Rhodes. You still at my fuck-pad in the Hamptons?"

"Shut the fuck up, Carter. I'm back in the city."

"Your dick broken already? That must have been some epic fucking. Lily must have some skills."

"Say another word about her and I'll choke the life out of you. Where are you anyway?"

"At the club. What's up? You don't sound too good."

"I'm coming over. Have a good bottle of Scotch ready in ten, not the shit you serve your customers." I end the call, drop a gear, and speed through the streets of Manhattan. I want to hunt down the C.E.O of Google and kick his ass. It's the nail in the coffin of my dating prospects. Women see me in the society pages, or my name on a new project and suddenly they know everything about me. Alexander Rhodes—free ticket to a life of luxury. Doesn't matter if they don't like me, they'd happily fuck me to reap the rewards. I know a lot of guys in my situation love no strings attached, but I've never been that guy. I've always been in love with the women I sleep with, or at least I thought I was in love with them at the time. Maybe that makes me a fool. Maybe it's time to take a leaf out of Carter's book and bang every hot girl who offers herself to me on a silver platter.

I pull up in front of Cube—Carter's nightclub. I hate clubs at the best of times, but his office in the back is a great place to get really drunk and talk shit. I throw my keys at the valet and give the doorman a nod as I walk inside.

The music is so loud it resonates in my chest, the bass thudding in time with my heart. There are half-naked women everywhere I look, but I don't even want to waste my time on some meaningless slut. I push my way through the crowds to Carter's office, and sure enough, he has a glass waiting for me. Scotch on the rocks.

"Hey, man. Thanks for letting me use the Hamptons house this weekend. Here's your key." I throw it down on the desk with absolute distain in my voice.

"What the fuck happened to you? Did this girl's pussy bite?"

I stare him down, furious at the mention of Lily. "Fuck off. I don't want to talk about it. I came here to get drunk."

"You're not the 'get drunk' type, so spill. I thought you liked this girl."

"I did... I do." I down my drink and swipe the bottle from Carter's desk, pouring myself a generous glass this time.

"Give me that." He pulls the bottle from my reluctant grasp and sits back in his chair, eyeing me warily as he fills his glass. "Talk to me.

You came here to get something off your chest. What is it? Was the sex bad or something?"

"Is everything about sex with you?"

A sly smirk creeps across his lips. "Fucking right it is! Take a lesson from my playbook. I'm the happiest motherfucker you know."

"I call bullshit on that one. You're just as miserable as me. The only difference is you've fucked your way through most of Manhattan."

"Enough praise. Spill your shit. I've got a club to run."

This is why I came to Carter. He's an asshole, who will convince me to forget about this girl. "I didn't sleep with her."

I don't think I've ever seen anyone's eyes as wide as Carter's right now. The mouthful of Scotch he was nursing has now been sprayed all over the papers on his desk. "What the fuck! You took her to the Hamptons, and she didn't put out?"

"I swear to God, if you talk about her like that again, I'm not kidding, I will murder you."

His smug chuckle irks me. "You like this girl! She's playing you. It's classic. If she makes you work for it, by the time she finally rides your dick, you're going to think it's the best sex of your life. Tell me you're not that gullible."

"It wasn't like that."

"That's what we all tell ourselves."

"She's a fucking virgin, okay!" My mouth is quicker than my brain. How could I betray her trust like that? "Shit. Don't you dare repeat that to another living soul." I drop my head in my hands, nervously running my fingers through my hair.

Carter and I have been friends since we were born. He knows I'm not messing around. He's serious now. "Okay. No one wants to be *that* kind of asshole. You're taking things slow to respect her. It doesn't explain why you're here getting drunk right now. Something else happened."

His words hang in the air, awaiting my reply. "She Googled me. She fucking Googled me! Yet again, I'm tantamount to a walking bag of cash. I'm sick of being Alexander Rhodes. I wanted to make something of myself. I didn't want to be the punch line for gold diggers." I steal the bottle of Scotch from the desk and swig it straight from the bottle. "What's the point of having all this success, and all this money, if I never have someone to share it with?"

"Stop being such a pussy. So, she Googled you—big fucking deal. What deep dark secrets is she going to find out about you, pretty boy?"

"How about everything there is to know about me and Natalie."

"Fuck her! You don't want to end up like me, do you? Then put on your big girl panties and man the fuck up. You're Xander-fucking-Rhodes. Of course, she knew who you were. Of course, she Googled you. You're an intimidating bastard! You want her? Then prove to her that you're more than a pretty face and a fistful of cash."

"You don't get it."

"Fuck you, man. I may not be as successful as the mighty Xander Rhodes, but I'm doing pretty damn well for myself. You don't think girls fuck me for what they can get? Sure they do. I'm just better at the game than they are. You don't want to play the game, then stop whining about it and win this girl over. Now go home and sleep it off. I'll have someone drop your car off in the morning."

I hate that he's right.

THIS WEEK FELT LIKE THE LONGEST OF MY LIFE. I CAN'T GET LILY OUT of my head. Her laugh, her smile, the way her body felt when I kissed every trembling inch of her skin. I'm haunted by the sweet sound of her moans, as every muscle tightened with orgasm. I don't usually go down on a woman until I know she's serious about me. It's an intimate act, but I couldn't control my desire to taste her, and she tasted so fucking good. I could lick her pussy for hours, just listening to her come, over and over again.

I haven't heard from her, not that I expected to, so I've thrown myself into work. Nothing helps—I can't forget. Maybe Carter's right. If I want her, I need to make it happen.

I'm Xander-fucking-Rhodes.

CHAPTER 8

LILY

I TOSS AND TURN, UNABLE TO GET COMFORTABLE, BUT I NEED TO SLEEP. Finals are this week and I've worked too damn hard to get distracted by a guy now, no matter how gorgeous and sexy and smart and wonderful he is. Damn it! I can't last ten seconds without thinking about him. I haven't slept since I left him on the sidewalk last week. I wanted to explain, but I couldn't find the right words. It's better this way—safer.

When I finally fall asleep, it's fitful at best and the nightmares are back, but this time it isn't my dad dying in my arms. This time the victim is tall, dark, and beautiful, with a stunning stare. I wake up screaming as the sparkle fades from his icy-blue eyes and the life drains from his body…

"No! No! No!"

I come to with Addi shaking me. "Come on, Lil, wake up… It's just a dream, honey… I'm here." She scoops me into her arms as I sob uncontrollably. "Is it the same nightmare about your dad?" I can't breathe, strangled by fear.

"No. Well, yes… but it wasn't my dad… it was… it was Xander." I break down, crying uncontrollably in the arms of my friend, unable to speak for what feels like hours.

"I can't do this, Addi. I need to stay away from him. I couldn't go through that kind of pain again. My dad was everything to me. Losing him broke me, and Xander deserves better. He deserves someone who isn't paralyzed by the fear of losing him."

She pulls me close, stroking my hair. "Lil, you need to let someone in one day, otherwise you'll never be able to truly love with all your heart. It's part of life. The reward of loving someone with every fiber of your being comes with the risk of losing them. If you could go back, you wouldn't want to love your dad any less, would you? He was worthy of your love, honey, and maybe Xander could be, too? Maybe you should call him and explain what happened last week?"

"Can we *not* talk about this? I appreciate what you're trying to say but I just can't deal with it right now. I have finals this week, and I haven't been a hermit for the past four years to throw it away at the final hurdle. I just need to focus on this and stop obsessing over a guy I barely know. I'm fine... really. Don't worry about me."

The look on her face tells me she doesn't believe a word of it, but I don't need her to agree with my decision, I just need her to accept it and let me do what I need to do.

I immerse myself in study, but unfortunately, most classic literature is based on love, whether it's love found or love lost, so it isn't the best distraction in the world. I only have three days until finals, and this is my last chance to excel at Columbia. I've decided to stay away from the library and just lock myself in the apartment. I'm happy with my progress come lunchtime and decide to give myself a break to grab a snack and listen to some music. As I dance around the kitchen to Katy Perry's *Firework* making myself a veggie sub, I'm stopped in my tracks by the buzzer.

A package has arrived, so I tell the doorman to bring it on up. I set the rectangular box on the table. It's black with a white ribbon and a familiar little envelope tucked under the bow. It's from Xander. I carefully untie the ribbon and open the card, my heart hammering in my chest.

I lift the lid and unwrap the tissue paper. Inside is a Monet repro-duction—one of his *Water Lily* oil paintings. It's exquisite. I can't believe he bought this for me. My heart soars at his thoughtfulness, but my head is fighting to focus on my decision to stay away from him. I pick up my phone and sit for the longest time, deciding what say.

> **Me:** Thank you for the Monet reproduction. It's stunning, but you shouldn't have. It's too much. Lily

> **Mr. P:** I'm glad you like it. It's not too much. I miss you.

> **Me:** I don't want you spending money on me.

> **Mr. P:** I'll bear that in mind in future.

> **Me:** There is no future. I messed up.

> **Mr. P:** So, let's talk.

> **Me:** I can't do this. It's safer for you this way.

> **Mr. P:** What do you mean? What's wrong?

> **Me:** Me.

My phone starts ringing. He's calling, but I let it go to voicemail. I know it's a cowardly thing to do but I can't hear his voice right now, it would lower my resolve for self-preservation. It rings another four times before my phone beeps.

> Mr. P: Why aren't you answering your phone? What did you mean by 'safer?'

I put my phone in the kitchen drawer and will myself not to answer him, because I know he would persuade me to change my mind. I hear it beep a few more times and then it stops. I'm relieved and a little sad at the same time. I sit staring at the Monet, contemplating what lies beneath. Xander might like what's on the surface, but if he finds out I was responsible for killing the only man I ever loved, he'll walk away, and I'll be crushed… again.

I don't know how long I sit lost in the memories that plague me, grief and guilt strangling me as if it all happened yesterday. I'm startled by banging on the door. As I stand to answer it, *his* voice comes booming through to me.

"Open the door, Lily." He pounds the door with his fists.

"Go away, Xander." I choke out.

"I'm not going anywhere until you explain to me what the fuck is going on. Unless you want everyone on this floor to witness me kicking your door down, I would suggest you fucking open it… Now." Shit.

I unlock the door and before I can open it fully, he bursts in, slamming the door behind him, his eyes wild and dark. He grabs me by the arms, spins me round and forces me up against the door. His breath is erratic, his face so close to mine I'm assaulted by the scent of him. It's so intoxicating, cologne, clean laundry, and him.

His hard, lean body presses up against me, covered in a black tailored three-piece suit that makes him even more appealing. His eyes are full of emotion, searching mine for answers I don't want to give.

He pins me against the door for what seems like hours, when in reality it could only be seconds, his mouth so close to mine I'm struggling to control the need to feel his lips.

He's on me, claiming me, his lips bruising mine with the intensity of his kiss. He curses under his breath. "Fucking hell." I try to stop him but he's having none of it. "Let me in, Lily… let me in."

He's kissing me with everything he has, and I can't fight it any longer. Parting my lips ever so slightly, his tongue ravaging me.

"You're mine. I want you so bad it hurts. You. Are. Mine. I know you feel it, too. Say it… fucking say it." He kisses me as he speaks.

"Xander. I can't." Tears fall from my cheeks.

He cups my face in his hands, his touch gentle as he kisses my tears away.

"Talk to me, please. I don't understand. I told you I wouldn't be able to walk away, and you let me taste you anyway. You have to tell me what's going on. I know I fucked up, but if you're staying away for my 'safety,' then stop." I crumple to the ground sobbing. He carefully scoops me into his arms.

"Where's your bedroom?"

I can't speak. I just point down the hallway and let him stride toward my room. I give in to the comfort of being in his arms and rest my head on his chest, letting the tears flow. He lays me down on the bed before removing his shoes, jacket, waistcoat, and tie, and climbs onto the bed beside me. He pulls me into his chest and strokes my hair as I cry, not saying a word, just letting me get it all out. Once I manage to compose myself, he speaks in a soft soothing voice.

"Please, talk to me, sweets. I want to help. I want you. I'm sorry I didn't give you a chance to explain last week. I was being an asshole. I'm so sorry." I know I have to tell him the truth, and I know he'll leave when I do, so I take a moment to hold him, memorizing his scent before I lose him for good.

"We can't be together. I don't want you to get hurt. That's what will happen if you get too close to me. I've already hurt you."

"That was my fault. I was scared."

"Let me get this out… while I have the courage to do it. I told you my dad died when I was fifteen, but what I left out… is that I killed him." His face freezes in shock, his body tense beneath me. I continue before I lose my nerve.

"It was Friday night and my parents wanted to have a family game night with me and my sisters. I was fifteen. I thought it was lame and I wanted to go to the cinema with my friends. My dad and I were close, so I knew he'd let me go if I asked him. He said it was fine as long as I called him to come get me, so we arranged for him to pick me up outside the theater in town at 10:30 p.m. I was the last one waiting outside at around 10:20 p.m."

I close my eyes, the memories flooding my mind.

"There was a guy standing across the street in the bus shelter, but I didn't think anything of it at the time. I started texting one of my friends and didn't realize when he wasn't there anymore. Before I knew what was happening, he was grabbing me, forcing me down into the alley. I punched and kicked as hard as I could, but he was too strong. He shoved me to the ground, and I hit my head. I remember the smell from the trashcans was foul. I still smell them in my nightmares. My head was swimming as I tried to struggle against him, but it wasn't doing any good. He was just getting angrier."

My voice begins to shake, my eyes misting with tears.

"He started hitting me and grabbing at my clothes. I remember thinking he was going to ruin my favorite shirt. How dumb is that? He had this disgusting look on his face, I could tell he was enjoying it. I tried to memorize his features in case I made it out alive so I could identify him. He had this nasty scar running from his eyebrow down to his chin on the left side. It was really jagged and red. He had tattoos all over his arms and neck, and I noticed one in particular, an animal skull with a dagger through it. He ripped my shirt off to get to my bra, then he was trying to get my jeans off. That's when I heard my dad shouting behind him."

I take a moment, the memory of my dad's voice booming in my ears.

"He grabbed the guy off me, throwing him into the trashcans, the noise deafening as they started fighting. He was shouting at me to get to the car and call for help. I scrambled to my feet and ran as fast as I could. I put in the call to 911, but I could barely choke out our location, and as I disconnected the call, I heard the most terrifying noise rip from my dad's throat. I will never forget that sound. It haunts me.

I ran back toward him, and the guy ran off shouting and swearing, calling me a dirty whore. When I reached my dad, I realized what had happened. That animal had stabbed him in the stomach. I tried to stop the bleeding until the police arrived. They called for an ambulance as I sat with him cradled in my arms, trying to stem the flow of blood. My dad was asking if I was okay. Even then... as he lay dying in the street, he was thinking of me."

I wipe the tears from my eyes.

"The ambulance arrived and three EMTs tried frantically to save him. They were shouting things I didn't understand and grabbing stuff from their bags. I moved round to let him rest his head on my legs, so he wasn't on the cold, dirty ground. I looked in his eyes as he took his last breath. It was the worst moment of my life. They caught the guy who did it and I was able to identify him. He was sent to prison for assault, attempted rape, and the murder of my father."

I stand, pacing the floor, letting Xander process everything I've just told him.

"It was my fault. I played on the fact that my dad and I were close, so he'd let me get my way. We never should have been there that night, and if I had stayed in, my dad would still be here. He was my... everything. I loved him more than anything in the world."

Tears stream down my cheeks.

"I've had nightmares ever since. After spending the night with you, and knowing I hurt you—I had the same dream, except this time, it wasn't my dad lying in my arms dying... it was you. Don't you see? I vowed I would never let anyone in like that again. I don't want to love someone so much that I live in fear of losing them. I would never forgive myself if something happened to you because of me. That's why it's best for you to walk away now."

He moves toward me tentatively, reaching out to envelop me in his arms. I'm so drained. I can't fight him. I don't *want* to fight him. He presses a gentle kiss on my forehead.

"I'm so sorry you had to live through that. I'm sorry you lost the most important man in your life. No one should have to deal with that, especially not at such a young age, but you need to listen to me right now. You. Are. Not. To. Blame. It wasn't your fault. It was the scumbag who attacked you, it was his fault that your dad had to protect you. It was his fault, he stabbed your dad. Lily, look at me." I gaze into his eyes, full of tenderness, glassy with unshed tears.

"Your dad loved you, and he would have done anything to keep you safe. Dying to save your daughter from a monster is something every good father would do. You have to forgive yourself. You deserve to be loved, and you can't live in fear that it will be taken away from you. No one knows how long we have in life, but you have to make the most of it. You *lived*, Lily. Now you must *live* your life. It's what your dad would want."

I can hear wailing, but it takes me a minute to realize that it's coming from my chest.

"Shh. I'm here and I'm not going anywhere. Don't you understand that from the moment I met you, I didn't have a choice anymore? You're mine, baby. Mine to cherish, mine to protect. I can't walk away because I'm already in too deep. That's what I wanted to tell you today. Let me cherish you."

We stay wrapped in each other's arms for hours, and when I've cried so many tears that my eyes hurt, I drift into an exhausted sleep.

WHEN I WAKE UP, XANDER'S GONE. I'M BEGINNING TO PANIC UNTIL I hear voices in the lounge. He's talking to Addi. He's still here, he didn't leave. I open the door to my room as quietly as possible, hoping they won't hear me. I know it's bad to eavesdrop, especially when he's been so understanding of everything I told him, but I need to hear what they're saying.

"I can't believe she's been carrying this around all this time, blaming herself."

"I can't believe she told you. She's never opened up to someone like that. Her family and me... we're the only people who knew what happened, until now. It was a massive deal for her to confide in you, so you better treat her right or I will hunt you down and castrate you. Got it?"

"You have nothing to worry about. I'm crazy about her. I stayed away because I was scared she didn't feel the same way. I would never intentionally hurt her, and I'll be around for as long as she'll have me. I just wish I could take all the bad stuff away for her. It kills me to see her like this."

He's crazy about me? For as long as I'll have him? How about forever? That would work for me.

I find myself welling up listening to him, and I can't stay away any longer. I make sure they hear me as I walk down the hallway, both of them turning to greet me.

"Hey, sleepy girl. How are you feeling?" He pulls me down into his lap, wrapping his arms around me.

"I feel a lot better. I'm sorry about earlier, I was a complete mess. I didn't mean to sleep so long either."

"Don't apologize, sweets. I'm glad you told me, and I'm happy to be here with you." He strokes my hair as his voice washes over me, so warm and peaceful. "I was thinking... maybe I could stay here with you tonight... if you want?" There's an endearing vulnerability in his tone.

"I would really like that, thank you, but, what about fresh clothes and work tomorrow?"

"I'll get David to drop by some of my things, and don't worry about work. That's the beauty of being the boss." A sly grin spreads across his face.

"Okay. Thank you. Do you want some dinner? I can rustle something up."

"How about I get David to drop in some Thai food for the three of us?"

Addi pipes in. "Sounds like a plan, Billionaire Boy. You paying?"

There's a look of amusement on Xander's face, as he takes her teasing in his stride. "Of course."

David arrives thirty minutes later with an overnight bag and our dinner. It's nice hanging out with Addi and Xander, chatting and laughing together, Addi telling stories about when we were younger. It's relaxed and comforting after an exhausting day, as if the past week never happened, Xander and I falling into a comfortable rhythm.

By ten o'clock, I can barely keep my eyes open. Xander offers to sleep on the couch, but I shoot that idea down in two seconds flat. I'm going to savor every minute of him in my apartment and in my bed. I hold out my hand, which he eagerly grasps, and I lead him down the hall to my room in silence.

Just holding his hand sparks electricity between us, a palpable energy in the room that consumes me. I'm oblivious to anything except *him*.

I'm rudely snapped from my daze by Addi yelling down the hall. "What am I, chopped liver? Don't I get a goodnight?" She's so funny.

"Goodnight, Addi. Love you."

As she walks down the hall, she peeks her head around the door.

"Love you, too, Lilliput." She thinks she's hilarious, and I can hear Xander chuckling in the bathroom. He better not start calling me that.

My breath catches in my throat when he emerges from the bathroom in only his Calvin Klein boxer shorts. I will never get used to the sight of his chiseled body. I swear I could stare at his chest and happy trail for days and not get bored.

"See something you like, sweets?" He says teasingly.

I know I'm blushing, so I quickly grab my PJs and slink into the bathroom. When I emerge in plaid sleep shorts and a red t-shirt, I'm met with the sight of Xander tucked up in my bed, having turned down my side to welcome me in. I scurry over and climb in. He pulls me close, nestling me into his chest. We fit together perfectly, like we were made for each other. I know that's corny, but what can I say? I'm a lost cause. He strokes my hair, kissing the top of my head as we lie here, content to just... be.

"Get some sleep. I'll take advantage of you in those cute shorts in the morning when I peel them off you in the shower." With that delectable promise hanging in the air between us, I drift into a wonderful dreamless sleep, peaceful in the cocoon of his arms.

CHAPTER 9

LILY

Xander makes good on his promise the next morning, and it's eleven o'clock by the time we shower and sit down to breakfast. We must have taken almost an hour and a half to get washed and dressed with his roaming hands and my unquenchable thirst for him.

I'm in no rush to get on with my day because I know I won't see Xander until after finals on Friday night.

I've organized to go out that night with friends to celebrate the end of exams, so I convince Xander to meet us after work for drinks, which he agrees to on the condition that he can organize a private celebration for me at the weekend. I'm not going to say no to seeing him on Friday night, and at the weekend! I'm excited and it's great to have something to look forward to, but we still need to talk about what happened when we left the Hamptons.

Xander leaves for work at around one o'clock, giving me a heart-stopping, ruin me for anyone else kiss, to get me through until Friday night. When I close the door, my apartment feels empty without him. Later in the day, I receive a gorgeous bouquet of pink roses with a card attached.

Thank you for giving me a second chance.
Xander

ALEXANDER RHODES

I'm in a good mood, and I get so much studying done before going to bed, snuggling into the pillow that still smells of Xander. He calls me just before I fall asleep. it's a great way to end the day, listening to his smooth, enticing voice. He could say anything and it would sound amazing coming from his lips.

Every morning I wake to a text telling me how much he missed the feel of me lying in his arms the night before. And every day I receive a different color of roses with a card attached. Wednesday's card reads:

Thinking of you, sweets. I'm jealous of your books today.
Xander x

ALEXANDER RHODES

We text throughout the day and speak before going to sleep. I don't like admitting it, but I'm really missing him.

Thursday is the beginning of finals and at 8 a.m. the buzzer goes off. There is a package. I thought it would be flowers but it's a box, with a card inside.

Good luck today. I know you'll be amazing.

Xander x

ALEXANDER RHODES

Inside is a bouquet of HB pencils and they're too cute for words. There are all kinds of stationery in a box marked 'Exam Survival Kit,' and at the bottom there's a small box marked 'Good Luck Charm.' I open it to find a Tiffany & Co pouch.

My hands shake as I untie the ribbon. Nestled inside is a stunning silver charm bracelet with a single charm attached—a four leaf clover. I must have the most ridiculous smile on my face as I clip it around my wrist. A reminder of Xander wherever I go. I text him immediately to say thank you.

> Me: Your package was so thoughtful, I love everything. Thank you so much. I will be taking my survival kit today and I'm already wearing the bracelet. It's beautiful. You really shouldn't have.

> Mr. P: You're more than welcome, sweets. You won't need luck today, but I like the idea of you wearing something from me while you ace your finals. Call me when you're finished. Xander x

Before I leave for campus, my daily bouquet of roses arrives— yellow. Thursday's card reads:

Could he be any sweeter?

After I finish for the day, I grab some dinner with Addi and head back to the apartment. I call Xander, and we talk for hours. He listens patiently as I drone on about my exam, and just laughs when I go on and on about how much I love the bracelet and my exam kit. I put the bouquet of pencils on my desk because I don't want to use them. This gets me no end of teasing. We say goodnight and I prepare for my last exam on Friday.

FRIDAY MORNING IS FINALLY HERE. TODAY IS THE DAY I FINISH FOUR years of hard work at Columbia, but I have to be honest, my excitement this morning is more to do with the fact that I'll be seeing Xander tonight. The butterflies have taken flight in the pit of my stomach once again. I'll be counting down the hours today.

Another package arrives this morning. A large Saks bag. This time the card reads:

I hope you'll be wearing this when I see you
tonight.

Xander x

ALEXANDER RHODES

Inside is an amazing Dolce & Gabbana dress—a short teal sleeveless lace shift. There's also a Manolo Blahnik shoebox, which contains a pair of peach patent leather sandals with a giant buckle round the ankle. I may have died and gone to heaven.

There's a Prada clutch in the same peach color at the bottom of the bag, wrapped in its own Prada cloth tote. The whole outfit is spectacular. I wave of guilt washes over me, uncomfortable at the thought of how much all this cost, but I can't wait to wear it for Xander. There's one more bag I haven't opened. It's from Victoria's Secret. Inside is some seriously sexy lingerie. I have to press my thighs together to contain the ache that swells at the thought of Xander's gaze on me wearing this. A gorgeous teal satin balconette bra with matching thong. Of course, they're the right size. Did he go through my drawers when I was sleeping on Monday? I call to thank him and he's as gracious as always.

As I get ready for my last final, it dawns on me just how momentous this day is. I will no longer be a student at Columbia, I will be going out into the big bad world and carving a path for myself. Hopefully a path that will include Xander. Before I leave for campus my daily roses arrive, white with crystals woven through them, and a card that reads:

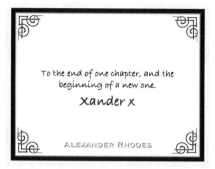

To the end of one chapter, and the
beginning of a new one.

Xander x

ALEXANDER RHODES

It amazes me that he seems to read my mind from miles away. I send him a quick text before I have to leave.

> Me: You read my mind. L x

Mr. P: I wish that were true, sweets. See you tonight x

I'm more than ready to close this chapter and embark on the next.

CHAPTER 10

LILY

THE ELATION THAT COURSES THROUGH ME AS I LEAVE THE EXAM HALL IS palpable. I did it. I made it through four years of hard work and dedication. I am ready to party! Addi's last final is today so I decide to wait in the student bar.

The look on her face as she walks toward me is beyond happy. We start jumping up and down like idiots, chanting, "We did it." Unleashing the crazy. Our friends aren't surprised by this kind of behavior, they've grown accustomed to it over the years. There has been a weight lifted from our shoulders, and the excitement for what comes next is in the air. Once we agree on a time and place to celebrate, I send the details to Xander so he can meet us there. He says he has a late meeting but should only be an hour late.

FOR THE FIRST TIME IN MY LIFE I FEEL TRULY BEAUTIFUL. THE OUTFIT Xander sent me looks fabulous, even down to the underwear. The only jewelry I wear is my Tiffany bracelet. My styling wand has transformed my unruly hair. It hangs down my back in soft golden curls that complement my outfit nicely. I've gone with smoky makeup with a touch of teal glitter on my eyelids, and it really makes them stand out.

When Addi sees me, she starts wolf whistling. "Damn, girl. You look H-O-T tonight. Xander is going to have a heart attack when he sees you. Or he could die of a perpetual boner!"

She looks stunning tonight with a barely-there black dress, the back of which is non-existent, ending so low down you can see the cute little dimples above her ass. "Looking foxy yourself, Addi. Ready to paint the town red?"

She interlinks our arms and grabs the keys to our apartment. "Hell yes, friend... hell-to-the-yes!"

We arrive at a great bar called Blue at around 7.30 p.m. to find the party in full swing. I guess our friends started early.

"You guys look phenomenal tonight." Our friend Matilda says, giving us a joint hug.

"Thanks. We're ready to party. Buy a girl a drink?" Addi is such a flirt—doesn't matter if it's a man or woman. If she knows they're attracted to her, she starts flirting. Matty has always been open about her sexuality, and Addi enjoys the attention.

"How could I refuse two beautiful women? French Martinis?" Everyone knows our poison of choice, especially when we're out to have an epic night.

As Matty makes her way to the bar, we join the rest of our group. There are about ten of us who finished up today and we're all ready to party. I think we have a bit of catching up to do with the drinking. I'm pretty sure most of our friends are already feeling the buzz.

The music is loud, the atmosphere charged in a way that you only find in Manhattan on a Friday night. This city sweeps you off your feet and all you can do is go along for the ride. I love it. There's nowhere else on Earth like it.

Matty returns with our drinks and parks herself next to us, reminiscing about our time at Columbia, laughing at some of the crazy nights we've had together. Addi is really laying the charm on thick with her tonight. I feel bad—she doesn't stand a chance. Addi will have her buying drinks all night then wave goodbye as she heads home with a guy. She loves cock too much! I lose track of her after a while, struggling to maintain a conversation with Matty above the noise in the bar. I lean in closer to hear what she's trying to say when I feel a warm hand on my shoulder. I know from the jolt of electricity coursing through my body that Xander is behind me. Even without seeing him, my body responds.

When I see the look on Matty's face I'm not sure I want to look into the icy-blue depths of his eyes. She looks scared. Tension emanates from him in waves as his mouth finds my ear, his voice edgy. "Hello. Aren't you going to introduce me to your *friend*?" I feel the whisper of a kiss on my cheek before he stands tall, his shoulders broad, extending his hand to Matty.

"Matilda, this is Xander. He's…" I don't really know what we are. It's not something we've spoken about, and I don't want to assume anything.

Xander jumps on my hesitation. "I'm her boyfriend. And you are?" Matty shakes his hand and introduces herself.

He snakes his arm around my waist, pulling me to his side, the heat in his eyes evident as he rakes his gaze over my outfit. Lowering his head down closer to mine, his sexy voice caresses my cheek. "You look astonishingly beautiful tonight, Miss Tate." Lifting my chin with his fingers he presses his lips to mine igniting a fire inside me that's been burning for days in his absence.

Everything around us fades into the background as our kiss becomes more passionate, his tongue teasing the crease of my lips to open, and I can't deny him, I don't want to. I part my lips and dart my tongue out to meet his, crashing into each other, hungry for a taste of what we've been deprived of. God, this man can kiss. I swear I can feel it down to my toes, his tongue tangling with mine in an exploration of our fierce attraction to one another. Xander pulls back before I do, holding my face in his hands.

"We need to stop now. I don't want your first time to be in a crowded bar, and if we keep kissing like this, I might not be able to convince myself to do the right thing."

I'm embarrassed to realize that I completely forgot Matty was standing next to me, looking dumbfounded by our combustible display. Xander has a cocky grin on his face, and I know—that kiss was tantamount to him pissing all over me. But let's face it, I loved every second of it. Women love a little caveman behavior, even if they don't admit it. It's sexy as hell. What I don't understand is why he's acting this way over one of my girlfriends. She makes her excuses and scurries off to chat with some other friends.

Xander pulls me into his arms, his masculine smell enveloping me —a delight to my senses. "How's my girl doing?" His fingers caress my cheek as he speaks.

"I'm better now that you're here. I missed you this week. Thank you so much for all the flowers and gifts, it was so thoughtful of you, but you shouldn't spend your money on me."

He holds up my wrist in his hand, inspecting the Tiffany bracelet he gave me.

"This suits your tiny wrist, sweets. But it's missing something." He dips his hand into his suit jacket pocket and produces a small Tiffany box.

"You can't keep buying me things."

Rolling his eyes, he places it in my palm and says, "Open it." A sweet smile forming on his beautiful, kiss swollen lips. Inside is an exquisite butterfly charm.

"It's gorgeous. Thank you. Could you put it on for me?"

As he attaches the charm he whispers in my ear. "For my beautiful girl who is about to spread her wings and fly."

My eyes well with tears, but before they escape, Xander's lips capture mine, giving me the softest, sweetest kiss. Pulling back, he pins me with his gaze.

"I hope I'm part of your next chapter." I'm lost for words. I just stand there dumbstruck and nod my head, my eyes unable to leave his blue depths.

Addi is at my side, and I hadn't even registered her. "Hey, dill weed. Let's get the drinking on the go and decide where we're going to hit next. I'm ready for some dancing."

Xander chimes in before I have a chance to speak. "A friend of mine owns Cube. How about I give him a call and get him to put us on the list? I can have him rope off an area for us. All of your friends are welcome, obviously."

I don't want to put him out, but Addi has other ideas.

"Get on that this minute, my good man. I love that place. I'll go tell everyone the plan."

"You don't have to do this for my friends. I don't want to put you in a bad position with your friend."

"Firstly, you're not putting me in any 'position,' as delightful as that sounds. I offered. My friend won't mind. Besides, I own the building. Secondly, I'm not doing it for your friends, I'm doing it for you, because I want you to have a great night celebrating an amazing achievement. Plus, I might be able to back you into a dark corner in there and have you all to myself for five minutes. My motives are purely selfish." He says winking at me. I don't believe that for a second.

He ducks out for a few minutes to make the call and when he walks back into the bar, I'm entranced by the full effect of him commanding the room. He's tall, broad, and lean in his charcoal suit. You can tell it's been tailored to his perfect body. His jacket is open showing a black fitted shirt, the top two buttons undone, a hint of chest hair peeking out. His dark clothing perfectly complements his complexion, his hair looking like he's just been fucked in the best possible way. But his eyes are the killer feature that grab you, shake you, and leave you breathless. Such a stark contrast to his dark hair, his eyes are pools of icy blue, sparkling with sex and mischief and a confidence that makes me weak at the knees. He's grinning as he makes his way to me.

"Keep looking at me like that and we'll never make it to the club." He knows exactly what he does to me, and I have no way of hiding the blush rising on my cheeks. I drop my gaze to the floor. "Don't be shy. I love that I can see how I affect you." He wraps his arms around my waist. "Would you like another drink while we wait?"

"We can just get a cab with everyone else. Don't go to any trouble for me."

"Or… everyone can just come with us." He's arranged for David to bring a limo so that I can travel with all my friends. I quickly shut down the swell of emotion threatening to overflow. It's too soon— definitely, too soon.

Thirty minutes later we're all bundling into the limo, Xander holding me close the entire time. I don't find it overbearing or proprietary… I find it… comforting. I usually feel like a fish out of water at the best of times, even around my friends. It scares me that I have such a sense of peace and belonging when I'm in his company. I'm enjoying my friends *more* because I'm more confident in myself. There's a niggling worry in the back of my mind that my confidence will be completely shattered into a million pieces, along with my heart when this ends—because *everything* ends.

When we reach the club, the queue to get in is around the block. Xander grabs my hand and pulls me toward the door. The guys on the door seem familiar with him, opening the rope to let us in, bypassing the line of eager clubbers. It never gets old seeing him so confident and commanding. He leads us through the crowds, parting the sea of sweaty, writhing dancers, to a staircase and up to the VIP lounge.

His friend has cordoned off half of the lounge for our party. It is the most luxurious club. There are plush purple velvet sofas and armchairs around the room, elegant glass tables, soft sensual lighting and walls covered in sumptuous deep purple damask. The bar in the VIP area is small, but sleek and modern with a bartender who could grace the cover of any magazine. Addi will have something to say about him. I've never been in a VIP lounge, and my earlier worries resurface.

Xander and I live in different worlds. He fits in perfectly here, surrounded by luxury. I quickly quash my insecurities with a shot of tequila and decide to enjoy tonight—there are no guarantees in life. Why waste the time I have with him right now?

"If you're going to do shots, you need to do them properly."

He speaks to the bartender and two minutes later there are two shots of tequila, two lime wedges and a saltshaker in front of us. He licks the back of his hand and sprinkles salt over it. Just the sight of his tongue has me pressing my legs together. He holds his hand out to me.

"Lick."

Every muscle in my body clenches into a tight ball in my stomach. With my eyes fixed on his, I lick my lips and lower my tongue to his hand. It's intensely erotic licking the salt from his strong, hard hand. I can see the fire burning in his eyes as he watches me, and I love that I affect him.

As I down the shot, Xander picks up the lime wedge and places it between his teeth. With a sly, sexy grin playing at the edges of his mouth, he lowers his face to mine. My heart is going to burst from my chest it's beating so fast. I slowly suck the lime while he holds it in his mouth, desperate to devour him, but he has other ideas. He's enjoying teasing me and grabs my hand holding it to my lips.

"Lick."

I do as he asks, watching in a haze of desire as he covers the back of my hand with salt, heady with anticipation of what comes next. The thrill that runs through my body as his tongue connects with my hand is exhilarating—a fire chasing the burn of tequila starting to take effect. I'm mesmerized as he downs his shot and holds the lime for me to take between my teeth.

I struggle to calm the storm inside that's causing my breath to hitch as his thumb caresses my lip. His rough palms hold my face still as he leans in, keeping his eyes on mine, daring me not to close them. His lips brush lightly against me as he takes the lime into his mouth and sucks the juice from it. I think if he wasn't holding my face, I would drop to the floor in a pool of raging hormones. Shots have never been so sexual. He pulls the wedge from my teeth and discards it on the bar before devouring my mouth with a passion so fierce I think I just forgot my own name.

His hands slide from my face, through my hair and down my body until they settle at the base of my back, his fingertips caressing the top of my ass. I get lost in the dance our tongues are performing, running my hands through his hair to bring him closer still, the taste of him intoxicating.

"Mmm, I like the way you do shots, Mr. Rhodes." I murmur into his mouth.

"I like it when you call me Mr. Rhodes." Pressing his pelvis against me, I'm acutely aware of what it does to him. He rests his forehead on mine, breathing deep and even.

"Okay, when my... problem subsides, I'm going to get us some proper drinks. Usual for you?" He doesn't wait for an answer. I'm so predictable! With a kiss to the tip of my nose he orders drinks, and almost immediately, I feel a hand grasp my arm and drag me in the direction of the dance floor downstairs.

"Come on, Lilliput. Let's show them what we've got." Addi says pulling me behind her.

I glance in the direction of the bar and sure enough Xander is tracking my every move. I give him my best 'I have no choice in the matter' face and a massive grin before heading down the stairs.

It feels amazing to let loose and move with the beat. The DJ is on fire and the dance floor feels like a living, breathing entity, everyone moving separately but together, lost in the music. With my best friend next to me we begin to dance. The energy of the crowd is tangible as the music courses through my veins. I suddenly feel a shudder run through me and I know he's watching. I glance up to the balcony to see Xander staring at me like he is the hunter, and I am his prey. The hunger in his eyes makes me feel sexy. I start to move just for him, holding his stare as I sway my hips to the music, running my hands over of my body, my feet moving effortlessly in this small space.

Addi and I start to move, our bodies well practiced together on the dance floor. As she steps behind me, I slink down her body, my hands moving up and down her sides, my eyes fixed on Xander as I wet my lips with my tongue. The look in his eyes is primal, running his hands through his hair as if he's going to pull it out. Biting his bottom lip, I can see the rise and fall of his chest as his breath quickens. It's intoxicating watching him react to my body.

I close my eyes and keep dancing, my arousal growing at the thought of him watching me. I'm feeling a buzz from the tequila and as song after song fills the air around me, my inhibitions fade. It's liberating and my mind starts to drift to thoughts of letting Xander make love to me, giving him every part of myself.

I feel Addi's hands sliding to grip my hips as I move. I let my head drop back, resting against her shoulder to steady myself. I feel breath on my ear. "You are hot as fuck tonight."

What the hell? I'm yanked from my drinking haze. My eyes fly open and I see Xander standing at the balcony, a murderous look on his face. His fists are clenched at his sides as he takes to the stairs. I whip round and push myself away from the body behind me... Matty.

"What the hell, Matilda? What are you doing?" I shove her aside to put some distance between us.

"Oh, come on, Lily. You know I like you. You can't tell me you were dancing like that for no reason. You want some attention, and I will *happily* give you it." Her speech is slightly slurred as she grabs me round the waist, grinding against me.

"You're drunk, Matty. Let go of me. We're friends, nothing else. You know that. Besides, I thought you liked Addi." I struggle against her, but I can't break free.

"She's okay for a tumble once or twice, but *you*... I could fuck you in ways you can't even imagine, and never tire of your sweet, innocent little cunt. Come on, Lil', we'd be so good together. I can please you in ways that no *man* every could." I'm getting angry now.

"NO! Let me go." Matty's grip loosens just enough for me to break free.

"I suggest you stay the fuck away from her." I'm scared by the terrifying tone in Xander's voice. I know he would never hit a woman, but his anger is tangible.

Matilda is obviously too drunk to care. "Fuck you. I've known her for years. You've known her what, all of five minutes?" She says, reaching for me.

Before she gets a hold on my arm, Xander alerts the female club security. "Is everything okay, Mr. Rhodes?" one of them asks, her gaze fixed on Matty.

"Yeah, thanks, Jen. She was harassing my girl. Drunk and doesn't know when to quit. She needs a safe ride home to sleep it off." He sounds calm, but his body language is tense.

"We'll make sure of it, Mr. Rhodes. If you would like to return to the VIP area, the boss will be with you in five." Xander grabs my hand and moves through the crowd and up the stairs so fast I'm practically running to keep up. Not easy in Manolos.

"You didn't have to make her leave. She's my friend."

He doesn't stop when we get to the lounge, continuing past the bar and over to the corner, to a door I didn't notice earlier. Without a word, we're in a small private room and the door is locked behind me. He's pacing in front of me as I lean back against the door.

"Jesus Christ, Lily! I have never felt this angry in my fucking life. I don't like feeling murderous towards a woman!" He strides over to me, his eyes wild, his hands pressing to the door at either side of my head. "Do you want her? Tell me. Is there something more than friendship between you? The way you were dancing with her… I can't contend with a woman if that's what you need to be satisfied."

I just stare at him. I can't believe he's even asking this question. I thought he knew how deeply he affects me. "You need to answer me. I'm going fucking crazy here."

Before I know what I'm saying, the words fall from my lips. "I'm yours. Only yours. You're all I want." His whole body slams against me, his lips capturing mine, bruising them with the ferocity of his kiss.

"Fuck. Lily…" He punctuates my name with a hard kiss. "I couldn't fucking stand seeing her hands on you. I want to kiss you everywhere her hands were, to make you mine."

I can barely contain my desire. "Do it. Kiss me all over." Eliciting a groan from deep within his chest, our kiss reaches fever pitch, our hands grabbing at each other.

I push his suit jacket off his shoulders and claw at the buttons of his shirt, desperate to touch the skin underneath. As I move to undo his fly, his lips start roaming over my neck, nipping at my ear, nibbling my shoulder. I hear his sharp intake of breath as I take his hard length in my hand, rubbing my thumb back and forth over the tip before gripping his impressive girth, slowly moving up and down the length of him.

"Oh, God. That feels so fucking good."

His strong hands move to cup my breasts, kneading them, squeezing them.

"Take me, Xander. I can't wait any longer." My voice is dripping with need, desperate to feel him inside me. He moves my hand, pinning it above my head.

His voice is a breathy whisper. "Not like this, sweets. Not here. Not now. You deserve better." I drop my gaze to the floor, the crushing rejection heavy in my chest. I just offered myself on a platter and he doesn't want me. "Baby, look at me." I can't. "What's wrong?" I'm embarrassed.

"I get it. If you don't want to it's fine." I try in vain to pull my hands free from his vice like grip.

"What the fuck? Of course, I want to! Look at me... feel me." He pulls my hands back down to his cock. "Does this feel like I don't want you? Tell me, Lily. What does this feel like to you?"

Like velvet-covered steel... and I love it, but I'm too embarrassed to answer. He grabs my chin forcing me to look at him.

"I have never wanted someone as much as I want you. I physically ache, but I don't want it to happen like this. I want you in my bed. I want to take my time, I want to savor every sweet inch of your sexy little body." He kisses me in a sensual slow dance.

"It's going to happen... soon. But for now, just let me make you feel good." His hands move down to the hem of my dress, pulling it up to reveal my satin thong. "Fuck me. These look amazing on you, it's almost a shame they have to come off." He slides his fingers underneath the satin strips and pulls them, lowering to his knees, his eyes fixed on mine with a look of pure sin. I step out of my panties and watch as he scrunches them into a ball and puts them in the pocket of his pants.

"Lean back against the door and lift your leg up onto my shoulder." I do as he asks, opening myself to him. His hands cup my ass, pulling my pussy to his mouth. "God... you taste so sweet, I could do this all night." The vibration of his words against my skin sends a direct current straight to my core.

I hear the sounds of the club outside, the thumping beat and the crowds of people, but none of that matters. There's only us—me, Xander, and the intense sensation his tongue creates on my clit. He sucks and flicks the hub of all my pleasure, swirling his mouth round and tracing what feels like intricate patterns over my flesh. He slides a hand from my ass and slips one finger inside me. "You're so fucking wet for me." Then there are two. "Fuck… so… tight." He's moaning as he laps at my folds, finger-fucking me to the same rhythm.

It's sublime, and as my orgasm detonates from deep within, he sucks my clit into his mouth, massaging it with his tongue, letting me ride it out on his face. I'm screaming his name, my hands in his hair holding him in place as I fuck his mouth. Every inch of my body is on fire, desperate for more of him. I need him inside me, but I know he won't give in.

"You are so fucking beautiful when you come. It's incredible." He fixes my dress but doesn't give back my panties.

"Did you forget to give me something?" I say with a grin.

"Afraid not. These are mine now," he says, patting the pocket he put my panties in. Knowing that he has them and is going to make me walk out into the club in my short dress, drenched and naked, makes the throbbing between my legs return.

I decide it's time to pleasure him when I notice a sofa in the corner of the room. "Take a seat." I back him toward it, my hands on his bare chest. His shirt is open from earlier so it's easy to pull it down his arms and drop it to the floor.

"That's much better, Mr. Rhodes." I can see that my choice of words excites him. When he reaches the sofa, he stops moving and I push him until he sits down. "Put your hands along the back of the sofa."

He does as I ask, a panty-dropping smile on his face—if I was wearing any.

"What do you have planned for me, Miss Tate?"

I hold his gaze as I lean over him brushing my lips over his ear before whispering. "I'm going to fuck you with my mouth." I pull back to look into his eyes. He looks like he's about to lose control, his erection straining against his suit pants.

I run my hands down his washboard abs, pulling at the waistband of his boxers. He lifts his hips slightly to let me move his pants and boxers low enough for his rock-hard cock to spring free. God, he is beautiful. I run my hands over the length of him, caressing him. He watches intently as I kneel between his legs, moving close enough for him to feel my breath without touching him.

His breathing becomes labored, the rise and fall of his chest a sign of how I affect him.

I plunge him into my mouth, taking as much of him as I can. Fisting my hand around his thick base. "Your mouth feels so fucking good."

I can see his hands curl tight around the back of the sofa from the corner of my eye. I sweep my hair to one side so he can watch me, looking up at him through my hooded gaze, the look on his face spurring me on. He tastes so good. I can't get enough.

I quicken my pace, swirling my tongue over the tip on every up stroke, moaning with desire as I lap the small drops of pre-come from his engorged head. A groan bursts from his chest and his hands fly to my hair, fisting handfuls of it, pulling me down onto him until he hits the back of my throat. Relaxing so I don't gag at the size of him, I let him set his own rhythm, using my mouth however he wants it.

He's thrusting hard and fast as he shouts my name, over and over. I feel the pulsing of his orgasm ripple down the length of him before a hot burst of come shoots down my throat. As his grip softens, I milk the rest of his orgasm, taking every last drop. His head slumps back onto the sofa as he regains his composure.

I lick my lips and move to sit next to him. "Was that to your liking, Mr. Rhodes?"

"Holy Fuck, that should be illegal. You are incredible. I can't wait to be inside you." He pulls me down onto his chest, stroking my hair and cuddling me close. We sit blissfully content for a while before he puts his shirt and jacket back on. It... is... bliss. I could stay here all night.

Looking far from innocent, I'm sure, Xander unlocks the door, and we head back out into the VIP lounge to find our friends. I'm surprised to find Addi sitting looking very cozy with his friend.

"Is that Carter with Addi?"

"Yes. He owns this club. He arranged all of this." I wonder how she felt when she saw him. I bet she never called him back after their wild night last weekend. When I catch her eye, she waves us over with a huge grin on her face.

"You didn't tell me this was the friend you were talking about *Xander.*" She says accusingly.

"I thought you already knew, I mean, you guys have slept together, right?" Addi turns crimson, leaning into Carter for comfort.

"Shut up, man. You're ruining my chances at an encore here."

Xander throws his head back and laughs. "Tell you what, why don't I get us all a round of drinks and we can catch up." He kisses me on the cheek and heads off to the bar.

Addi pulls me down next to her. "Lilliput, you totally have sex hair and a glow that only comes from a great orgasm. What the fuck? Where have you been?" It's my turn to blush.

I lean in so Carter won't hear. "There's a private room in the corner. He dragged me in there and... well... apparently my face and *hair* tell you the rest."

She's doubled over laughing. "Oh my God. You really do go from zero to a hundred. Good for you."

We both have a good giggle before Xander returns with the drinks. The four of us have a great night—we drink, we talk, we dance into the early hours. Xander on the dance floor is a sight to be seen, the man has moves. I'm wet just watching him, and when he pulls me close and starts moving our bodies as one, I think I'm going to pass out from the electricity sparking between us—around us.

I lose track of everyone else over the course of the evening, but we have such a fabulous time it doesn't really matter. We stay until the club closes and the four of us go back to our apartment. As the car pulls up in front of the apartment, I'm exhausted, and a little drunk, my body refusing to correspond to my commands. Xander jumps out first to help me out of the car, but I struggle to keep myself upright, the street spinning a little as I stand up. He drapes his jacket over my shoulders and lifts me into his arms. I'm not cold, but I realize he's trying to cover the fact that I'm not wearing any panties because of him! I don't want to give Addi and Carter an eyeful.

I snuggle into his chest and fall asleep on the way up to the apartment. He takes us straight to my room and I wake up as he lays me on the bed. He disappears out into the hallway and returns two minutes later with a tall glass of water and two aspirin. "Here, take these and drink all of this." As I swallow them, he strips down to his boxers, before finding some PJs for me. He carefully undresses me, obviously rethinking the PJs as he discards them on the floor. "I like you naked." He crawls in next me, caressing my cheek. "Get some sleep, sweets."

CHAPTER 11

LILY

WHEN I WAKE ON SATURDAY MORNING, OR SHOULD I SAY AFTERNOON, I'm pinned to the bed by Xander's beautiful body, and before I can move his eyes are open.

"Morning."

"Afternoon, Mr. Rhodes." I snuggle into him.

"Seriously? Shit. I've got stuff to do today." A pang of sadness tugs at my heartstrings. He's already thinking about leaving.

"I'm sorry. If I'd known, I would have set an alarm."

"Don't apologize. I just have some stuff to sort out for our date later." A cheeky grin spreads across his face.

"Oh, really. What kind of stuff?"

"You'll have to wait until later. You know what they say... anticipation is key." He's wiggling his eyebrows at me suggestively and I can't help but laugh.

"Okay. Well, how about we grab some breakfast and then you can go do whatever it is you need to do? Smells like Addi is already cooking up something nice. I'll go see what she's up to. Come on in when you're ready." I grab my favorite hoodie and head out to the kitchen.

Addi is cooking up a storm. It looks like she's making enough food to feed our entire building. This is not a good sign. When something is wrong, she cooks, and cooks and then cooks some more.

"Hey. Everything okay?" I ask tentatively.

"I'm fine. You hungry?" Her voice is sullen.

"Yeah. Xander will be out in a minute. Where's Carter?"

"Still asleep, I guess." She continues to cook, avoiding my questioning gaze.

"What's going on? Did you guys have fun last night?"

"Yes, we did. Don't read into it. It was just that… fun. When he gets up, he'll leave and that'll be the end of it. Carter being friends with Xander doesn't change that." I don't get a chance to respond before the boys appear, joking around, shoving each other.

It's cute seeing Xander acting like a boy. He's looking sexy and a bit naughty wearing last night's clothes. Coming up behind me he wraps his arms around my waist and nuzzles my neck. Carter does the same to Addi and I'm surprised to see her flinch before melting into his touch. It's obvious to me that he has it bad for my friend. He seems like a good guy and he's Xander's best friend so I'm hoping she doesn't break his heart. I'm worried about her. She doesn't seem like herself this morning. I'll need to have a proper talk with her when we're alone.

The four of us sit and enjoy a massive breakfast together, the boys having second and third helpings of everything. I have one of my favorite muffins and a giant cup of coffee. She also made pancakes, eggs and freshly squeezed orange juice. Wow. She's in a bad way.

After gorging himself, Xander has to leave. I walk him the ten feet to the door, and he gives me the sweetest, chaste kiss before entering the elevator. With a sly grin on his face as the doors close, he says, "I hope you're ready for me later, sweets. I'll be here to pick you up at seven." And then he's gone. I can't wait to see him in five and a half hours.

As I head back over to the kitchen, there's a deafening silence between Addi and Carter. She's completely shut down.

"Do you have any plans today, Addi?" Carter asks tentatively.

"Yes. I'm busy all day with Lily." Her tone is so curt it makes me cringe.

"I better get going then. Walk me out?" She stands from the table, her eyes glassy.

"It was really nice to see you again, Lily." I give him a small smile.

"You too, Carter. And thanks for everything at the club last night." I feel bad for him.

"Anytime." With his hands tucked into his pockets and his head lowered, he makes his way to the door. Addi is already holding it open for him—she may as well have 'fuck off' written on her forehead. He stops in front of her, seeming a little unsure of himself. Totally different from the guy we were hanging out with last night.

"So, I'll call you?" He leans in to kiss her, and I try to give them some privacy, but I want to see what she'll do. She grabs his face in her hands and deepens the kiss like her life depends on it. When she pulls back Carter has a goofy satisfied look on his face. Without another word, he turns and heads for the elevator. She doesn't wait for it to close before shutting our front door.

"What the hell was that, Addi?" I'm confused.

"I don't want to talk about it." She's agitated and I think she's about to burst into tears. I know her well enough to know I can't push her just now.

"Okay, but you know I'm here if you need to talk."

"There's nothing to say. We had a tumble, it's done, end of."

"Bullshit. What was that kiss at the door then? You looked like you wanted to eat the poor guy." Okay, knowing I can't push her when she's sad, and doing it when she's being downright obnoxious, are two different things entirely.

"It was goodbye." Without another word, she strides toward her bedroom, slamming the door behind her. What the fuck? I have no clue what just happened here.

∾

ADDI STAYS IN HER ROOM THE REST OF THE DAY AND I TAKE ADVANTAGE of having the remote to myself, watching trash TV for a few hours before getting ready for my date with Xander. While I'm in the shower, I hear my phone beep.

> Mr. P: I want you in a dress tonight, Miss Tate. Bring an overnight bag. X

> Me: Overnight bag? Presumptuous much? L x

> Mr. P: Yes. Finals are over, baby. You're all mine now. X

A rush of excitement blossoms in my stomach, unleashing the swarm of butterflies. I take his wardrobe advice and find a dress to wear. May is a beautiful time of year in New York and lends itself to any fashion statement a girl wants to make. Another reason to love this city!

I go with a figure-hugging cap sleeve navy dress, falling just below my knees, with a side split up to my thigh. Teamed with simple navy lace peep-toe heels and matching clutch, I'm feeling good. I've packed an overnight bag with some sexy lingerie, PJs, and a change of clothes for tomorrow, as requested. As if on cue, the buzzer sounds.

When I open the front door, Xander is leaning against the door jamb, arms over his chest with his legs crossed at the ankle. He looks incredible, like he's walked off a Paris runway and into my life. He's wearing a navy pinstripe three-piece suit, crisp white shirt, and a powder blue tie. My mouth is watering... literally.

"Well, well, well, Miss Tate. We match again. You look devastatingly beautiful tonight. I might have to cancel our plans and take you to my offices. You're putting me in the mood to live out a very naughty secretary fantasy." I like the sound of that.

"Anything you say, Mr. Rhodes." He slowly eases past me, picks up my overnight bag and takes my hand in his.

"Let's go." I shout goodbye to Addi as I close the door behind me.

David is waiting at the entrance to my building. Xander hands him my overnight bag and starts walking away from the car, tucking me into his side.

"Where are we going?" I'm so excited to be out with him again.

"That would be telling... we'll be there soon. It's a surprise."

It's a great night for a stroll in the city. The sun is shining, it's lovely and warm but with just a light breeze—the city is alive with possibilities. Xander occasionally lifts our interlaced fingers to his mouth, pressing a gentle kiss to my skin. It's a small gesture, but I love how cherished it makes me feel.

We make our way into Central Park, one of my favorite places in the world. The tranquility that can be found in here is such a juxtaposition to the hustle and bustle of the city streets. It's like being transported to paradise. I'm beginning to wonder where he's taking me when I stop in my tracks. There are no words for the inexplicable swell of emotions slamming into my chest. It's breathtaking—magical. It's everything I could hope for in a fantasy and more.

"Do you like it?" He seems almost nervous waiting for my reaction.

"Oh my God." I'm choking up. It feels like I've got a golf ball stuck in my throat. "I've never seen anything so beautiful in my life. It's perfect."

Xander has brought me to Shakespeare Garden for dinner. It's filled with only flowers mentioned in the works of Shakespeare. This was one of my favorite places to come when I was planning out my thesis. It's gorgeous on a normal day, but tonight it is exquisite in its beauty.

There are white twinkling lights everywhere covering every bench, every tree, and woven throughout the flowerbeds. It's like walking into a dream. There's an intricately carved gazebo covered with lights and climbing roses set up close to the bronze statue of my favorite playwright. Inside there's a table set for two. Wow. I thought the beach was romantic, but this is something else entirely.

I'm so taken aback by everything around me I don't even realize I'm crying until Xander cups my face in his hands, wiping my tears.

"Please, tell me these are happy tears?" His eyes are twinkling under the stunning lights.

"Yes. They're happy tears. I'm overwhelmed that you would go to so much trouble just for me. This is... God, I can't even find the words to describe how amazing this is. Thank you."

"Of course, I would do this for you. You deserve so much more. I wanted to find a place that could look half as beautiful as you. You're enchanting, Lily, I can't get enough of you. I'm completely enthralled by you." He leans down and ever so gently licks my lips with his tongue, entreating me to open to him. I part my lips and let his tongue consume me, mine reflecting his every movement. It's as if I was made to kiss this man.

I don't know how long we stay like this. However long it is, it will never be enough. If I wasn't sure before this moment, I know now without a doubt—I am in love with Alexander Rhodes.

He pulls back, and a light, satisfied hum emanates from his throat, his eyes half shut, the picture of contentment.

"Come with me." He leads me over to the table where a waiter is pouring two glasses of chilled Cristal. He ushers me to my seat before taking his and lifting his glass to make a toast.

"To you, Lily Tate. Congratulations on finishing your degree. Here's to the next chapter, may it bring you everything your heart desires and more. Cheers." The champagne is delicious. Everything about this night so far is perfect.

The waiter lifts the silver domes from our dishes to reveal a simple and completely scrumptious Caesar salad appetizer, followed by the best steak I've ever tasted—medium rare, on a bed of spinach, topped with goat's cheese, olive oil and balsamic vinegar.

The conversation flows easily between us—as if we've known each other for years. He tells me a little about his family—an only child, with a mom and dad who are very much still in love, and who are very proud and supportive of his achievements. He's a poster child for a happy upbringing. He knows better than to talk about my family tonight. The last time we talked about them, I cried for hours. Instead, he seamlessly steers me onto my plans for the future.

"So, Miss Tate. What lies in store for you now? Is there something you've always wanted to do?" God, I love his smile.

"It's silly, but I always dreamed of becoming an author. I love everything about literature, reading it, writing it, and studying it. To make a career for myself doing what I love would be incredible. Obviously, I'll need to find a job that pays the bills just now, but if I can work on a novel in my spare time then who knows what the future could bring." His eyes light up.

"That's amazing. You will be a fantastic writer." He leans under the table, bringing a rectangular box back up with him. "I hope this will help you make your dream come true." He hands it to me.

"Xander, you don't have to buy me stuff. I just want to spend time with you."

"I know that. I saw this and it made me think of the day I met you looking gorgeous with all those loose papers fluttering down around you like feathers from heaven. Please, open it." I lift the lid on the box to find a stunning burgundy leather notebook with an engraved white-gold plaque on the front. It reads:

MY SWEET LILY:

HEAR MY SOUL SPEAK.

OF THE VERY INSTANT THAT I SAW YOU,

DID MY HEART FLY TO YOUR SERVICE.

XANDER X

He can quote Shakespeare? Not just any Shakespeare—*The Tempest*. It's one of my favorite plays. I wipe the tears that are forming at the corners of my eyes.

"It's beautiful. Thank you so much. I love it." His face is brimming with joy at my reaction.

"I'm glad you like it. Maybe you could use it to write down ideas for your novel."

"That's exactly what I'm going to do."

"In some small way I'll have contributed to helping you make your dreams a reality." There's a vulnerability in his eyes.

I forget to engage the filter. "I'm pretty sure you could be a huge contributor to all of my dreams coming true." My cheeks flush at my confession. Xander takes my hand in his, grazing his thumb back and forth over my knuckles, holding me with his intense gaze. My heart is racing, my eyes fixed on his, a charged silence crackling between us.

Dessert is a delicious crème brulee, but the best part is watching as he licks it from his spoon. Who knew dessert could be so sexy?

He stands from the table, holding out his hand. "Dance with me?" Music begins to play in the background, ethereal and haunting. I don't even want to think about how he pulled all of this off, I just want to dance with him. The band is playing an acoustic version of Adele's *Make You Feel My Love*.

He pulls me close, holding my hand to his chest as he wraps his other arm around my waist. We sway in unison, moving effortlessly, my head resting on his chest, listening to the lyrics. I want to remember every moment of this evening. The sound of Xander's heartbeat against my ear, the smell of his cologne and the feel of his body moving against mine as a peaceful hum escapes my chest. He holds me tighter, his voice a sultry whisper in my ear.

"I would consider it a privilege if you'd stay with me tonight, Lily, and do me the honor of letting me make love to you."

His heart thunders against my hand, my own quickening to keep time. I look up into his eyes, pure reverence shining back at me. I'm nervous, but I know I don't want this to happen with anyone but him.

"Yes."

It's all I can manage past the lump in my throat. Moving my hands up into his hair, I guide his lips to mine, and with a tender kiss, confirm my answer.

"Yes."

CHAPTER 12

LILY

DAVID IS WAITING FOR US AT THE ENTRANCE TO THE PARK WITH A TOWN car. Xander opens the door for me.

"I thought you might not want to do anymore walking with those heels on... which I love by the way." His eyebrows wiggling suggestively at me.

When we're settled in the backseat together, David pulls into traffic toward the Upper East Side. I don't care where we're going, I just want to be with him. We don't speak, the weight of our decision hanging in the air between us. He gently strokes my hand, his touch eliciting a wave of excitement at what's to come.

We turn onto 5th Avenue, and David pulls up in front of Xander's building. Carved into the granite above the lobby doors, is the name Suffolk Tower. It screams money. I mean, I live on the Upper West Side, but I could never afford something like this. I've been living on my inheritance from the sale of the ranch while I've been studying. That won't last forever, another year at best. Then I'll be looking for a slightly less expensive apartment.

Xander ushers me through the impressive glass doors into the lobby, where a distinguished looking man greets us.

"Good evening, Mr. Rhodes. Miss." Xander smiles and says hello as we pass to the elevators. Once inside he pulls a key card from his pocket, inserting it into the panel before punching some numbers into the keypad. We're going to the penthouse. Even the elevator is stunning, refined and elegant with soft lighting and decadent decor.

Clutching my hand in his, we arrive at the lobby of his apartment. There's a chunky marble table in the center with at least ten dozen roses arranged in a giant crystal vase. Absolutely gorgeous. He unlocks intricately carved oak doors and ushers me in. Wow. Apartment is not the word for this place... Kingdom, maybe.

My eyes are immediately drawn to the wall of windows framing Central Park in all its majesty. It's beyond breathtaking, and I can see how he must feel like a king standing here looking out over Manhattan. Xander snakes his arms around my waist from behind.

"It's an amazing view." He isn't staring out the window, he's looking directly at me, as if he's looking into the depths of my very being.

"It's spectacular."

As I turn in his arms he slowly caresses my waist, his hands traveling up, skimming the sides of my breasts as he makes his way to my face. My nipples harden, my breath quickening as I look up into endless pools of ice-blue heaven staring back at me. His hands cupping my face as if I was made of glass.

"Lily, the only thing in here that is spectacular is you. You take my breath away. I lo... I..." His gaze hungry, he groans as his mouth takes mine. Our lips and tongues moving in perfect harmony. I can't stop myself from moaning into his mouth, the sensation of his tongue stroking mine sending waves of pleasure throughout my body.

I start to shake, my nerves getting the better of me. Xander moves his arms around me, pulling me close to his chest.

"What's wrong?" he whispers, trailing kisses up and down my neck.

"I don't know what to do. I don't want to disappoint you." My gaze drifts to the floor.

"Look at me, Lily. Please." When my eyes find his, there is only tenderness shining back at me. "There is nothing you could do that would disappoint me. We don't have to do this tonight. There's no rush, sweets. I can wait."

"It's not that. I want to. I want to… with you. But I have no experience and I want you to enjoy it. You have so much more experience than me. How can I compare?"

He lets out a small chuckle. "How many women do you think I've slept with? I'm not a player. What's with the *so much experience?*" I'm embarrassed now.

"Look at you. Women must throw themselves at you all the time. You could have any woman you want."

"Wow. I didn't think this was where our conversation was heading, but I guess we're talking about this now. Take a seat and I'll grab a bottle of wine from the fridge." I could kick myself. I completely ruined the moment. This is not what I wanted it to be like after the wonderful date he arranged for me tonight. I wanted it to be perfect.

Xander returns with a bottle of Prosecco and two glasses. He pours a glass for each of us and hands me one before sitting across from me. Shit. He doesn't even want to sit next to me now. I've made a total mess of this, and yet I continue my verbal vomit without thinking.

"I'm so sorry I ruined this. I didn't mean to put you off."

He cuts me off. "Calm down, Lily. You haven't ruined anything. You certainly haven't put me off. I just want to take it slow and put your mind at ease. I don't want you to be worrying. I want you to relax and enjoy yourself." A small smile touches the corners of my lips.

"I'm not some player from a romance novel. I haven't slept with hundreds of women. I've never done the one-night stand thing. It's just not who I am. I'm not a bad boy. If that's what you're looking for, I'm not it. I've slept with a grand total of five women, and I was in what I would consider a long-term monogamous relationship with each of them. I'm not a manwhore. Was I in love with them? Looking back now, no. I cared about them, and I thought one of them was true love."

"What was her name?"

He runs his hair through his hands. "Do we have to talk about this now?"

"I've already killed the mood. You may as well tell me."

"You haven't killed anything. I just want tonight to be special for you."

"It will be."

With a sigh of resignation, he rubs the scruff on his jaw. "Her name was Natalie. We dated for three years, which ended a year ago. I thought we were in love—that we had a future together. But she had other ideas. She realized my money and business contacts weren't going to get her what she wanted. She was an aspiring model. I found out she'd been sleeping with any guy who said he could get her on a magazine cover. Of course, she didn't leave me until one made good on his claim. She left like it was nothing, and the next thing I knew, she was on the cover of *Sports Illustrated*."

"I'm so sorry." I don't know what to say.

"She's the reason I got upset when you said you Google searched me. I was so humiliated. There are years of press coverage and photos of me looking like a love-struck puppy. She was cheating the whole time and when the gossip rags got hold of the truth, they tore me apart." I move to comfort him, resting my hand on his thigh. "I should never have done a search on you. I didn't see any pictures. I was too intimidated just knowing how successful you are."

"I haven't dated anyone since, until I met you."

My heart breaks for him. I'm happy he's not with her anymore, but I know it's selfish, and I can't help wondering if he still loves her. "Why me? I'm not special."

"Constantly underestimating yourself, Miss Tate."

"Do you... still have feelings for her?" My voice wavers as I choke out the questions I'm not ready to hear the answer to.

He swears under his breath. "She doesn't deserve to breathe the same fucking air as you. What we had wasn't real, it never was."

"Three years is a long time, Xander. How can I compete with that?"

"Yes, but three weeks with you has meant more to me than she ever did. There is no comparison. I have never been so drawn to a woman in my life. The stuff we've done together so far has felt better than any sex I've ever had. Yes, I have experience. I'm going to make you come in ways you never thought possible. Trust me, it's going to be amazing between us. How could it *not* be?"

He places his glass on the table, before kneeling between my legs. I couldn't speak even if I wanted to. As he takes my hands, I gasp with the tangible force passing between us—up my arms, through my body and straight to my core.

"Do you feel that, Lily?" He says in a low breathy rasp. "That's why sex between us is going to be mind-blowing." He nibbles my neck. "Are you sure about this? Because once I take you to my bedroom and strip you out of this dress, I *will* make love to you."

My heart is going to scatter to the winds when this is over, but I love him... and I want him more than I want my next breath.

"Make love to me, Xander."

He leads me from the living room, down a beautiful hallway and up a flight of stairs into the master suite. It's stunning. He walks over to the massive bed and sits me down on the crisp white covers. It's so soft and plush and the pillows look so plump and inviting. I watch as he removes his jacket and tie, setting them over a chaise on the other side of the room, loosening the top few buttons on his shirt.

He kicks off his shoes and socks, removes his watch, placing it on a table by the windows that boast the same spectacular view as the living room. He stalks toward me, the muscles in his arms flexing under his shirt. He rolls up his sleeves showing his corded forearms.

"Let's get these pins out of your hair." He crawls onto the bed behind me, running his hands along my shoulders and up my neck, nibbling with his teeth. "May I?"

I drop my head to the side giving him better access to my neck, and he very carefully removes the pins, running each loosened tendril through his long fingers. I take a moment to absorb my surroundings, relishing the feel of his hands.

The room reflects Xander perfectly—masculine yet sumptuous, decadent yet comfortable. The wall of windows is the perfect back-drop for any room. The other walls are a rich teal color, and they almost look like velvet. There are elegant large framed black and white photographs on the wall behind the bed. They are stunning pieces, sensual and erotic without being tawdry. You can't see anything explicit, but you can tell that the bodies in the photos have intimate knowledge of each other, their connection leaping out of the frame. It's what makes them so beautiful.

"You like?" He removes the last pins from my hair.

"They're wonderful. The connection between them is almost tangible, so sensual and tasteful. I love them." He's nibbling my neck as I speak, his fingers moving to unzip the back of my dress.

"The connection is what drew me to them…" I don't think he's just talking about the art on his walls. "Do you feel the connection, Lily?"

He rains open-mouthed kisses down my neck as his fingers blaze a trail down my back unzipping me. Even the smallest touch of his hand has me on fire.

"Yes, Xander, I feel it." How could I not? No one has ever elicited such raw desire in me. He slips my dress off my shoulders, kissing every inch of my now exposed skin with reverence. I feel completely worshipped.

"Stand up and turn around to face me." I do as he asks, trying to tame my raging nerves as I stand. My dress falls to the floor and as I turn, I step out of it, but I can't resist the urge to shield my body with my arms as much as possible. I'm standing in front of this picture of perfection in my bra, panties, and high heels, feeling self-conscious without a clue what to do.

"Don't hide from me, sweets. You have nothing to feel insecure about. Your body is stunning… simply stunning."

I drop my arms to my sides and let him look at me. Raking his gaze over every inch of my body he crawls down off the bed, picking up my dress and laying it over a chair. He walks around me, slowly, making his appreciation known with little groans.

"God. You are going to kill me with this tight little body of yours." He stands in front of me. "Now, undress me." Oh. My. God.

My hands are shaking as I unbutton his waistcoat and push it over his broad shoulders, letting it drop to the floor. As I put my hands on his chest to unbutton his shirt, I can't disguise the trembling. He clasps my hands in his, holding them to his warm, hard chest.

"Breathe, Lily. I've got you. Just relax." The sound of his voice is soothing, calming my nerves.

I lift my eyes to his, smoldering back at me. He dips his head and kisses me, gentle at first, coaxing me to open for him, and as our kiss deepens my fingers make short work of his buttons. I run my hands up his muscled torso before ripping his shirt over his shoulders and throwing it to the ground.

As our tongues grow hungry and urgent, I move to his pants, unzipping and letting them drop. He steps out and moves me to the bed without breaking our kiss.

"Lie on the bed." He takes my hand to steady me as I do what he asks. "You are a vision. So pretty. So beautiful."

He crawls between my legs, spreading them to accommodate his imposing frame. He lifts each leg in turn, removing my heels, running his fingers over my instep and up my calf. He continues up my thigh, stopping short of where I want him to focus his ministrations. He does the same with the other leg, teasing me as he leaves me wanting more, my panties growing damp.

Just the sight of him in nothing but his Calvin Klein's is enough to make me wet, but combine that with each sensual touch and I'm more than ready for him. He truly looks like a God with his sexy tanned skin, and broad shoulders tapering down to a slim waist and hips. Every muscle is perfectly defined, strong thighs and solid sinewy arms. Every inch of his body screams that he can control me, and I want him to.

He drinks me in from head to toe. I've never felt so desired.

"I'm going to kiss every inch of you, Lily Tate, claiming you as mine."

His arms come down to rest at the sides of my head and his mouth lowers to mine. My hands begin to explore his back, feeling each taut muscle move under my fingertips. His skin is soft but covers a body so hard and perfect he could be one of Michelangelo's masterpieces.

"You taste so sweet."

Holding his weight above me with one arm, his other hand drifts to my breasts, kneading them through my lace bra, and it feels so good. My nipples begin to harden at his touch as his fingers slip inside one of the cups, pulling the lace out of the way, exposing my breast.

"Such pert little rosebuds. So responsive." His tongue replaces his fingers, sucking my nipple into his warm mouth, swirling his tongue around the tip.

"Oh… Xander." His fingers move up to release my other breast, rolling my nipple between his thumb and index finger, hardening it further. He moves his tongue over to lavish the same attention on each nipple sending lightning bolts directly to 'little Lil'.

My hands are fisting in his hair, pulling him close, but it's never enough. He places a tiny bite on my nipple and my back arches off the bed in pleasurable pain. In a split second his hands are under me, unfastening my bra and peeling it down my arms. He twists it around my wrists and pushes my hands above my head.

"You're so fucking beautiful." He runs his hands down my arms, followed by whispers of open-mouthed kisses and flicks of his tongue, leaving behind a trail of want and desire that has me panting for more. He kisses his way down, laving every inch of me with attention, his fingers teasing the edges of my panties, occasionally dipping a finger underneath to torment me.

"You've had these on long enough, sweets."

Biting his lip, he hooks his fingers under the sides of my lace panties and drags them down my legs torturously slow, never taking his eyes from mine. God, his eyes are gorgeous. He dips his gaze to my exposed sex, his breath quickening and his length hardening at the sight.

"God, baby, I can see how wet you are for me, and it's so fucking hot." It's indescribably sexy watching him harden further under his boxer shorts just from looking at me.

"Take your shorts off. I want to see all of you." His eyes widen at my words and a sinful smile spreads over his lips. He leaves me sprawled on the bed, my hands bound with my bra above my head.

Standing at the foot of the bed he slowly pushes his shorts down, his impressive length springing free, as they drop to the floor. He just stands there for a moment, his eyes locked on me, watching as I memorize the perfection of his body. I can't pull my gaze away from his delicious V, his happy trail leading down to his beautiful cock, hard and ready because of me. I am so turned on. I sit up on the bed to get a better view of him, my hands draped in between my legs where heat radiates from my sex.

"Make love to me, Xander."

His sexy smile drops, an intense stare taking its place on his stunning features. He crawls back onto the bed and pulls my bra from around my wrists.

Itching to touch him, I grab his face in my hands, the scruff scratching my palms. I pull his lips toward mine. His arm snakes around my back, lowering me to the bed with tender precision, his body hovering over me—the promise of something amazing in the air between us.

There's an unspoken dialogue, my body begging for Xander with every breath. As the weight of his body presses down on me, I feel his hard length pressing against my thighs. I open my legs, letting his cock caress my folds. I want to thrust my hips up to take him in, but he pushes my hips down into the bed.

"I want to make sure you're ready for me, sweets. I don't want to hurt you." He flicks his tongue out to lick my bottom lip before moving down my body. His strong, callused hands grasp my thighs and push my legs apart, as wide as they can go, exposing my sex. He runs his nose from my entrance, up my folds, to my clit, nuzzling the small patch of hair left after waxing.

"God... you smell so good, I can't wait any longer. I need a taste of you... now." His tongue follows the same path as his nose, in one long, hard lick.

"Fuck, Lily. You are so wet for me... and this sweet little pussy of yours tastes as good as it looks." Groans escape my chest in a plea for more.

His tongue feels magnificent, sending electricity sparking to every nerve ending in my body. The now familiar pull begins to build, heralding something explosive that only his touch can elicit. As the pleasure becomes more intense, his fingers gently open my folds, alternating between raining open-mouthed kisses around my clit and darting his tongue out to flick the small bundle of nerves that hold the key to my undoing.

When his tongue quickens—harder and more urgent—satisfied moans escape him, vibrating against my clit. I can't hold back any longer. A myriad of sensation explodes in my core and radiates throughout my body, causing wave after wave of pleasure.

I'm screaming his name, grabbing fistfuls of his hair, holding him to me, riding his face as the aftershocks pulse through me. It's so intense, but it leaves me wanting more. I want to feel him inside me. I want to connect with him on the deepest level possible.

"Oh my God. I need you… please… Xander."

"I've got you." He thrusts his fingers inside me, his movements vigorous, stretching me, stroking just the right spot inside and it has me on the edge of another soul-destroying orgasm. I physically can't hold back.

"Oh God."

It rips through me, quick and hard. He pulls out his fingers and slides them in his mouth, sucking on them. "So sweet. You look so fucking beautiful when you come, Lily. I want all your pleasure to come from me."

He reaches under the pillow, producing a condom packet. As he moves to rip it open with his teeth, I find a confidence I didn't know existed. "I don't want you to use it. I want to feel all of you."

His breath catches in his chest, his eyes fierce. "Do you know what you're asking of me? Are you on the pill?"

I hold his gaze. "I know what I'm asking. If you're not comfortable with it, it's okay. I've been on the pill for years, and you know I'm a virgin so I'm clean. I want to feel you, Xander."

His forehead drops to mine. His voice a sexy, breathy rasp. "I've never done this without a condom before. I'm clean, and I want to feel you skin on skin, but only if you're certain.

I clasp his face, gently kissing his lips. Pulling his ear down to my lips, my breathing shallow, and my heart racing.

"Yes."

I pull back, gazing into his eyes to convey my sincerity. He stares back at me in awe and wonder, as he drops the packet. He grabs the back of my neck, pouring so much passion and hunger into this kiss. His other hand slides down between our writhing bodies, grasping his hard length he positions himself at my slick entrance.

"This will probably hurt a little, sweets, but I'll do my best to make it as pleasurable as I can." He pushes just the tip inside of me. "Are you okay?" I nod, biting my lip.

He eases slowly inside, stretching me, filling me. When he's halfway inside, a guttural roar rips from his throat.

"Fuck... Lily... You feel unbelievable!"

He thrusts the rest of the way, causing a tearing sensation and a jolt of pain, but the overwhelming fullness is mind-blowing. He drops his lips to mine.

"There is no better feeling than this, than being inside you. Mine... Lily... Mine." He starts to move, slowly at first, his strong arms flexing above me, his muscles rippling as he holds himself over me thrusting his hips, his hard cock moving deep inside me before pulling out almost to the tip.

He creates a delicious rhythm as he teases my G-spot with every movement. I grab his ass and pull him in to the hilt, wanting to take every last inch of him as deep as I can, causing him to cry out.

"Fuck!"

I can't get enough of this man. Our kisses are demanding, wild, our tongues fucking to the rhythm of our bodies. Writhing, sucking, pulling, and pushing us toward our joint release. His pace quickens, becoming more urgent. His thumb moves down to circle my clit as he loses control, hammering into me, harder and harder. I adore it.

"Come with me."

His words are my undoing and I shatter into a million pieces, my muscles clenching around him with each wave of pleasure. He closes his eyes, throwing his head back as his own release consumes him. He has never looked so beautiful. Everything about his face and his expression is exquisite.

"Fuck, baby. Oh my God, Lily... Fuck." His warm come spills inside me.

Tears well in my eyes, the emotion of what has just transpired between us too much to contain. I feel so connected to Xander, an overwhelming barrage of emotions washing over me, unlike anything I've felt before.

I am so completely in love with him.

He brushes my hair back from my face, kissing my tears away.

"What's wrong? Did I hurt you?" His eyes search mine.

"I'm perfect. That was... astonishing. I have never felt so connected to anyone in my life. It's like you're a part of me now."

He feathers kisses all over my face, nibbling at my neck and shoulder.

"I know exactly what you mean. It has never been like this for me before. You're different... we're different. You speak to something deep in my soul. I can't get enough of you." As he pulls out of me, I'm bereft at the loss of physical contact. His come spills out of me and I'm crushingly embarrassed until he speaks. "That is the hottest thing I have ever seen." He runs his hand over my entrance, spreading his come all over me, claiming me as his. When he's finished, he jumps off the bed and disappears into the bathroom.

He emerges almost immediately with a damp washcloth, and a towel, but I've already pulled the sheets up to cover myself. He peels them down, exposing blood and come everywhere. I'm mortified. He sits down and gently starts cleaning me.

"You don't have to do that. I can go to take a shower." I try to push his hands away.

"I want to look after you, sweets. Let me." He is so tender and genuine, so I push aside my unease and let him clean me.

"I'm really sorry about your sheets. I'll buy you a new set."

Xander grabs my chin between his thumb and finger, forcing me to look straight into his gorgeous eyes. "Don't *ever* apologize for this. You just gave me such a precious gift that I will always treasure. I can't express what it means to me that you wanted me to be your first." I jump into his arms and wrap my legs around his waist, hugging him with all my strength.

"Thank you."

He stands from the bed with me wrapped around him like a little monkey, as if I weigh nothing, walking me into the bathroom. There's a stunningly deep freestanding roll-top bath with cascading waterfall taps and bubbles everywhere. He must have started it running when he left me to get the washcloth. The lighting is soft and sultry, the floor and walls a stunning grey granite with white granite around the top, accentuating the lights perfectly. It's masculine and beautiful, reflecting its owner.

There's a ginormous shower. You could fit ten people in easily, with multiple oversized shower heads and a tiled bench seat running along one wall. My mind starts to wander, thinking of Xander and I together in there.

He kisses my neck, still holding me tight against his gloriously naked body. "Bath?"

I nuzzle into his neck. "Perfect."

He gently lowers me into the luxurious tub and steps in behind me, settling against the tub, pulling me back to rest against his chest. He wraps his arms around my waist and rests his scruffy chin on my shoulder. It's total bliss. I don't know how long we bask in the silence, just enjoying each other's company, resting together, as our chests rise and fall in unison.

CHAPTER 13

LILY

I wake up to Xander nuzzling my neck, whispering in my ear. I must have nodded off listening to his heartbeat.

"Wake up, sweets. Time to get out the tub. I don't want my little spider monkey pruning beyond repair." I love him when he's like this, —it's so cute.

"Is it okay if I just quickly wash my hair?"

"You can do anything you want. You don't have to ask." He stands, stepping from the tub. I watch the rivulets of water, jealous of their journey down his toned flesh, rippling over muscle after perfect muscle. I want to lick every last delicious drop from him. "Plenty of time for that. Go shower and I'll be waiting for you."

I let out a little chuckle. "Are you a mind reader or something?"

"No. The look you're giving me right now is telling me everything I need to know. I think maybe you need a rest. You'll be sore after what we just did, and I don't want to hurt you." Wrapping a towel around his waist, he gives me a chaste kiss on the lips and leaves the bathroom, closing the door to give me some privacy.

I take my time, enjoying the cascading water from the giant shower heads, easing my aching muscles. Xander was right, I am sore from our exploits, but I love every delicious twinge and throb. It reminds me of what we just shared. A night I'll never forget. It was everything I had hoped it would be and more. I've lived my romantic life vicariously through the works of Shakespeare, Austen, Brontë and countless others for years, afraid to let anyone close, afraid to let anyone touch me. I never expected to find someone who would make me feel this way about sex, about love, or what my future could be.

I use Xander's shampoo and shower gel, consumed by his scent. I grab some towels, wrapping my hair and body before heading into the bedroom. I don't know why, but I feel nervous being in his bedroom with him again. I squash my worries and open the door, my breath catching in my chest at the work of art in front of me.

He's stretched out on the bed, his hand behind his head, a heart-warming, brain-melting smile on his face and a twinkle in his eye. He's changed the bedding. Lying in crisp, fresh white sheets, they're draped carelessly but suggestively, highlighting his happy trail. I want to rip the sheet off the bed to see the rest of him.

There's a hairdryer laid out on the table in front of a beautiful, gilded mirror. It's cute that he thinks I could do anything with the brush he left for me! I grab my PJs from my overnight bag. I know it's silly when he's seen every inch of me, but I still duck into the bathroom to put on my tank top and shorts.

When I emerge, Xander's laughing. "Seriously? We've just done the most intimate act possible between two people and you can't put your PJs on in front of me? You're so damn cute. Get over here." His arms are spread wide for me, and I jump at the chance to get close to him... literally... I'm a little over enthusiastic! He tucks me into his side and pulls the covers over us, smoothing my hair from my face, running his thumb up and down my cheek, completely at ease with our intimacy.

"Are you okay? Was it... okay for you?" There's a vulnerability in his voice that betrays his cool, confident exterior.

"Are you kidding me? Xander, it was earth-shattering, life-changing, mind-blowingly amazing. I know I have nothing to compare it to, but I'm sure if it felt this amazing for everyone, I would be supplied with triple the amount of detail from Addi than I already have to endure." He lets out a heartfelt belly laugh, making my spirit soar.

"I'm flattered. And if I have my way, you won't *ever* have anyone else to compare it to." I literally stop breathing. I want to believe that he means it, and it's not just post-coital nicety, but I don't know the things people say to each other after sex, but I can't imagine ever wanting to experience this with someone else.

He lets out a contented hum. "Mmm. You smell like me. I like it. Not as much as I love your smell, but I like you covered head to toe in *Eau de Me*."

I giggle. "Is it weird that I like smelling of you?" His hold tightens around me.

"God, you're perfect for me. You even enjoy my caveman tendencies." He plants a soft kiss on my forehead as he speaks. "How did I get so lucky?"

"I guess we both got lucky." I retort with a mischievous grin.

Xander's demeanor turns solemn. "I'm serious, Lily. I don't deserve you, but here you are. I've spent so long shutting people out and questioning their motives. Do they want my money? Or my connections? Do they want media attention? Do they really want to be friends with me? And with women... after Natalie I lost faith that any woman would want me for me. I was afraid of getting hurt again"

I cuddle closer, trying to give him some comfort as he continues.

"Then you literally crashed into my life and turned it upside down. I can't explain why I haven't felt any of my usual reservations with you. From the moment I met you, I've wanted to make you mine. Even after our misunderstanding early on, I knew... I had to have you. I've never felt this close to someone in my life. The trust you put in me tonight really overwhelms me. Thank you."

Tears prick at the back of my eyes. I lift my head from his chest, pulling his head down to mine, sealing his honesty with a kiss. I pour all the emotion I can't put into words into this one kiss, hoping that he understands what I can't convey. It's not that I don't *feel* it, I'm just not ready to put it into words, making it real and opening myself up to being hurt. I know it doesn't work like that, but I'm doing the best I can.

I slowly move my body on top of him, marveling at how our bodies fit together like two pieces of a puzzle. I can't help myself, my thirst for him unquenchable. Our kisses become all consuming, ravaging each other with our tongues, our hands desperate as we trace every line and curve of each other's body. I can feel the discomfort from earlier between my legs, but I want him so badly it's a physical ache in my chest, much worse than any other pain in my body. As I lean over, he grabs my hair and deepens our kiss, bruising my lips with his intensity. In a split second I find myself beneath him, his strong frame looming over me.

"Tell me you're mine, Lily." The words drip from his lips in an enticing command, the yearning in his voice pulling at every cell in my body.

My answer is effortless. "I'm yours. Only yours. I only *ever* want to be yours." His mouth captures mine. "Make love to me. I'm yours."

He steadies his breath, trying to control the urge to take me as hard as he can. "I don't want to hurt you. You're already sore from earlier."

I gaze into his icy blue depths. "Xander. I need you. I want you so badly it's a physical ache. Please… please… make it go away. I need to feel you inside me. I *need* you." Any control he was fighting to maintain is gone.

He makes love to me again and again, each time with more reverence than the last. He worships my body with every kiss and caress, taking me to new heights of ecstasy, holding off on his own release, allowing himself to come only when I fall over the edge with him. Sometime after 3 a.m. we fall into an exhausted sleep, our bodies tangled together—a perfect fit.

Tonight, there are no nightmares, just a beautiful sleep with an extraordinary man.

❧

XANDER'S BED IS RIDICULOUSLY COMFORTABLE. I WAKE UP SWADDLED IN his arms, his chest rising and falling gently underneath my head, his steady heartbeat a beautiful sound. I try not to wake him, but I want a peek. I slowly shift myself in his arms, tilting my head to gaze at the perfect plains of his face.

He looks so peaceful, young, and carefree in his sleep. He's breath-taking. His long black eyelashes almost kiss his sculpted cheekbones. His eyebrows naturally shaped and masculine. Slight curls in his hair sitting haphazardly on his brow. He really is a work of art. A bronzed God lying under me, holding me tight even while he sleeps. My heart swells in my chest at the realization that he wants to be here with me.

"Morning, sweets. Like what you see?" He peeks one eye open, a cheeky grin on his face, his voice low and raspy. I shy away, not wanting to go too close before I brush my teeth. I really don't want to inflict morning breath on him.

"Sorry. I didn't mean to wake you. I'm just going to go brush my teeth. Be back in a minute." I try to pry his arms off me, but he tightens his grip.

"What? No good morning kiss?"

"Not before I brush my teeth."

He starts teasing me. "Oh. Go on. Just one peck. I won't let you go until you do."

"No. It's gross." He starts tickling me.

"Are you calling me gross? You're going to pay for that." He's not lying. I hate being tickled and he is relentless. I'm wriggling all over the bed trying to get away from him, with no success, so I finally give in.

"Okay. Okay. Okay. You win." I choke out through giggles. "A peck on the cheek. That's my best offer."

"I'll take it." He says with a smug smile.

I peck him on the cheek, but he grabs me, pinning me to the bed. He looks sexy as hell hovering over me, his sex-mussed hair looking like it's been styled to perfection. He holds my arms at the sides of my head rendering me helpless. Lowering his lips to mine, his tongue licks along the seam of my mouth, coaxing me to open for him.

I want to refuse and run to the bathroom to make myself minty fresh, but I just can't say no. Our kiss is gentle, yet passionate, a lazy morning wake-up call to my libido. Only Xander could taste good first thing in the morning. After he works me into a frenzy, he stops and moves off me.

"Off you go then. Leave me all lonely and go to the bathroom." He's so playful. It's unbelievably cute. As much as I enjoy the kiss, I jump out of bed and head for the bathroom. Wow. Sex hair is not becoming on me! I must have given Xander a fright when he opened his eyes. I quickly brush my teeth and try to tame the bird's nest.

It takes me about ten minutes to get it under control before I can put it up in a quick messy bun. When I head back into the bedroom there's no sign of Xander—just a note on the bed.

Gone to rustle up some breakfast.
Come find me when you're ready.
Xander x

I find my way down to the kitchen, following the sound of him singing along to my favorite Pharrell song *Happy*. He's ridiculously cute and sexy at the same time, shaking his ass as he cooks, dressed only in black pajama bottoms. I stand just out of sight, watching his carefree display, but it doesn't last long. He spins around to grab some tomatoes from the kitchen island and stops in his tracks before doubling over laughing.

His response has me giggling uncontrollably. I crumple on the floor, my laughter fueled by his. When I manage to calm myself enough to get up, I run over and jump into his arms, kissing him all over his gorgeous face.

"If I knew I'd get this response, I'd make an ass of myself more often."

"You didn't make an ass of yourself. That was quite possibly the cutest thing I've ever seen. Even cuter than puppies." I peck him on the nose.

"I don't want to be cuter than puppies. I want to be a sexy caveman." He growls, capturing my mouth with a groan.

"Trust me when I say this. Everything about you is manly and caveman and one hundred percent sexy." He claims me, body and soul. Thoughts of anything but him flee from my mind at his kiss. There is only us and the connection we share. It's a rush I never want to end, but we're pulled from our own little world at the smell of burning eggs... gross.

"Shit." He puts me down and darts over to the frying pan. "I *was* making you a Spanish omelet for breakfast, but I'm going to go out on a limb and assume you don't want to eat this burnt monstrosity."

"How about... you come shower with me and then we can head out and get some breakfast/brunch somewhere?" A sly grin creeps across his face.

"Mmm. A shower with you... better make it dinner. This could take a while. You're very dirty, and I personally won't rest until I've cleaned every... single... inch of your filthy little body." His gaze is intense as he stalks toward me. Grabbing my hand, he pulls me behind him in silence.

He doesn't drop my hand—he doesn't speak. He just starts stripping me, gliding his hands gently over my naked flesh, leaving a trail of goosebumps in his wake. The juxtaposition of the cold sensation on my skin with the fire burning inside me is thrilling.

I feel dirty in the best possible way as I stand in front of him... naked and unabashed... for his eyes alone. I feel sexy. Reveling in it, I lift my hands up into my hair, dropping my head back as I run my hands down my neck, along my collarbone and down toward my breasts. Xander's eyes are fixed on my every move, wide and burning with desire. He gives me a confidence I've never had before. I tweak my nipples and watch as he bites on his knuckle.

"Stop biting and kiss me. I'm yours. Only... For... You." I've unleashed something from deep inside him. I can see it in his eyes. He loses all control, ripping his bottoms off before dragging me into the shower. As the hot water cascades over our intertwined bodies, he grabs me and presses me against the shower wall.

The cool tiles send a shiver down my spine, my nipples pebbling against his chest. He ravages my body, kissing every inch of my wet skin before taking me hard. After we chase our release together, I slump into his arms, the intensity of my orgasm too much for my body to deal with.

"I've got you. I'm sorry, baby."

"Don't apologize, that was… incredible."

"Wrap your legs round me." He carries me out of the shower, engulfing the two of us in a soft, fluffy white towel.

"Why did you say sorry?" I burrow further into his chest as I ask.

"Because I can't believe I was so rough with you. You're still sore from last night. Are you okay? Did I hurt you?" He lifts my face, searching for the truth and I offer it freely.

"You didn't hurt me. Yes, I feel the effects of last night, but… I kind of love it. Is that weird?"

He strokes his thumb down my cheek, adoration in his eyes. "It's not weird… it's… lovely. You're lovely. Never forget that." He gives me a gentle kiss, squeezing me close to his bare chest.

"Where would you like to go for brunch?" I ask, changing the subject. If I don't steer us toward a safer topic, I'm going to blurt out three words that will change everything, and I can't say it after only a few weeks. Has it only been that long? I feel like Xander has been a part of my life forever. I can't imagine my life without him in it.

"Earth to Lily." Oops.

"Sorry. Wandering mind of an aspiring novelist, I guess." Good save. I pulled that one out of my ass.

"Why don't we just get ready and head out… see where the day takes us?" His voice is playful and carefree.

"That sounds excellent. We'll let the Big Apple decide."

We get dressed together, my earlier shyness gone. This man wants to be with me and seems to *really* like my body. It's a revelation, and it's liberating. I sit down to dry my hair and Xander takes the opportunity to head to his office to make some calls. Once I'm in the ballpark of presentable, I go in search of him.

The door to the study is wide open and Xander is sitting at a stunning antique mahogany desk, large and imposing, just like the man behind it with his feet up on the desk. He's still on the phone so I signal that I'll leave him to finish, but he ushers me in and gestures for me to sit down on the leather sofa against the back wall. This office is bigger than my bedroom.

I wonder just how many rooms there are in this apartment. I take a moment to wander round his study, taking in the stunning works of art on the walls. Behind the desk is his degree from Columbia. Guess that partially answers why he was there the day we met.

My gaze is drawn to a particular piece—it's a Monet water lily oil painting. It's not the same as the reproduction he bought me. I think there are about two hundred and fifty different paintings Monet did in that series. It's stunning.

"Do you like this one better?" His arms wrap around my waist from behind, his nose nuzzling into my neck, drinking in my Chanel.

"I love mine. I've only seen a few of them in books and museums. They're stunning up close."

"I think so, too. I bought two at auction several years ago. Cost a small fortune but they were worth it, especially now that they have a deeper meaning. When I sit in here and look at this one, I think of a certain someone who has me quite enchanted." He's so smooth.

"Isn't it strange that you should have this particular Monet? Wait... you said you have two. Where is the other one?" As I wait for his answer, it dawns on me. There is a space on the wall next to the Monet... a space for the one that's hanging in my apartment. It's not a reproduction. He gave me a real Monet! I am such an idiot. I thanked him for the 'reproduction', and he didn't correct me. I spin round in his arms.

"Please tell me I'm not right. That you didn't give me a real Monet?"

"Why does it matter? It's a painting. I wanted you to have it."

"You have to take it back. It's not right. It's too much." He grabs my shoulders, holding me steady.

"Listen to me very carefully. I want you to have it. I won't take it back. Even if you left here today and never spoke to me again, which I really hope you don't, I would still want you to have it." I know I'm not going to win this argument, and he senses my wavering resolve as my shoulders slump in defeat.

"Good, that's settled. Thank you." His warm callused palms cup my face as his lips caress me, sending a delicious and now familiar jolt of electricity straight to my core.

An hour later, we head out to see the sun shining and the city buzzing with happy couples, families, and friends, all of them enjoying the weekend and everything this wonderful city has to offer. We do exactly the same and have a fabulous day together, chilling out, chatting about anything and everything. We must walk at least five miles, stopping for coffee, soaking up the sun, lying out in the park for a few hours, grabbing brunch and then later in the day when the sun begins to set, we have a lovely dinner before heading back to his apartment. Once there, I realize our magical weekend is at an end, but I don't want to leave him. Lucky for me he has the same idea.

"I was thinking. If you're not sick of me yet, maybe I could stay with you at your apartment tonight?"

I run into his arms and squeeze him with all my might. "I'd love that. I don't think I could ever get sick of you."

We spend the next three weeks, living in our bubble, only apart when Xander is at the office, and even then, we have a habit of texting *all* the time. When he works from home, I cozy up next to him reading a book or searching for a job online. We fall into a comfortable routine, not having to ask the question, 'are we staying together tonight?' It's a given. I don't think I could sleep without him next to me. And the sex... has been mind-blowing. He wasn't kidding when he said he would make me come in ways I couldn't imagine. There hasn't been a day that he hasn't taken me to the heights of pleasure and jumped off the cliff with me. Every kiss, every touch, sparks a thirst that only he can quench.

This has been the most amazing three weeks of my life, and I couldn't be happier. To cap it off, I graduate tomorrow, and I got confirmation this morning that I got the job I interviewed for last week. I start a week from Monday, so I have a week of freedom after graduation before I join the ranks of the New York employed!

CHAPTER 14

LILY

My mom and sisters are coming to graduation today. This will be the first time I've seen them since I met Xander. He desperately wants to see me graduate, so this will be the first time they all meet. I'm not worried in the slightest that my family won't love him. If anything, I'll need to keep an eye on my sisters' flirting. I'm more worried about how he will react to them, especially when he notices that I'm not exactly close with my family.

My mom and younger twin sisters Catherine and Olivia are all really close. Cathy and Liv still live with mom, and they do everything together. I used to be part of that, but after my dad died, I think they blamed me for what happened, and we just sort of drifted further and further apart as the years went by.

When I met Addi, she became my sister. She's the one I talk to about everything, who accepts me and loves me, knowing the good and the bad, including what happened with my dad. It's only since meeting Xander and telling him what happened that I've started to realize my dad wouldn't want me to blame myself. I didn't kill him. A massive burden has been lifted from my shoulders and allowed me to enjoy my time with Xander, letting him get close both physically and emotionally. I'm a little worried the guilt will resurface when faced with the blame I see reflected in my family's eyes, but if I can just get through a day with them, they'll go home, and Xander and I can get back to our bubble... hopefully.

Jason has organized a dinner at La Cattedrale tonight to celebrate Addi and me graduating, which is great, because I haven't seen him in a while. I've been so busy with Xander, and Jason has been flat out at the restaurant which is a good thing. Business is booming and I couldn't be happier for him. Addi's family will be there, along with my mom and sisters, Xander and a few people Jason has invited to join the party.

Xander gave me a stunning black off-the-shoulder dress last night and a pair of classic black Louboutins. I've given up telling him no— he never listens!

I sit in front of the mirror thinking about how my life has changed in the past month. I feel like a new person, alive and truly happy for the first time since my dad died. As I clasp my bracelet around my wrist, I dreamily trace the elegant clover and butterfly Xander gave me.

I think today is the day I'm going to tell him how I feel. As my decision fortifies, Addi knocks on the door.

"Hey, stranger. Looking foxy for graduation, Lilliput. How's the demanding billionaire?"

"He's great. Coming to graduation and dinner at Jason's, so you can ask him yourself." I apply the finishing touches to my makeup and turn to see her sitting on the edge of my bed.

"Wow. Addi. You look stunning. Graduation agrees with you." Her hair is tousled to perfection, her makeup flawless. She really is gorgeous.

"Thanks, friend. I can't believe we survived. Just got to find myself a job now. What about you?"

"I've got news on the job front actually. Remember the interview I went on last week—the one at T Magazine? Well... they contacted me yesterday and offered me a job as a blogger. Three more letters and I'll be working for *Time*! I'll be writing for a living and posting reviews on the magazine website. The pay isn't great, but I'm excited, and hopefully I can make some good contacts. It's flexible hours, so I'll be working on my novel in my spare time and see what happens."

She jumps off the bed and grabs me into a crushing hug. "That's amazing, Lilliput. Congratulations. This is definite cause for some major celebration tonight."

"Not going to argue with you. Looking forward to hitting a bar after I deal with the family reunion. I'll probably need more than a few drinks after that." She gives me a sad smile, knowing I don't get on with my mom and sisters anymore. We don't fight. we just don't really get involved in each other's lives.

"I don't get it. Why are they so cold to you? You're awesome, and your dad would kick their asses if he could see their indifference." Addi gets very protective of me around my family. I'll need to make sure she doesn't go postal on them tonight when she's had a couple of drinks.

"Promise me you'll be nice to them. I don't want Xander to see how dysfunctional we are."

She gives me the evil eye, but she can't resist my pouty face. "Okay. I'll play nice. Only because you asked me to… and I love you." We're hugging it out when there's a knock on the door. "That'll be billionaire boy. I'll get it while you grab your bag and make a grand entrance." She shoves my shoulder.

The doorman and Xander have become fast friends over the past few weeks. They're on a first name basis now after all the deliveries and tips Xander has given him. Plus, I told him just to let him in whenever he visits. I grab my bag and take a last look in the mirror. I'm ready to graduate.

Xander's face as I enter the lounge is satisfying to say the least. His jaw drops at the sight of me, his eyes filled with desire.

"Wow. You look… Incredible. Seriously… Wow." The thrill of his reaction sends a shiver down my spine.

"You look pretty *wow* yourself." I saunter toward him, an extra sway in my hips.

He really is breathtaking—standing tall, oozing sex from every pour in his three-piece pinstriped suit.

He slinks his arms around my waist, pulling me flush against his body. He smells divine. Is it weird that I love to sniff him? Not that I care if it is, I'd still totally do it!

He gently bites my bottom lip, before engulfing me in a kiss. Sparks fly as we lose ourselves in each other, our tongues dancing together in a practiced yet surprising waltz.

"Seriously, guys. I'm in the room." Addi breaks the spell, making me laugh into Xander's mouth.

"To be continued… Miss Tate."

Why do I love it so much when he calls me that? It's so formal, but so intimate at the same time. He threads our fingers together as we head off to Columbia for the last time.

I LEAVE XANDER TO GO AND FIND MY SEAT WITH ADDI. I'M WORRIED about her. She's not been herself recently—not since Carter. She obviously likes him, and he seems keen, but any time I try to talk to her about it, she shuts me down instantly. I'm going to have to talk to Xander about Carter if this goes on much longer.

I spy Xander in the crowd with a massive grin on his face. I give him a little wave and blow him a kiss before turning my attention to the ceremony. As the dean takes to the podium, the crowd of graduates and proud spectators go silent, but the air of excitement is palpable. We sit through some lengthy speeches that aren't as snooze worthy as I thought they would be. Let's face it, we all just want to grab our diploma and celebrate.

As soon as I hear my name, Addi is shouting from her seat. I make my way up the steps onto the stage, praying I don't fall on my ass in these robes. That would be so humiliating, and so like me! As my foot hits the stage, I glance in the direction of where I know Xander is sitting. He's standing, clapping and whistling, a massive grin splitting his face. It warms my heart to see him in a sea of thousands, standing alone to applaud my accomplishment. With a renewed confidence I stride over to the dean, accept my diploma, and shake his hand.

As soon as Addi's name is called, I'm on my feet, shouting and clapping for my best friend, my heart full of pride. She gives me a sly wink as she struts across the stage to accept her diploma, and as she rocks her robes, the male graduates show their appreciation, catcalling and whooping. She doesn't so much as blush, relishing the attention. There's the girl I know and love.

We sit through the rest of the ceremony, clapping where appropriate, putting in some extra effort when it's a friend of ours. The whole time, I want nothing more than to run to Xander and share this moment with him. As soon as the ceremony ends, Addi makes her way to me, giddy with excitement that we finally graduated together. I throw my arms around her and join in the crazy reveling. We congratulate our friends for a few minutes before scanning the crowd for our relatives.

Addi spots her mom and dad, making a beeline for the proud parents. It's heartwarming to watch. Her mom is crying, and her dad has the biggest grin on his face. As my mind starts to contemplate how my dad would have reacted today, warm arms snake around my waist from behind. With a kiss to my cheek and a squeeze, Xander lifts me off the ground and spins me round. "I thought I was going to burst when I saw you up there. I'm so damn proud of you. I wanted to tell the whole stadium that you're mine."

When he puts me down, I turn around and pull his face down to mine in a ravenous kiss, scared my love for him might burst out of my chest if I don't tell him right now.

"Xander, I…"

I'm interrupted by a familiar voice berating me from behind. "Calm it down, sis. You're in public, you know?" Of course, my family would ruin this moment for me.

I pull out of Xander's arms, put on my happy face, and turn to greet Cathy. My mom and Liv are with her. We all exchange 'hellos' and they offer their congratulations. My mom looks like she's been crying, but it's so unlike her, so I don't mention it and just give her a hug and a kiss. She holds me close—longer than a standard hug. I wish my dad were here. I pull back and reach for Xander, instantly soothed by the warmth of his hand.

"Mom, I'd like you to meet my boyfriend Xander."

He switches on the charm that has every woman he meets melting at his feet. "I'm the very lucky man who dates your beautiful daughter." He holds out his hand. "Very nice to meet you, Mrs. Tate." The megawatt smile is in full force now.

"Please, call me Jocelyn. It's a pleasure to meet you, Xander." My mom is blushing like a teenager. If it weren't so humiliating, it would be funny. He then turns his attention to the twins, who are already a pool of hormones at his feet. I swear there's drool on Liv's chin. They both thrust out their hands to shake his in unison.

"One at a time, girls. Hi, I'm Xander." Liv is doe-eyed and ridiculous, turning to give Cathy a shit-eating 'he picked me first' grin. How am I related to these people? This is just embarrassing, and he's enjoying making them feel uncomfortable.

"H… Hi. I'm Olivia. And this is my sister, Cathy." Cathy holds out her hand, forcing him to drop Olivia's.

"Nice to meet you, Cathy." He quickly extricates himself from the twins and takes his place at my side. I'm instantly relieved to have his arm around my shoulder in a casual yet possessive way. I love my family, but I always feel bad about myself when I'm around them.

"You must be so proud?" Xander asks, his tone demanding an answer.

My mom speaks up. "Yes. We're so proud of Lily. She's been through a lot and her dad would have been so happy to see her take the stage today." I'm stunned.

She takes me by surprise, engulfing me in a tight hug. "You've done well for yourself. It's lovely to see you achieve your goal." I don't remember the last time my mom hugged me like this. The girls join in, and we have a strange, but nice family moment. I'm struggling to hold back tears. I don't want to get my hopes up that they've finally forgiven me for my dad's death, but in this moment, I feel loved, and I've missed it.

Things feel a bit awkward after my mom's declaration, but Xander steps in to make small talk, giving me a minute to compose myself. He explains the plan to dine at Jason's restaurant with Addi and her family. As if her ears are burning, she bounds toward us with her parents in tow. This provides a great distraction for me as her parents catch up with my mom and sisters, exchanging all the usual pleasantries. She can tell I'm a little overwhelmed and comes to my rescue.

"You okay, Lilliput? Is this big chump looking out for you?" She can always make me smile.

"I'm a chump, am I? So nice to see you again, Addi." Xander is trying to stifle a laugh. They have a funny kind of friendship. Addi makes fun of him, and he takes it, pretending he doesn't find her crazy nicknames funny. They seem to like each other but she gives off the 'you're still on probation' vibe. I do love how she looks out for me, but I don't think she has to worry. I can't imagine him ever hurting me.

XANDER GUIDES ME INTO THE RESTAURANT WITH HIS HAND AT THE BASE of my back. It sends a jolt to 'little Lil' every time he does that. It never gets old. I'm touched by all the effort Jason has put into today. The place looks even more amazing than it normally does. There is a gorgeous banner with 'Congratulations Addi and Lily' over the bar area. The place has hundreds of balloons hanging from the ceiling, making it look magical. The entire restaurant is lit with what must be hundreds of candle lanterns. The tables have been set into one long banqueting style table in the center of the room, and it's decorated with stunning arrangements of roses, with crystals woven throughout the foliage. It has Xander written all over it. There are place cards for everyone, seating Addi and I at either end of the table. It gives us a good vantage point to make crazy faces at each other throughout dinner.

As I walk around looking at the names next to each place setting, I notice Carter and Logan's names. Addi is going to blow a gasket when Carter gets here, and as if by magic, I watch that very scene play out in front of me. The door to the restaurant swings open and in walks

Logan, followed closely by Carter. As she looks toward the entrance, her expression drops and panic spreads across her features, the color visibly draining from her face. I'm guessing they are the friends Jason invited to join us. He welcomes them both before anyone else gets a chance. I turn to Xander.

"Did you know they were going to be here?" He looks puzzled.

"Yeah. Why? Is there a problem? Jason and I thought we could all go out later after the families disperse, do some real celebrating. What's wrong?"

"Things between Addi and Carter are... well, I don't actually know what they are, but from what I saw when he left the last time, it's not good."

"But he only has good things to say about her." I pull him off to the side so no one can overhear us, especially not Addi.

"If I tell you this, you have to keep your mouth shut. I suspect she likes him more than she's ever liked a guy. I'm pretty sure it spooked her because they've not known each other very long. She hasn't been her usual flirty man-crazy self since she last saw him. I've tried to talk to her, but she shuts me down every time."

"Why? If she likes him, she should just give him a chance."

"She had a bad experience freshman year with a total creep of a guy, and she's never let anyone close since. I was hoping if she met someone worthwhile, she would let her guard down, but that's not happening, as you can see." We both turn in her direction. She is completely blanking Carter. I feel so bad for him. It's obvious to everyone in the room, there's something going on between them.

Jason urges everyone to take their seats for the appetizers, and Carter takes the opportunity to find his seat next to Xander—a friendly face. He looks crestfallen by Addi's lack of acknowledgement. Logan is next to Carter, and my family are across the table from them. My sisters are eyeing the latest man candy, and they waste no time in trying to charm the pants off both men. They seem to be having fun and the conversation flows freely.

My mom is further down the table next to Addi's mom Marjory. It's nice to see her laughing and joking with friends. It warms my heart to see her happy. Addi, on the other hand, is shooting daggers at my sisters and Carter from the bottom of the table. As the waiters take our drink orders and bring out dessert, I catch her attention to accompany me to the bathroom. We're best friends. One look and she knows what I'm trying to tell her— 'Get your ass to the bathroom now.'

I excuse myself and drag her by the hand, down the hall and into the restroom. I lock the door behind us.

"What the fuck is going on?"

She leans against the marble sink, her eyes focused on the fascinating tile pattern on the floor.

"I don't know what you mean." So, this is how she's going to play it.

"Okay. Have it your way. I haven't pushed you until now, but you need to get a grip. It's obvious that you like Carter, and yet you don't seem to want to give him a chance even though he's given you no reason to doubt that he's totally into you."

She interrupts me with her weak excuses. "Yeah, right. Have you *not* seen the way he's shamelessly flirting with your sisters? I wouldn't be surprised if he tries to take them both home tonight."

"Firstly, What the Fuck? They're my younger sisters. And secondly, they are the ones who are shamelessly flirting. From where I'm sitting, he's been very polite, but he can't stop staring at you every five fucking seconds." She's not happy at that last statement.

"Shut up, Lily. You don't know what you're talking about." Did she just tell me to shut up?

"Get a grip, Addi. Xander told me Carter really likes you. It's written all over his ridiculously handsome face. If you keep blowing hot and cold, you'll lose any chance you have with him. Make nice tonight, but don't lead him on if you're not interested. He's a nice guy, and he doesn't deserve the way you're treating him." I know it's harsh, but she needs someone to set her straight.

"You're supposed to be my best friend. Not Carter's."

"Don't talk shit! I'm saying this because I love you. I don't want you to miss out on a great guy because of that douchebag Gavin."

With her words left hanging in the air, I unlock the door to the restroom. "Don't let Gavin win."

I hope I wasn't too blunt, but I feel like it's the only way I'm going to get through to her. I leave her to think on that before coming back to the table. We're supposed to be celebrating graduation together, so I really hope she's not mad at me. I take my seat next to Xander. He can tell something just happened. I quietly assure him that everything is fine before taking a long swig of my Prosecco. Not my most feminine moment, but I really need a drink.

Addi emerges five minutes later, her makeup touched up and her head held high. She comes up behind me and gives me a hug, whispering in my ear. "Thanks, friend. Love you."

I clasp my hands on top of hers, giving them a squeeze. "Love you, too." She gives me a peck on the cheek and heads back to her seat.

Carter's eyes are on her the entire time, and amazingly, when he finally catches her eye, she gives him a genuine smile. He looks like the cat that got the cream for the rest of dinner. It's sweet, actually.

CHAPTER 15

XANDER

I AM SO FUCKING PROUD OF MY GIRL. WATCHING HER TODAY WAS LIKE an out of body experience. Being an only child, I've always been the center of attention, my achievements at the forefront of our family. It's been the same way in business—people falling over themselves to lavish me with praise. I thought I knew what it was to feel pride—I've never been shy about my accomplishments—but today I felt a sense of pride that far surpassed anything I've ever done.

Lily was transcendent when she took to the stage. I thought my heart was going to explode it was beating so fast. And when she sought me out in the crowd, flashing me her sweet smile—fuck me. I would have shouted to the entire stadium that she's mine, if I didn't think she'd die of embarrassment. I wanted to steal her away and have her all to myself, but it meant a lot to her to have her mom and sisters here today, and I'll do anything to make her happy.

Thankfully, dinner is over and so is family time. Now, I get to take her to Cube. I'd rather be taking her back to my apartment, but having her grind against me on a dance floor is a close second.

"Come on. You're riding with me. Carter's arranged a car for the rest of them. They're going to wait on Jason." We say our interim goodbyes and leave.

As soon we pull into traffic, I put up the privacy window and wrap my arms around Lily. It's so good to have her alone, if only for a few minutes.

"I got you a graduation present. I hope you like it."

She always gets this shy smile when I give her a gift. It's so fucking cute. "You didn't have to get me anything. You've already done so much for me today." I love that she never expects anything of me.

"Just open them." I'm really fucking nervous about this gift. She's either going to love it, or think it's way too soon, and freak out about us. Nothing with her is too soon. I want it all, and I want it now, like a greedy schoolboy with no self-control. I take a deep breath to steady my nerves before handing her an envelope and a Tiffany's box.

"I love it. Thank you." I got her a silver graduation cap.

"Just so you know, I'm not some crazy guy who's going to buy you a charm every time I see you. You just happen to have a lot of significant achievements going on in your life right now." Why the fuck do I sound like an idiot around her?

"I would never think you're crazy. It's lovely." She opens the second pouch, puzzled by what's inside—a silver and Tiffany blue double-decker bus charm.

"Open the envelope and it will make sense." Now I'm nervous. She opens the envelope painstakingly carefully and removes the contents —two first-class tickets to London, leaving on Monday.

Fuck. She's not saying anything. "Baby… talk to me. Are you happy?" I thought there would be screaming, or jumping, or… something.

"Oh my God, Xander. I can't believe you did this. This is amazing. I've been dreaming of going to London my whole life." I breathe a noticeable sigh of relief.

"Good. For a minute there you had me worried. You did *not* look happy."

I grab her face in my palms and kiss her with everything I have.

"I'm beyond happy. I can't believe I get to see London… and… I get to see it with you." Then I see the cogs starting to turn. "What if I don't have a passport?"

"Don't you know me by now? I have my sources." I wink at her before explaining. "I called Addi before I bought the tickets to check, I wasn't going to book tickets to somewhere you couldn't go!"

She pulls me into a fierce kiss, and I lose myself to the passion I feel for this woman. I take control, gently lifting her into my lap. This kiss is urgent and full of fire. I want her so badly right now, my dick hardens underneath her as I fuck her mouth with my tongue.

My hands begin to roam all over her toned little body, palming her breast over her dress, my other hand sliding under the hem. I stop in my tracks when I feel the lace of stocking tops.

"Fuck me, baby. You're wearing stockings. I need to see this." I pull her dress up to her waist, revealing delectable stockings, black garter belt and matching lace panties. "Fucking hell, Lily. That is the sexiest thing I have ever seen."

I grab her ass in my hands and kiss her with a ravenous hunger, setting a punishing rhythm with my tongue, desperate to take her right here. I feel like I might explode if I don't slide my cock inside of her, fucking her to the same rhythm as this kiss.

"God, Xander. I need you. Please… please, fuck me… Mr. Rhodes." I lose all control at those words, barking through the intercom for David to take us to my office. I know I should be at least a little embarrassed by how much I want her in this moment, but I'm not. Her words are like fire. "I want you now."

"As much as I would love to, I am *not* fucking you in a car, with my driver close enough to hear you come. That sound is for me." Thank fuck, we've arrived. The moment the car stops, I throw open the door and bark orders at David, telling him to wait for us. Lily looks mortified as I grab her by the hand and pull her through the doors and across the marble lobby. The security guards smile as I disappear into the elevator, pushing her against the wall and kissing her with everything I have, impatient to get her into the privacy of my office. It's strange in here at night, all dark corners and silence. It's exhilarating. "In there, now!" With a slap of her ass, I chase her into the confines of my office.

My lips find hers the moment the door closes behind us. I move quickly, taking Lily with me. I sit on the luxurious, hard wood of my desk, and within seconds, she's straddling my thighs, her dress around her waist. I quickly unbutton my suit pants and slip them down just enough for my cock to spring free. I yank the lace of her panties to one side and thrust two fingers inside of her as she drops her head onto my shoulder.

"You're so ready for me, sweets, and it's so fucking sexy." I'll never get enough of her. She's always ready for me—slick, wet, and inviting. I position myself at her entrance, drawing her down onto my cock, hard and fast. Being surrounded by her sweet pussy is intoxicating, I can't get enough of her, and I can't stifle the guttural moan that escapes my chest.

I devour her mouth with my tongue, fucking her in time with each delicious thrust of my cock. It's amazing, and I can feel her quickly building toward release.

"Oh God, Xander. I'm so close. I'm going to come."

I speak in between kisses. "Not. Yet. Sweet. Girl. Not. Until. I. Say. So… Your. Orgasm. Is. Mine." My voice is thick with desire. I try to hold back but I don't know how long I can last. She's so close. I start pounding into her harder and faster. "Yes, baby. That's it. Oh, fuck. Come for me now. Come *with* me." On command, she crashes over the edge, and I embrace the immense pleasure coursing through every nerve ending of my body. We scream and groan, riding out the after-shocks of our joint release. It is raw and primal. "Holy Shit! You are the sexiest woman alive. I don't think I'll be able to stand, let alone function in the club around other people."

"How do you think I'm going to face everyone with this obvious sex hair?" We both burst out laughing, my cock still pulsing inside her.

"I don't care what anyone thinks, baby. You look fucking breath-taking right now." I lift her up and place her down gently beside me, straightening her dress before attending to my own attire. We cuddle into each other for a few minutes, enjoying the post-coital bliss before making our way down to the car. I instruct David to take us to Cube. On the drive back toward the club, I take the opportunity to attach the new charms to Lily's bracelet.

When we arrive outside Cube, poor Lily can't look David in the eye as he opens the door for us. I think it's funny. He's the most professional man you'll ever meet, but I know he has a good sense of humor when it comes to something like this. We bypass the queue and head to the VIP area.

Addi is on Lily in seconds, trying to steal her away from me. I don't like to share, but Addi is a good friend to Lily, and it warms my heart to heart to hear Lily so excited as I leave them to go in search of Carter.

"Xander is taking me to London for a graduation present." I'm pretty sure even over the thundering beat of the music in here, the queue outside heard her scream, jumping up and down like a lunatic. It makes me laugh, and I am so genuinely excited to be taking her to the home of the *Globe Theater*. They look like kangaroos, high on speed, but it's cute to watch.

Lily didn't even notice I left to go get drinks. I tap her on the shoulder, handing them each a French martini each. Addi gives me a sloppy kiss on the cheek before punching me in the arm and saying, "Good work on the London trip."

I snake my arm around Lily's waist, pulling her close. Addi rolls her eyes at us and without a word disappears into the crowd, her drink in hand.

I see Carter watching her every move from the bar and as she loses herself in the music, he strides through the crowd and claims her as his. I'm getting a little hot under the collar just watching the way his hands are moving her, pulling her tight against his body. Lily's eyes are transfixed on them. Their connection is almost a visible aura around them. I trace the line of her neck and along her collarbone distracting her from her blatant voyeurism.

"You like that? Watching them writhe against each other as if there is no one here but the two of them. You can feel the sexual energy between them, can't you? Is it making your panties wet, Lily?"

She wants to say no, but everything I said is true. I know that look in her eye. My own sexual appetite awakens again, sated only thirty minutes ago, my desire is sparked watching their bodies move together, knowing how earth-shattering it feels when my body collides with Lily's. Anticipating how much pleasure we will wring from each other. She drops her head back onto my shoulder, allowing me unfettered access to her neck.

I kiss behind her ear in the spot I know drives her wild. I want her, right here, right now, and as I tease her with my tongue, I let out an uninhibited moan.

"I want you, Xander." Those four words are like a red rag to a bull.

My excitement spikes at the memory of the last time we were locked in the private room here, listening to hundreds of people on the other side of the door as we lost ourselves in each other. Before I realize what I'm doing, we're already locked inside.

She hasn't said a word to me yet, but I can see the pure, unadulterated lust in her eyes. I leave her standing at the door, striding across the room to sit on the sofa. I leisurely throw my arms across the back of the sofa, but my eyes give me away, greedily devouring every inch of her as she stands before me... waiting... wanting.

"Take off your clothes, Miss Tate."

"What?"

"You heard me. Now take your clothes off so I can look at you."

I'm in a dominant mood. I want to drink her in slowly, raking my eyes over her naked flesh before I devour her.

She slowly removes her dress, letting it drop to the floor. When she steps out of it, she flicks the dress with her shoe, landing it right in my lap. It's so damn sexy. I gasp as I take in the sight of her half-naked body, dressed only in stockings, a garter belt, lace panties and a matching bra. Fucking perfection. She moves to take off her heels, but I stop her.

"Leave them on. You look so fucking sexy right now, I just want to bend you over the desk and fuck you until you're screaming my name."

"What are you waiting for? Fuck me, Mr. Rhodes." Holy fuck! My restraint shatters in an instant and I'm up, tearing off my jacket and waistcoat, shirt and tie. I rip open my slacks before moving to the desk. The sight of her makes me lose all control as she bites down hard on her lower lip.

"Do you want me to touch you, Miss Tate?"

"Yes."

A sly grin slides across my lips. "Come here." I'm desperate to own her, body and soul. I back her against the edge of the desk before staking my claim on her mouth. Our lips and tongues crashing together in perfect symmetry. She rakes her nails down my back, and it's all I can do not to pound into her as hard as I can.

Our kiss becomes all-consuming, my hands fisting in her hair, clutching her ass, palming her breasts. We can't get enough. I make quick work of removing her bra, guiding her back to lie on the desk, her gorgeous, full breasts heavy with arousal, on display just for me.

I move my head down, caressing her already hardened nipples with my lips. I take one into my mouth, kissing, suckling, tugging on it while forcefully grabbing the other in my hand. Her skin is silky smooth on my tongue, sending a pulse straight to my cock. I slide one hand beneath her panties as I turn my attention to her other breast, teasing it with his mouth. I unleash a guttural groan as my hand meets with the evidence of her arousal.

"Miss Tate, it would appear that you are more than ready for me." Her back arches off the desk as I thrust my fingers inside of her. She feels so fucking good.

I tease her with a few deep, delicious thrusts before pulling out. With the speed of a cat, I flip her onto her front, legs on the ground spread wide. Her naked breasts are pressed against my cold hard desk. I grab my cock, letting it loose from my boxer shorts as an ache begins to build.

"As pretty as these are, I'm afraid they have to go." I rip her panties, throwing them to the floor, exposing her slick, throbbing sex to my gaze. A groan of approval escapes her throat as I grab her hair to anchor her in place as I rub my cock up and down her wet folds, coating myself in her arousal. Without warning I thrust into her, right to the hilt. The stretching feeling of her tight pussy around me is exquisite. I halt my movements, taking a moment to control my breathing.

"Do you want me to fuck you, Miss Tate?"

Her answer drips from her lips, a plea for me to take her.

"Yes."

One sharp, hard thrust.

"Are you mine, Miss Tate?"

"God, yes, Xander."

"Yes, who?"

I tug on her hair. A second delicious thrust inside her.

"Yes, Mr. Rhodes. I'm yours." I love it when she calls me that. It's such a turn on I can barely control myself.

"MINE."

I set a punishing rhythm, taking her hard and fast, my desire animalistic. As I thrust deeper and harder, I find her clit, rubbing in circles, complementing every sweet thrust of my hips. It's only seconds before she's screaming my name, and I let her ride out her orgasm before chasing my own, her walls clenching around me, milking every possible ounce of pleasure from my cock.

I collapse against her back, feeling the sheen of sweat between our bodies. The smell of sex is in the air as I kiss up and down her spine, gently caressing her side with my hand, the other holding my weight. I pull out of her, watching my come run down her leg.

"Stay right there, baby. You look so incredible right now with my seed running out of your sweet little pussy. So fucking hot."

I grab a handkerchief from my pocket before dropping to my knees, taking care to gently clean Lily, making sure to wipe the tops of her stockings, covered in my come. When I'm finished, I place a sweet little kiss on her ass before standing and pulling her up into my arms.

"You are so beautiful, Lily. I can't get enough of you." I nuzzle her neck, losing myself in her scent, but I'm startled from our tender moment by a bang on the door. I hurry to grab Lily's bra and dress, thankful that I locked the door when we came in. The banging continues.

"Xander. Man, we have a problem. Put it back in your pants and get out here." It's Carter.

Shit. He wouldn't come looking for me if it wasn't something important. I zip Lily's dress, making sure to pick up her torn panties as we head to the door.

"This better be fucking important, Carter." I usher him away from the doorway to let Lily make a quick exit without having to talk to him.

I follow Carter downstairs through the crowd, anxious to know why I was dragged away from a very hot, naked Lily.

You've got to be kidding me. My blood runs cold seeing who's standing at the bar... fucking Natalie. Carter leaves us to talk, but I wish he hadn't. The way she's touching me—running her hands up and down my biceps—makes me want to vomit. We have a short and not so sweet discussion before I send her on her way.

I go in search of Lily, but she's nowhere to be found. Addi finally tells me she went to the restroom but hasn't returned. Fuck!

I quickly make my way down the hall, stopping in front of the door. It's locked and there's a line of angry women outside waiting to get in. I know she's in there, so I bust the door open to find Lily with tear-streaked cheeks.

"What the hell, Xander? This is the ladies room in case you hadn't noticed."

"You've been in here for twenty fucking minutes. I was worried about you."

"Why didn't you send Addi in to check on me then?" Her tone is exasperated.

"She's dancing with Carter, and I wanted to check on you myself."

"Well, I'm fine, so you can leave, and I'll be out in a minute."

I turn to leave when I hear her mumbling under her breath. "I'm surprised you noticed I was gone."

I spin back around, anger in my eyes. "What the fuck? What's going on? Of course, I would notice. You're all I fucking think about 24/7." Did I not just show her how much she means to me?

"I'm just saying... you disappeared, and I'm surprised you noticed I was gone." I'm relieved. For a moment I thought she saw Natalie. That's the last thing we need right now. "What did Carter need you for?"

I feign innocence. "Just a staff problem. It's sorted now, so I'm all yours for the rest of the night." I move toward her.

"I didn't realize your *ex* works here. You lying sack of shit!"

I pace the floor, running my hands through my hair in frustration. Why did I just say that? "Fucking. Fuck. Fuck… She fucks everything up. Listen to me, baby. Natalie turned up downstairs and Carter thought it would be better if I went down and asked her to leave so she didn't come up here and make a scene. I didn't want her to ruin your night. I was going to tell you about it tomorrow… after we had a good night celebrating your graduation."

"You just lied to my face, Xander. Why should I believe you now? Were you down there laughing at how gullible I am? I was begging you to fuck me ten minutes before she was running her hands all over you. Well, fuck both of you. I'm not going to be second best, or the other woman, or whatever the fuck I am to you." She tries to force her way past me and out the door, but I won't let her. I'm fucking livid.

"Wait just a goddamn minute. I told you why I didn't want to tell you she was here. I wanted us to enjoy tonight. And as for the rest of the shit you're spouting, I'm going to assume that's the work of the alcohol and your ridiculous Google search, because if you don't know what you mean to me by now then I'm obviously doing a fucking pathetic job here."

As I reach out to touch her face, she shirks from my hand, stabbing a dagger through my heart.

"Please, don't pull away from me. I made a mistake, but it was to protect you. I'm sorry, it won't happen again. I promise." When I reach out again, this time she lets me soothe her. I press a tentative kiss to her lips. "You could never be the other woman, or second best to anyone. Any man lucky enough to know you, knows you're the one you don't let get away. The one who makes you stop noticing other women altogether. The only one who thinks you're second best… is you. You. Are. Amazing. There is no one who compares to you, Lily.

Not for me. Please believe me when I tell you, you're number one with me. There is no number two, or three. You're the only one. The only one there's ever going to be."

The kiss that follows is a plea, a heartfelt request for Lily to believe me. I implore her to open up to me, licking my tongue over the crease of her sweet seductive lips. She tastes so intoxicating. I pull her flush with my body, connected from chest to hip, my heart thundering against her breasts as our kiss deepens. I can feel her heart hammering, confirmation that I affect her, a comfort to the ache I feel in my chest.

We could have been standing like this for a minute or an hour and I wouldn't know, I'm so lost to the sensations and emotions she stirs within me.

I break contact just long enough to pull her out of the ladies room and back her up against the wall in the hallway. I relish the feel of my body pressed against her, my sole purpose to bring her pleasure. There is a strange calm surrounding our frenzied connection in a club full of people who doesn't make sense. Everyone around us disappears, everything we've been fighting about vanishing. There is only this, only us—our bodies, our mouths, and the tangible bond crackling between us. After what seems like hours, we pull apart, our breaths ragged. I press my forehead to hers.

"Please, hear me. Please, believe me. You have *nothing* to worry about. You are *all* I see, *all* I want. How could you *not* be?" I lift her face, forcing our eyes to meet. With an unspoken understanding that we are on the same page, we head back into the VIP. lounge to spend some time with our friends.

To bring us back down from our rollercoaster ride, we are greeted by the sight of Logan being... what I can only describe as mauled by Lily's twin sisters on the dance floor, but to be fair to them, he seems to be enjoying every minute of it.

I spot Addi and Carter in a dark corner looking cozy. I hope she gives him a chance, he's a great guy and he's crazy about her.

I order a bottle of champagne from the bar, and we find our own quiet corner to celebrate in. The rest of the evening is more chilled.

We dance, we laugh, and talk about what we're going to do when we get to London. I'm so excited. In three days, I'll be in London… with Lily.

By 2 a.m. she can barely stand after dancing for hours and having far too much champagne and cocktails. I decide it's time to take her home. I'm pretty sure Addi is taking Carter home to their apartment, so I take Lily back to the penthouse, and she is more than happy to oblige.

CHAPTER 16

LILY

I WAKE UP CONFUSED. THE LAST THING I REMEMBER WAS GETTING IN the car outside the club. When I take in my surroundings, I realize that I am tucked into Xander's side, snuggled in his huge comfy bed, wearing one of his t-shirts and nothing else. Wow. I must have been really drunk last night not to wake up when he was obviously taking such good care of me. He squeezes me closer.

"Go back to sleep, sweets. We have nowhere to be today. You're stuck with me." That puts a smile on my face—as if anyone would feel 'stuck' with Xander Rhodes.

I kiss his warm chest and snuggle in, wrapping my legs over his and drift back into a peaceful sleep until lunchtime. When we finally wake, we spend another hour lazing in bed planning what we need to do today to get organized for London. I have shopping and packing to do. I can't go to London without some new clothes! Xander doesn't have much to do because he already knew we were going so he's decided to take me wherever I need to go today. Eek! I'm so excited. I don't think I'll believe it until we're standing in front of Big Ben.

We spend the day in Saks, and Xander insists on paying for anything I so much as look at. He's crazy adorable, following me round like a walking clothes rail, holding everything, giving me a running commentary of the naughty things he plans to do to me in each outfit. I let him *think* that he's going to pay for all this stuff, but I have a cunning plan.

He's a great shopping partner, he doesn't moan, keeps me laughing, gives his honest opinion of the clothes I show him, and makes me stop for regular treats and drinks. Once I've gotten everything I need for our trip, we head to the cashier, and this is where my plan comes into play. Xander sets down all my lovely purchases on the counter.

"Could you go pick up those sunglasses I saw earlier? I meant to go back for them. The Dior ones." He gives me a peck on the forehead and off he goes with a smile on his face.

I turn back to the cashier and tell her what I need. "Can you ring this up as quickly as possible, please? If you don't, he'll insist on paying."

She laughs. "Gorgeous and generous. Let him pay, honey. He's a keeper." He definitely is, but I don't want him for his money, and I need him to understand that.

"Please, just ring it up. I really want to pay for it myself." She does as I ask, and I sign my name on the dotted line just as Xander returns.

"Miss Tate, what do you think you're doing? Did you actually intend on buying these sunglasses, or was I just sent on a wild-goose chase?" He's sporting a disgruntled but amused smirk.

"Sorry, but I had to pay for this stuff myself. You're paying for the trip. It wouldn't feel right if you paid for all of this as well, and I know you wouldn't have let me if I hadn't sent you away." I give him my best puppy-dog eyes and a saccharin sweet smile. He can't resist, grabbing me by the face and setting a smacker of a kiss on me right in front of the cashier.

"Oh, honey. Where did you find him? I need to get me one of those."

I giggle. "Sorry. I'm pretty sure he's one of a kind."

When my stuff is all bagged and ready to go, Xander brushes past me and puts the sunglasses on the counter. "I'll take these, please." He can't be serious.

"What are you doing?"

He doesn't so much as glance in my direction as he answers. "I am not a man who gets sent on pointless errands, Miss Tate. I'm buying these sunglasses for a woman I happen to be taking to London on Monday. Please don't interrupt me, it's very rude." I can't see it, but I hear the smug grin plastered all over his face. I don't have the energy to fight a battle that I will inevitably lose. I decide instead just to kiss him on the cheek and say, "thank you."

He unburdens me of my bags, and we decide it's time to go home. I was lucky enough this morning that Xander had arranged for some casual clothes and my favorite toiletries to be at his apartment. Of course, I didn't think of that when I was getting drunk last night. I really don't deserve to feel as good as I do today.

He gave me some concoction to drink that made me feel great.

When we make our way outside, I don't know why, but I'm surprised to find David waiting for us with the SUV. Xander puts the bags in the back before ushering me into the car.

"I'm sure we could have walked back to your apartment." He laces our fingers together pulling me closer as we start moving.

"Well, I figured you'd have a few bags, and I thought you might want to go to your apartment to get organized for Monday."

"Okay. Thanks." My obvious disappointment is thinly veiled.

"It's not that I don't want you to stay at my place. Heck, I'd keep you there permanently if I had my way." What the hell? I know it's way too soon, and it was probably just an off the cuff remark, but my heart soars. I try to hide my elation.

"I just figured you need to get packed, and you'd probably want a night with Addi before we go. It would be easier if you stay with me tomorrow night so we can just head to the airport when we get up. Obviously, if you want to stay on your own tomorrow night as well, then I'll come pick you up a bit earlier on Monday morning." He sounds sad, and I'm a little over eager.

"No... no... NO. I am completely okay with staying with you tomorrow night. Thanks for thinking of me and Addi. I hope she's free tonight." The look on his face tells me he's already checked. "She's free, isn't she?" I can't help but smile. He really does think of everything.

"Yeah. I just wanted to make sure you got to see her before we go."

"You're a control freak you know that, right? Lucky for you I find it quite sexy."

He's on me in seconds. "Oh, Lily. If it's control that does it for you, you ain't seen nothing yet." He kisses me, pinning me to the spot, helpless but to acquiesce to his desires. I'm breathless when we pull up in front of my building. I don't want to leave him, and he seems nervous as he rubs his thumb over the back of my hand.

"I was wondering if you want to have Sunday dinner with my parents tomorrow. I'd love for them to meet you." A shy little boy stares back at me.

"That sounds lovely. Guess I better go and get my packing sorted then." He senses I'm not ready to leave him yet and gets out to open my door—offering, or rather demanding, to bring my bags up to the apartment. I let him because I'll take any extra time. I'm addicted to him.

As I open the door, Addi comes barreling down the hallway, enveloping me in her arms. "Friend! Girls' night in tonight. I get you all to myself. Woohoo!" She peeks around my shoulder. "No offence, Xander." That makes him laugh.

"None taken. I know I'm stealing your girl away for the better part of a week so this was the least I could do." He sets down my bags and takes my hand, leading me out toward the elevator.

"I'll miss you tonight. Call me later?" As soon as I say yes, his lips capture mine in a tender but intense kiss. His tongue teasing mine in a gentle rhythm. I run my hands up his back, losing myself to the sensation of his soft lips, his delicious tongue and his muscles rippling under my fingertips. His scent surrounds me. I'm bereft when the elevator arrives and he steps inside. He holds my gaze, his stunning ice-blue eyes never leaving mine as the doors come between us. When they finally close and he's out of sight, I just stand there like an idiot, staring at the doors. Addi comes out and throws her arms around my neck from behind.

"You've got it bad, Lilliput. Dang girl, he must be phenomenal in bed." We burst out laughing and head back into our apartment for a night of wine, Chinese food, and some good old chick flicks. We have a great time, and eventually she mentions her night with Carter.

"Okay. I'm going to choke this out, so don't be an asshat about it. You were right." Oh. Holy. Mother. Of. Pearl. That is the first time… ever… that Addi has admitted I'm right about anything. I'll be damned if I'm not going to milk it for all it's worth.

"What was that? I didn't quite hear you. Please… *Please*… tell me again."

"Ass-hat it is then. You were right, you loser. I was punishing Carter for Gavin's mistakes and he didn't deserve it. He stayed last night, and we're planning to go out tomorrow on our first proper date. You happy now?" I can tell she's excited at the prospect of going on a date with him. Her eyes are sparkling, and her cheeks are glowing.

"Of course, I'm happy… for you. I don't want that douche Gavin wasting any more of your time. Carter is *nothing* like him, and he's obviously into you. Did you have a good time last night?" Her sly siren smile creeps onto her lips. Oh damn, I've just opened myself up to hear every last detail of their sexcapades, and she doesn't disappoint. I hear a play-by-play of all the places I'll need to disinfect because they've apparently had sex everywhere in this apartment. Where do these boys get their stamina from, it's ridiculous?

We stay up talking into the early hours. Gladly, at some point during our nonsense we moved to my room and Addi helped me pack.

"I can't believe he's taking you to London. What a flashy bastard." I know she's just kidding around but I still feel the need to defend him.

"He's not a flashy bastard. He's just really generous with what he has. And I'm not just talking about his money." I say wiggling my eyebrows. That has both of us in a wine induced giggling stupor for a good fifteen minutes. It must be after three before we get my packing finished and collapse on my bed.

I wake in the morning to Addi's hand on my face. Then I remember our late night and copious quantities of alcohol. I glance at the clock—it's already 11 a.m. I am in dire need of coffee. I grab my phone off the sofa and start making a pot of coffee. As I wait for the machine to supply me with my much-needed hit, I check my phone. Oh crap. I was supposed to call Xander last night. I have a missed call from him and quite a few texts.

12:01 a.m.

> Mr. P: Hey, sweets. Haven't heard from you. Tried calling. Call me when you get this. Miss you. X

12:59 a.m.

> Mr. P: Did you forget about me, Miss Tate?

3:23 a.m.

> Mr. P: I don't like being ignored.

Shit. I immediately dial his number. He answers on the fourth ring. "Xander Rhodes." Wow, he's mad. He knows it's me.

"Hi… it's Lily."

"Remembered me, did you?" I feel bad. I obviously hurt his feelings. I would feel the same if he had said he would call me and didn't bother.

"I'm sorry, honey. I lost track of time and we ended up collapsing on my bed after packing for the trip." Silence. That can't be good.

"If you're looking to get back into my good books by giving me a mental image of you and Addi in bed together… it's working." Okay, maybe he's not so mad.

"Not like that, you pervert! We were exhausted." He's chuckling now.

"Can't blame a guy for dreaming."

"Anyway. I am sorry I didn't call. I actually really missed you. What did you do last night?"

"I hung out with Carter. We played some pool, drank some beer. Guy stuff. We didn't collapse in bed together in case you're wondering." I take a moment to create that visual in my head. Two gorgeous men in Xander's bed. Mmm.

"Thanks for the mental picture. I'll treasure it."

"You better not be thinking about anyone in a bed other than me. I mean it." He's jealous of a joke. I love him.

"You're jealous."

"Fucking right I am. I don't want you thinking about any man other than me. Especially not Carter. I would hate to have to kick his ass." I let out a full-on belly laugh.

"You're not serious? You would punch your best friend if *I* thought about him in a sexual way?"

"YES! Let's stop talking about this, I want to punch him right now, just because of this conversation." He sounds genuinely upset.

"You're so adorable, honey."

"I like it when you call me that."

"Good. *Honey.* What time are we going to your parents' house for dinner? I need time to make myself beautiful."

"Without seeing you I can tell you're already stunning." Such a smooth talker. "I'll pick you up at three, if that's okay?"

"That's great. I can't wait to see you."

"Me too, sweets. I better go get some work done before we go. See you at three."

"See you then." I'm already counting the hours until he's at my door.

I fuss and deliberate for at least an hour about what to wear to meet Xander's parents, and keep my makeup minimal. I don't want his mom to think I'm trashy.

The time flies by and before I know it, he's standing in my doorway, sexy as hell in a crisp white shirt with the sleeves rolled up, blue jeans and his mussed-up hair. I could lick him all over.

"Keep looking at me like that and you can explain to my mom why we're late for dinner." How can he make me blush within two minutes of arriving? He hasn't even set foot inside. He leans in and places a chaste kiss on my lips.

"I missed the taste of you last night."

I kiss him back. "I missed you, too. I'm kind of used to you now." He deepens the kiss, unleashing the butterflies in my stomach.

"Good, because you're stuck with me."

Addi pipes up behind us, "I think I just got diabetes watching the two of you."

"Oh, be quiet, Addi. You'll be the same with Carter tonight so don't give me any of your crap."

Xander has a boyish grin on his face. "I was hanging with him last night. He has quite the night planned for the two of you. Of course, I can't tell you anything because he'd kill me. I'm just saying... be prepared." He thinks he's funny winding her up.

"Leave her alone. It took this long to get them on a date. Don't mess it up or you'll be dealing with me."

"Oh, baby. That's not a threat. I'll *deal* with you any time, any place."

"Right, let's go and leave Addi to get ready for what I'm sure will be a lovely evening." I hug her goodbye while Xander grabs my bag for London.

"Call me as soon as you land so I don't worry."

I give her an extra squeeze. "Of course, I will. Love you, friend. See you next week."

"Look after her... or you'll be sorry." Xander smiles.

"Of course. Precious cargo. I'm aware. Have a good night and be nice to *my* best friend. He's a good guy."

We head down to his car, and I'm surprised to find no sign of David today. Instead, his pride and joy is sitting on the curb—his Ferrari. He just manages to shoehorn my case inside before opening my door. The car roars to life as we set off to see his parents.

I'm going to meet Xander's parents.

Shit.

CHAPTER 17

LILY

THE DRIVE TO HIS PARENTS DOESN'T TAKE LONG, ESPECIALLY THE WAY HE drives. I try to take my mind off how nervous I am by asking how he knows Carter. Turns out they've been friends their whole lives. Their dads own a very successful law firm together. Their families have always been close so they're more like brothers than best friends.

It's nice to hear him talk about when they were growing up together and all the fun stuff they've done. They both went to Columbia, which led to an answer to my question 'Why were you on campus the day we met?'

"I was going to meet an old professor of mine. I try to meet up with him at least once every few months. That's where I was going when you came crashing into my life."

I'm so glad I did. I can't image my life without him. I ponder that as we make our way to Staten Island. Bruno Mars is playing on the radio, and I don't think he realizes he's singing along, so I keep quiet, listening to his voice. I've always thought it's sexy when Bruno sings *Billionaire*, but hearing Xander is infinitely sexier. He has a good voice, deep, breathy, and sinfully sexy. I think I just came a little. Oh. My. God. I have a stupidly goofy grin on my face when he sneaks a glance in my direction.

"Are you laughing at me? Is my voice that bad?" He's playing with me. He knows exactly how he affects me.

"Definitely not. I've always thought that song was kind of hot, and you singing it has most definitely secured it as the sexiest song of all time."

I thought he was going to be the one laughing at me after that comment, but he doesn't. He simply keeps singing. I watch and listen, captivated by his voice, the very last line dripping with sex. I feel like I've just been seduced.

I need to get my mind off Xander and the word 'fucking' before I meet his mother. I don't want to meet her with this buzzing feeling between my legs.

"Is that your theme tune? Seems fitting." I'm rewarded with his soft chuckles.

"Ha ha. Not quite."

"If you can't joke about being a billionaire, what can you joke about." I like teasing him.

"Not what I meant and you know it, Miss Tate." He squeezes my thigh, sending a jolt of electricity straight to my already throbbing sex. "I just mean… I never wanted for anything growing up. My dad is successful, and I've always had money available to me. I'm not a rags to riches story. I guess I'm just motivated. I didn't want to live off my dad. I wanted to make my own mark on the world. I'm not being big headed when I say, I'm very good at what I do, and I've put in a lot of hard work to get where I am now. I enjoy the game, the risk, the gamble. Plus, it's nice to be able to share the wealth, you know? I've been able to set up charities and invest in projects that give less fortunate kids a chance to make something of themselves and get the support they need to achieve it."

Could he be any more perfect? It's sickening. Every time I find out something new about him, he only intrigues me further.

"It's even more impressive that you didn't *need* to be this driven. You could have lived off your dad's money, but you didn't. It's amazing."

"Thanks. What about you? You live in a rather nice apartment on the Upper West Side. What's your story?"

"Well, I don't come from mega-money if that's what you're asking. When my dad died, my mom sold our ranch. She kept the money and the insurance policy payout and put it into a trust for me and my sisters. My mom is a successful book editor at one of Manhattan's biggest publishing houses, so she was able to raise us more than comfortably on her salary. I decided to use my inheritance to go to Columbia, and I get to stay in a nice apartment with Addi because her parents are *very* well off, and they pay half the rent. I was reluctant to accept their offer, but they wanted to make sure that we lived in a good area, close to campus. We split the other half of the rent between us. It's been amazing to focus on my studies without worrying about getting a job during term time. I still worked summers to top up my funds but I'm aware that they won't last forever so I won't be living on the Upper East Side for too much longer. I want to be self-sufficient after I graduate and get a little place of my own that I can afford."

"Here's a question for you. If your mom is so well connected in the industry you want to be a part of, couldn't you give your manuscript to her to submit?" I give him a disapproving look.

"You of all people should understand that I want to do it on my own merits. My job at T Magazine will allow me to make my own contacts and learn how the industry works. When I finish my manuscript, it will go to someone *I* choose, and if they like it, it will be because it's good." His grin is huge.

"I know that. I'm proud of you for wanting to make it on your own terms. I know you'll write a *New York Times* best seller one day. You're my girl, and you're phenomenal." I blush at his words.

"Thanks. I appreciate the vote of confidence. I might need you to tell me a few times along the way about the whole *New York Times* thing!" With a chuckle he agrees. We pull up to a huge set of iron gates. They have an intricate design along the top and the view up to the house is stunning. House is playing it down, this place is a mansion, and it's absolutely gorgeous.

Xander drives carefully up the gravel driveway, winding its way toward the massive double door entrance, muttering under his breath about the gravel scratching the paintwork on his car. I feel a rush of nerves as he switches off the engine.

"We're here. You look like you're about to vomit. Are you okay?" Silence. "Lily. Look at me." I manage to pull my gaze from my hands wringing restlessly in my lap.

"I'm just a bit nervous. What if they don't like me? They'll know I'm not good enough for you." Xander grabs my face, his own radiating anger.

"They will love you. Don't ever say you're not good enough for me. I'm the one who's thanking my lucky stars every day that you want to be with me. Please, don't make this difficult on yourself. Just be… you… and everything will be great." A sweet, tender kiss calms the raging storm inside me, giving me peace in the knowledge that Xander wants me, and if he says it will be fine, it will be.

He takes my hand to help me out of the car and keeps a firm, reassuring grip as we make our way to the front door. Before we get the chance to ring the bell, the door flies open, and a beautiful woman has her arms held out to welcome him.

"Sweetheart. It's so lovely to see you." She envelops him in a hug that only a mother can give.

"You look great, Mom. A lot better." He holds her at arm's length, really studying her. After a moment, he turns to me.

"Mom, I'd like you to meet my girlfriend, Lily Tate." I hold out my hand to greet her, but she pulls me into a warm embrace. It's a lovely feeling, if a bit disconcerting.

"It's so nice to meet you, Lily. I've heard so many wonderful things about you." He's been talking to his mom about me.

"It's a pleasure to meet you, Mrs. Rhodes."

"I'll have none of that. Please, call me Lizzie." I already love this woman. She's so warm and inviting, just like my mom used to be with me, before…

"Let the poor girl go, Lizzie. She's not even in the door yet and you're smothering her." A low, jovial voice that sounds very much like Xander, comments from inside the house. His dad comes into view.

He is a distinguished looking gentleman, very handsome in his own right, but he doesn't look like his son.

Xander takes after his mom. She has the same stunning eyes and hair. Her skin is not quite as tanned, but she really is a beautiful woman. Not what I expected, though. She has short, cropped hair, and I don't know why, but I expected her to have a long braid down her back. She lets go of me to usher us into the house. Xander gives his dad a handshake and a pat on the back—a man hug.

"Hey, Dad. I'd like you to meet Lily."

"Very nice to meet you, Lily." His dad gives me a quick hug. "Come on in and we'll get you a drink."

"Thank you, Mr. Rhodes. It's lovely to meet you, too."

"Call me Jonathan."

Xander leads me into a spacious living room with stunningly high ceilings and large windows looking out over the yard, and by yard, I mean acres upon acres of land. The flowerbeds are perfectly pruned, and the trees are trimmed, the expansive lawn is immaculate and there are wonderful decking and patio areas with soft lighting and a gorgeous outdoor eating area.

With his hand on the small of my back he moves me toward one of the sofas and we take a seat. He laces our fingers together and gives me a warm smile as I struggle to calm my nerves.

"You have a beautiful home, Lizzie."

She thanks me as she takes a seat on one of the sofas. Jonathan moves over to a small bar area in the corner of the room. "Would you like a drink?"

"White wine if you have it, please."

"I'll have the same. I'm driving, so just a half glass for me." It's nice to see Xander in this setting. He's so relaxed. Jonathan organizes drinks for everyone before sitting down across from us, next to Lizzie.

"So, Xander tells us you're off to London tomorrow." I hope they don't think I'm after his money.

"Yes. He organized the trip as a graduation present. I told him it was far too much, but he wouldn't hear of it. We went shopping yesterday to get everything we needed, and I managed to trick him into letting me pay." They both laugh at my statement. Xander chimes in to tell his side of the story.

"She's the only person I'd let dupe me and get away with it. She sent me on a wild-goose chase for sunglasses she didn't want while she paid for everything else. I bought the damn things anyway. I knew it would drive her crazy. She even put up a fight about that." His dad gives me a warm smile. He understands the point I was trying to make.

"I think you've met your match in this one, son." Xander nods, squeezing my hand.

We sit like this for a while before dinner is served. There is a delicious looking roast in the center of the table surrounded by platters of vibrant colored vegetables and a yummy looking gravy. The roasted potatoes look positively mouthwatering, and as we take our seats, I compliment Lizzie on such a wonderful spread.

"I'd love to take credit for it, dear, but I catered in today. I'm not quite up to full-strength at the moment and wanted to make sure we had a nice dinner. I hope you enjoy it."

"Well, it certainly looks delicious." Lizzie gives Xander an odd look which he reciprocates before eating his dinner. The conversation flows naturally, and Jonathan tells me some great stories about Xander when he was young. I bet he was super cute. I also got some dirt on Carter to share with Addi.

Xander tells them about our plans in London. When they ask about my family, his face contorts with worry. I know his parents notice but I decide to play dumb and give them the short version of my life. I just don't mention my dad, and they're gracious enough not to ask. Xander's phone rings just as we finish our meal and when he looks at the caller display, he's not happy.

"Sorry, guys, I have to take this. Work stuff. I'll just be a minute." He excuses himself and heads out into the garden. I track his movements as he gets further and further away from the house, pacing back and forth, looking more and more frustrated as the conversation goes on. Xander's mom tries to distract me.

"Why don't I give you a tour of the house while he finishes up?" I readily accept because something in my gut tells me it's more than a work problem.

We wander from room to room, and I listen to Lizzie as she gushes with pride for her only son. It's lovely to hear.

"You probably noticed Xander was a bit awkward earlier when I mentioned I wasn't feeling a hundred percent at the moment."

I nod, "I didn't want to pry."

"I know, dear. He knows I don't like people to feel sorry for me, which is obviously why he didn't tell you. I'm recovering from breast cancer surgery." I'm shocked.

"I'm so sorry, Lizzie. How are you?" I'm genuinely worried about this woman I've just met—the woman who brought Xander into the world.

"I'm doing much better now, thank you. Unfortunately, this is the third time I've had to fight cancer. It's tough for Xander and Jonathan watching me go through this over and over again, but they are both amazing men and they've supported me every step of the way." I'm left speechless at what this family has had to deal with.

"Feel free not to answer if it's too personal, but when was the first time you found out?" Lizzie pats my shoulder, a small smile on her lips.

"Of course. You can ask anything you want. I was first diagnosed when Xander was five. We had been thinking about having another baby for a while, but I had been putting it off, enjoying my time with Xander too much. I started to feel unwell, but I didn't think anything of it until I found a lump on my left breast. I immediately made an appointment to see a consultant and by the end of that week I was having chemo and radiation. I managed to beat it, but the radiation left me unable to have more children, so I consider myself extremely blessed to have Xander. He was such a strong little boy, even at five, he helped me through a very difficult time and asked for nothing in return."

My heart breaks for a scared five-year-old Xander, terrified of losing his mommy, but being strong for her.

"Then I found a lump in my right breast when he was sixteen. He should have been out with his friends having fun and being a normal sixteen-year old boy, but not him, he came to every chemo session, rubbed my back when I was sick, and looked after me every day without complaint. They caught it early enough that time. I had the lump removed and the treatment got anything they might have missed. I really thought that was the end of it."

I haven't noticed a single room on our tour of the house, but I understand that Lizzie wants me to know what Xander has been through.

"A year ago, I found another lump, and I immediately had a double-mastectomy followed by chemotherapy. Now, I've come through it, and I had reconstructive surgery two months ago. I'm healing well but I'm still a bit tired out. Xander worries too much, but I can't really blame him. He's been through a lot. It's lovely to see how happy he is lately, and I'm certain that you're the reason behind it." I know I'm blushing uncontrollably.

"Thank you, Lizzie. He's made a huge difference in my life in the short time I've known him. He means the world to me."

"I know." She gives me a gentle squeeze before we head back to the living room.

Xander and his dad are deep in discussion when we walk in, but as soon as they see me the conversation stops dead. There is definitely something going on. After a second, Xander puts on his best panty-melting smile and stands up to greet me, wrapping his arms around me he nuzzles into my neck.

"Where have you been? I came in and you were gone. You been having fun with my mom?" I glance to Lizzie who smiles warmly back at me.

"Yes, your mom and I had a really nice chat, and I got some dirt on you and Carter into the bargain."

"Oh, really? I'll torture it out of you later. Anyway, we better get going, we've got a big day tomorrow and I want you to get a good sleep so you can enjoy London when we get there."

His concern is sweet, but I can't shake the feeling that something is off. It takes us thirty minutes to say our goodbyes, his mom and dad wishing us well for our trip, asking me to visit again soon. I really like them. On the drive home Xander is quiet.

"Are you okay?" He immediately snaps out of his funk.

"Of course. My parents loved you and I get you to myself in London for the better part of a week. I've just got a work problem to sort out before we go. Nothing for you to worry about, sweets. I just want to make sure nothing interrupts our time away." I can't help but probe further.

"Is that what you were talking to your dad about when I came in earlier? You stopped talking as soon as you saw me. I thought maybe I had done something wrong."

He looks pained as he answers. "You haven't done anything wrong. I was talking to my dad about a problem, and he was giving me advice, that's all. Honestly, you have *nothing* to worry about. I promise I'll be more fun when we get to London and work is a distant memory." I take him at his word and leave it at that.

He had a point about getting a good sleep. By the time we make it back to his apartment I'm exhausted. My night with Addi must be catching up with me. I quickly get ready for bed. Xander has to work for a while, but comes to lie next to me, telling me he'll get it done in his office after I fall asleep.

"You can go. I'll be fine." He kisses the top of my head as he curls me around his body.

"I missed you last night. I want to stay with you until you fall asleep. No arguments." I'm too tired to fight him, so I nestle against his chest and fall asleep in his warm embrace.

I'M STARTLED AWAKE AT FOUR BY THE SOUND OF THE FRONT DOOR. I reach over to wake Xander, terrified there's an intruder in the apartment. He isn't here. His side of the bed hasn't been slept in. I'm cowering beneath the covers praying that I'm just having a bad dream when the door creaks open. A strangled scream escapes my throat.

"Fuck! Lily, it's me. It's just me." I think my heart is about to explode. "I'm so sorry I frightened you. I was trying to be quiet."

"Where were you? It's 4 a.m." He strips off his clothes and opens the door to the master bathroom.

"I had to go into the office. I'm sorry. It's all fixed now. We can go away and enjoy a break from everything. I'm just going to take a quick shower and I'll be right in."

Five minutes later he's under the covers, sliding in next to me, pulling me close to his hard body.

"I'm all yours for the next five days, no work, I promise. It's not always like this. I don't want you to think that life with me is going to be all phone calls and crazy hours."

"It's fine. Let's just get some sleep, we have a long day ahead. I'm glad you got whatever it was done."

"Me too..." I sense there is something more to that statement, but right now I just want to calm my frayed nerves with the warmth and comfort that being in Xander's arms provides.

"Kiss me." No other words are spoken between us.

He claims my body and soul with his kiss, before gently making love to me, our joint release intense, slow, and earth-shattering. We fall asleep wrapped in each other's arms, all worries or reservations forgotten.

When the alarm goes off at nine, there is nothing I want to do less than get out of this nice cozy bed.

"Time to get up, sleepy girl. London awaits." That gets my attention. I'm up like a shot, jumping up and down on the bed, much to his amusement.

"I can't believe we're going to London today. I don't think I've ever been so excited." He's got an amused look on his face.

"You mean you're more excited than you were on our first night together? I'm deeply wounded by that, Miss Tate." The fake pouty face he's sporting melts me.

"How can I make it up to you, Mr. Rhodes?" I stand astride of him on the bed.

"Oh, I'm sure I can think of something." He pulls me down on top of him and shows me exactly how excited he can get me.

Xander reluctantly leaves me sated and happy in his bed to go and take a shower. The sight of him striding to the bathroom, gloriously naked with a sheen of sweat from our love making covering his toned body, is enough to get me worked up again.

"I'll be in to join you shortly."

He turns to give me an incredibly sexy grin. "I'll be ready for you." I know he will.

I lie for a few more moments, enjoying the quiet. That's when my phone starts ringing. I grab it from the nightstand—it's my mom. It's a bit early for her to be calling me, but I totally forgot to call and tell her I'm going to London today so it's good timing on her part.

"Hey, Mom. I was just about to call you. Xander is taking me to London today for five days as a graduation present. Can you believe it?" Radio silence. I wait for her to say something, but it doesn't come. "Mom. Are you still there? Is everything okay?" I'm starting to worry now.

"I'm here. I'm so sorry to have to tell you this when you're going on vacation, but it's probably a good thing you'll be out of town." There's another pause as she tries to calm the obvious upset I can hear in her voice.

"Just tell me, Mom. Are the girls okay? What's happened?"

"...Ron Peterson escaped from prison last night. The police just called to tell me. They have units out tracking him down as we speak, but they had to inform us." I fall to my knees on the floor. The man who killed my dad, the man who assaulted me, is on the loose. "Lily, darling. Are you there?" I'm shaking so badly I drop the phone. I scramble around trying to find it through my tears.

"I'm here, Mom." It's all I can say.

"I know this is scary, darling, but they are going to catch him and put him back where he belongs. By the time you come back from London he'll be behind bars." I know she's right, but I can't control the terror ripping through every fiber of my being. "He's already taken so much from you. Don't let him spoil your time with Xander in a city you've been dreaming about your whole life. I just felt you had a right to know. I promise I'll let you know as soon as he's found. Promise me you'll go and enjoy yourself. You deserve it more than anyone." I deserve it? I start sobbing into the phone.

"I'm sorry, Mom. I should never have gone out that night. I'm so, so sorry."

"Lily Tate, you listen to me. You did nothing wrong. None of this was your fault. It's that monster's fault and only his. Do you hear me?" I've wanted to hear those words for so many years. The instant relief that washes over me is gravity defying, a massive weight lifting off my shoulders.

"I hear you, Mom. Thank you. I really needed to hear that. I thought you blamed me for what happened to dad." My mom is crying.

"My darling baby girl. I have *never* blamed you. I just never knew how to reach out. I'm sorry. I was lost when your father died. I should have been stronger for you."

"I love you, Mom."

"I love you, too, sweetheart... so much. Now enough tears. We've both shed more than enough at the hands of Ron Peterson. You go to London and have a fabulous time, and when you come home, everything will be fine. Okay?"

"Okay. I'll let you know when I land. I better go and get ready. Love you, Mom."

When I hang up the phone I crawl up onto the bed and into the fetal position. I think about everything my mom said, and she's right. I'm not going to let that monster ruin what should be a magical trip with Xander. I'm going to put it out of my mind and enjoy myself. I can't tell him right now. I'll do it when we get back, and by then there won't be anything to worry about.

"Where did you get to? Did you fall asleep on me?" Xander crawls up the bed toward me. "What's wrong, sweets? You've been crying."

I settle on a half-truth. "I just called my mom to tell her about our trip and we had a good talk. It got a bit emotional, but things are so much better between us." He searches my face for answers I can't give him.

"Well, that's great. I'm glad things are good. Are you sure you're okay?"

"I'm sure. Take me to London. Take me away from here." He lifts me into his lap and strokes my hair.

"I can do that. Let's get you ready and then you're all mine… in London." True to his word, he helps me get organized, treating me like glass, as if I might break at any moment. I know he can sense there is something I'm not telling him, but he doesn't push. He just looks after me, showering me with affection.

The ride to LaGuardia is quiet, but Xander's hand in mine soothes the twister of emotions raging out of control inside me.

"You ready, sweetheart? Let me take you to London." I stare into the depths of his stunning blue eyes, and I know I'm exactly where I need to be.

"I'm ready."

I take his hand and leave my worries behind. Ron Peterson will not take this away for me. We move swiftly through the airport and into the departure lounge. London here we come.

CHAPTER 18

LILY

FLYING FIRST-CLASS WAS EVEN BETTER THAN I THOUGHT IT WOULD BE. I had the most comfortable seat and a nice blanket to snooze with during the flight. We watched a few in-flight movies and spent a lot of time talking. Even the food was better than I expected. My only problem was the flight attendants—they were practically drooling over Xander. It was nice to get away from them when we disembarked.

I can't believe I'm actually here. I've wanted to come to London since I was a little girl. My mom loves British literature and raised me reading all the classics. The history here is so fascinating. I'm speechless on the way to the hotel. I want to soak in everything around me. I'm like a kid on Christmas morning as we drive through the city.

The car pulls up outside a stunning looking building—Brown's Hotel. Wow. Of course, we didn't take a taxi from Heathrow Airport. Xander had arranged a private transfer to the hotel, and now I can see why. I wouldn't want to pull up in front of this place in a standard black cab. I'm desperate to take a ride in a hackney black taxi while we're here, though.

The staff are beyond helpful, and everything is taken care of without fuss. Before I know it, Xander is opening the door to a pent-house suite, ushering me into the definition of English decadence.

"Xander…" I am literally dumbstruck at how beautiful this place is.

"Pretty nice, huh?" His smug grin is beyond adorable.

"Nice… this is breathtaking! I can't believe you did this." His arms are around my waist from behind before I finish the sentence.

"Breathtaking? I plan on giving you multiple *breathtaking* moments in here, Miss Tate." The featherlight kisses he trails down my neck send shivers down my spine.

"You deserve the best of everything, Lily, and I want to give it to you. My Princess needs a palace for her slumber while she explores the *many* delights that London has to offer."

He closes the door and leads me by the hand into a grand master bedroom with a huge four-poster bed covered in sumptuous cream and gold bedding. I instantly forget that I'm in London—my dream city. I lose myself to Xander as he shows me some of the many delights *he* has to offer.

It's a few hours before we leave to explore some of the city. I bought a cute little pop-out map of London at the airport that tucks into the back pocket of my jeans. I'm hoping I won't look like such a tourist—fat chance. I'll be walking around with a stupid grin on my face the entire time!

The weather is warm, not like New York, but lovely all the same. We've got the whole afternoon ahead of us with the time difference. I'm ready for adventure.

First stop is Buckingham Palace. We spend the afternoon around the palace area, taking a long stroll through Hyde Park and watching the Queen's swans. The atmosphere is electric. Obviously, London is a bustling world city, but it's strange just how different it feels compared to New York. Its energy is different, and I'm loving just milling around, soaking it in. We do a whistle-stop tour of the major sights before dinner. Big Ben, Westminster, and Trafalgar Square.

I want to save The Globe for tomorrow when I'm rested and can spend the whole day steeped in Shakespearean history. Plus, I don't think Xander will be able to drag me away from it once I'm there. Seriously!

He takes me to a great restaurant for dinner called Vertigo 42. It's a champagne bar and I'm completely underdressed, but he makes me feel like the most beautiful woman in the room, and all of a sudden, I don't really care about what I'm wearing. Of course, every woman in the place notices Xander. Dressed in scruffy jeans, a black fitted t-shirt and leather jacket, he is still by far the most stunning man in the restaurant. The way he carries himself, with such an air of confidence, commanding the room as if he owns it, is sexy as hell.

Dinner is amazing and we have a great time chatting about every-thing we've seen today. I know Xander has been to London before, but he's as excited as I am about being here. We laugh a little too loudly at some of the selfies we took today at each landmark. You know the kind I mean—the ones you regret almost as soon as you've taken them. I seem to have an inability to just smile like a normal human being in photos, but crazy face, pout, cheesy grin—I'm your girl. Xander looks mouthwatering in every picture, even when he's pulling silly faces next to me. While we're playing around with the photos, I receive a text from my mom.

> Mom: No news yet. Will keep you updated.
> Have a wonderful time. Love you. X

That brings me swiftly down from my high. I had put him out of my mind as soon as I set foot on British soil. I just pray that they find him before we get back. I'm hoping I won't need to tell Xander what's going on. I look up into the eyes of this wonderful man and try to quell the unease in the pit of my stomach, immersing myself in his carefree laugh as he sends some pictures to Carter.

After dinner we take in the city lights as we leisurely make our way back to the hotel. It's surreal to be here in London, nestled at the side of the most amazing man I've ever met. I keep wondering when I'm going to wake up and go back to my humdrum existence.

"What are you thinking about, sweets?" How does he always know? Do I have a beacon on my forehead?

"Just how amazing it is to be here with you. It's like a dream I don't want to wake up from." He stops dead in the street, turning me to face him, lifting my chin to meet his intense gaze.

"I want to make all of your dreams a reality if you'll let me." If I were a cartoon, I would be melting into a puddle at his feet right now.

"Kiss me."

I can't pull my eyes from his as he moves in to meet my demand. Every touch of his lips is like manna in the desert. I'm starved for his kiss, every single brush of his lips a lifeline to sate my hunger. It's beginning to get indecent when we remember where we are. All thoughts of Ron Peterson obliterated from my conscious.

"Hotel. Now." His breathing is ragged, his voice filled with desire. We don't say another word as he pulls me by the hand back to the hotel, like a caveman—taking what he wants without question. He has a brief lapse in control in the elevator on the ride to the top floor, which I welcome. Every lick of his tongue on my neck and every nibble of my ear, is a teaser of what's to come.

As soon as the door to our suite opens, Xander becomes animalistic in his pursuit. He has me stripped bare in seconds and splayed on the bed for his eyes to devour every inch of my naked flesh. He doesn't wait long enough to undress himself before he's over me, capturing my mouth with his. It's a thrill to be naked for him, and it makes me wet with anticipation. He runs his warm callused hand down my chest and in between my legs, spreading them wider as he goes.

"You like that, baby? You are soaking wet. You feel naughty, don't you? You like being naked for me?" I moan in reply. He lifts his fingers to his mouth, spreading the evidence of my arousal on his lips.

"Do you want to taste your sweet little pussy?"

I'm so aroused I would do anything he asked without hesitation. I dart my tongue out to lick the seam of his lips, tasting myself. A satisfied groan rips from his chest before he pins me to the bed, my chest arched off the bed begging for his attention.

"I've got you, sweets."

His mouth captures my nipple, teasing and twisting it into a tight bud of sensation. He moves his hand, roaming all over my body, leaving a feather light trail of desire on my flesh, strengthening with each stroke of his fingertips. I'm shamelessly writhing beneath him, begging him to take me, but he pulls away, leaving me bereft.

"Not yet, baby. You still have to undress me."

I don't need to be told twice. I'm desperate to feel his warm taut skin against mine. I make short work of pulling his t-shirt over his head before slowly undoing the buttons of his fly. I hold his burning gaze as I lower his jeans and Calvin Klein's to the floor. I know exactly what he wants.

"Open your mouth, sweets. Clasp your hands behind your back." A shot of fire races straight to my core and I do as he asks, licking my lips in anticipation. Dominating Xander is back, and I want every hard, throbbing inch of him.

He takes a firm grip of my hair, guiding his cock into my mouth. I greedily lap at his swollen tip, licking the dewdrop of pre-come from his silky skin. With no control of my hands, I hum my delight, inviting him to thrust deeper. He drops his head back shouting my name as I take him to the back of my throat.

"God… Lily. Your mouth is so fucking sweet."

I run my tongue up and down the length of him, letting my teeth graze his hard shaft as I move back and forth, hollowing my cheeks to suck him a little harder—faster. He grabs my head with both hands, pumping in and out of me, taking control with his punishing rhythm. I give myself over to the heady sensation of pleasuring him in this way, watching him come apart under my ministrations, flicking my tongue over his engorged head on each thrust.

I feel the surge as Xander finds his release, his hot salty come shooting down my throat. I suck every drop before he stills my head, his body struggling to absorb the pleasure. He's hard in my mouth when he rasps his command.

"Get up and bend over the bed. Spread your legs wide for me." I stand on shaky legs and make my way over to the four-poster bed. I bend over, spreading my legs, holding onto the bed frame to steady myself.

"I could look at you forever. You're so fucking pretty. Everything about you. Your face, your tits, your tight little ass, and that slick pussy just begging for me to taste it." He drops to his knees behind me, grabs my thighs and parts my folds, running his palm up the length of me before teasing my clit with his fingers. He slides his fingers back down and rams two fingers inside me.

"So wet. I fucking love that about you. You're always ready for me." He pumps his fingers in and out until I'm panting his name, eager to reach my own release. He pulls out abruptly before devouring me with his tongue, the scruff of his chin adding to the intense pleasure he rips from my body.

He holds my legs steady as they begin to tremble, the familiar build of an explosive orgasm coiling in my core. He places open-mouthed kisses along my folds, suckling my tender flesh into his mouth. When I think my legs are going to give way underneath me, Xander holds me firmly around the waist with one strong, muscled arm, his hand splayed on my stomach. He begins to flick his tongue vigorously over my clit before thrusting three fingers inside me. Together with his tongue he sets a glorious rhythm, pushing me higher and higher until I detonate.

I writhe against his face, ridding out the aftershocks of my orgasm, enjoying the almost painful sensitivity of my skin against his scruff. He finally lets me slump onto the bed, turning me onto my back. As he crawls over my body, I can see my arousal dripping from his chin. He wipes it with the back of his hand, a sensual grin spreading across his lips.

"I'm not done with you yet." He captures my mouth with his. "Are you mine, Miss Tate?"

I know the answer to this question without hesitation—absolutely and irrevocably. "Yes. I'm yours. Only yours. Always." He slams into me, hard as steel. My body was made for him.

"Every delectable inch of your body belongs to me."

His words together with his relentless pace whip us into a frenzied, fierce, and extremely intense release, screaming each other's names as we spiral out of control together.

Xander curls me up in his warm embrace and shifts us up the bed until he can move us under the sumptuous sheets, wrapping us back in our little bubble. He drifts into a peaceful sleep, our limbs tangled, our hearts beating together as one.

"I'm so in love with you, Xander Rhodes. I always will be."

Today is the day I finally visit The Globe Theater, and I am truly excited. I'm like a kid at Christmas. The anticipation is killing me. I choke the life out of Xander's hand as we head out of the hotel into the sweet summer air. It's a beautiful day for an adventure with the one you love. I just have to tell him... when he's awake... and can hear me.

We skip breakfast in the hotel in favor of grabbing something en route to my Mecca.

"You're so adorable when you're excited, sweets."

He pulls me into his side, snaking his arm around my waist. I'm practically jumping up and down as we cross the Millennium Bridge, but I stop dead in my tracks when The Globe comes into view. I'm frozen to the spot, overwhelmed with emotion, tears spilling down my cheeks.

"This is supposed to be a happy moment. What's wrong?" He wipes my eyes as I try to explain.

"These *are* happy tears. I just can't believe I'm actually here. It always seemed like a dream that would never happen. Thank you so much."

I bury my head in his chest, embarrassed by my outburst. He leads me the rest of the way to the entrance, and I savor the moment, taking in everything around me, trying to soak it into my pores.

It is truly breathtaking. It's everything I thought it would be and more.

We spend hours wandering around, reading all about Shakespeare and this phenomenal theater. Xander disappears for five minutes while I steep myself in the history of the ultimate playwright. When he returns, he pulls a silk scarf from his pocket and without a word, covers my eyes. Taking my hand in his, he coaxes me away from the exhibition area—to where, I don't know.

After a few minutes of Xander leading me around blindfolded, he stops, brushing his hands down my arms before placing a tender kiss on my lips. "I want you to trust me and leave the blindfold on for a minute." I nod in agreement. "From the moment you came crashing into my life, nothing has been the same. You've given me something I thought I would never have. I want things with you that I haven't wanted in a long time. You've given me hope for the future. I want to give you the world, but I'll start with The Globe. I love you, Lily Tate."

He gently removes the soft silk from my eyes, but I don't comprehend anything around me. All I see is him—the man who just told me he loves me. As we gaze into each other's eyes the connection between us sizzles, waiting to explode with the brilliance and beauty of fireworks.

Xander gently cups my face before lowering his lips to mine. I have *never* been touched like this. The tender passion, the gentle intensity, the *love* conveyed through a single kiss, astounds me and humbles me at the same time, awe-inspiring in its purity. When I open my eyes again, I realize we are standing in the middle of The Globe itself.

"I love you, Xander. So much it's a physical ache in my chest." The smile lighting up his face is magnificent. He lifts me off the ground and spins me round in the center of the wooden O, with a laugh of sheer joy, but as he sets me down his mood becomes serious.

"I've wanted to tell you that since the moment I met you. Until now there has never been a time and a place that seemed worthy of you. It feels so good to finally say it out loud. I love you, Lily Tate." We stand lost in our bubble—our Globe—for what seems like an eternity, absorbing this moment, committing it to memory.

"Say it again. I want to hear you say it." His whispered plea tugs at my heartstrings and I gladly oblige.

"I'm so in love with you, Xander Rhodes. I. Love. You." He captures me in a hungry kiss, claiming me as his own.

"I need to make love to you, sweets. Let me take you back to the hotel. Let me show you how much I love you."

"I'm all yours."

He promptly finds the exit, and before I can take a breath, he's hailed a black hackney cab.

On the ride back to the hotel, he continuously lifts our interlaced fingers to his lips, kissing my fingers one at a time, darting his tongue out to make the briefest contact with my skin. My body is aglow, ready to make love, to connect to the other half of my soul.

CHAPTER 19

LILY

WE SPEND THE FIRST HALF OF WEDNESDAY CATCHING UP ON SLEEP, BUT as soon as I wake, molten blue eyes are staring back at me. Xander has been watching me sleep. God, I hope I wasn't snoring or drooling.

"I have a surprise for you today." I know he's going to draw it out, so I don't even bother asking him to tell me.

"Excellent. I'm sure whatever it is will be great." I think he's surprised I'm not probing him for more information.

"What would you like to do today, Miss Tate?" He starts tracing his finger in circles around my belly button.

"I don't mind, I'm easy." I catch the mischief in his eye as soon as the words leave my mouth.

"Oh, I *know* you are. It's one of the reasons I adore you." Mischievous and sweet in one sentence—I never stood a chance against him. We enjoy another amazing day, taking in the sights and sounds of the city, before having a delicious dinner in a trendy Chinese restaurant right in the center of town. Then he takes me to a great little bar. It's cozy, modern, and has a stage for live music. The place is packed and there's a great vibe. There must be a band playing tonight.

That's when it dawns on me. "Are we here to see a band?" He nods his head slowly, taking a swig from his bottle of Staropramen. "Cool."

He's sporting a sly grin—he knows who's playing. "Is it a band I've heard of?"

"Flaming Embers are playing here tonight." Oh. My. God.

"How did you know? They're my favorite British band! I love their debut album. This is amazing. I'm so excited." As the words leave my mouth, the crowd around us erupts at the commotion on stage. He pulls me tight against his chest in a protective stance and positions me for a perfect view of the band. The lead singer pulls the microphone to his lips.

"Hey, everyone, thanks for coming out tonight. Bit of an impromptu gig for us. A friend of mine told me one of our fans from America is in London this week, so we thought we'd give her a show. Put your hands together for Lily Tate, everyone." He just said my name. No... fucking... way! The crowd goes wild, clapping and whistling.

"What did you do?"

"I may have spoken to Addi last week and then made a few calls to Logan. They just signed with him, and he pulled some strings. The boys were more than happy to put on a gig for the fee I'm paying." Oh my God! He hired one of my favorite bands just for me.

"Thank you so much. This is so thoughtful. I love you." He gently tilts my head backwards to capture my mouth as the band starts playing.

"Enjoy."

I focus my attention on stage as the band kicks off the gig. They sound even better live and play all my favorite tracks. I lose myself in the music, Xander holding me a little tighter. With a kiss below my ear, he speaks just loud enough for me to hear. "God, I love you, Lily."

We enjoy the rest of the set, jumping and dancing with the rest of the crowd, the whole place alive with energy. When the band finishes, we demand an encore, stomping our feet, clapping as loudly as we can. They give us what we want and before they leave the stage, the lead singer, Campbell McCabe, shouts through the microphone.

"Thank you, you've been a great crowd. Hope you enjoyed the show, Lily! We're Flaming Embers. Goodnight and God Bless." Every girl in the place screams as they all jump off stage and make their way into the back room.

Xander has another surprise up his sleeve. He takes me backstage to meet the band. I get a signed copy of their album and manage not to make a complete idiot of myself in front of them, so I consider that a triumph!

I'm so jazzed from the gig that I don't want to go back to the hotel. So instead, we hit a few more bars and a club, dancing the night away before stumbling back to the hotel at about 4 a.m. I'm out cold before my head hits the pillow. What a great night. Xander never ceases to amaze me with the surprises he manages to pull off. He puts so much thought and effort into our time together, it makes me feel special beyond words.

I'm a little worse for wear today, but I want to make the most of our last day in London. I have a list of things I want to see and do and Xander obliges without complaint. First stop is Harrods. I buy a few gifts for Addi and maybe a few items for myself. I make sure not to give him the opportunity to buy me anything, but he still manages to pull me into Tiffany's.

"I know what you've been doing but I want to get you a charm in London to remember our time here. You can pick whatever you want."

Normally I would protest but his sentiment is heartfelt, so I just thank him as I follow him into the store. We're not in there very long before I spy the perfect charm—a solid silver heart with a letter 'X' engraved in the center. I gave my heart to Xander in London. He smiles as I point it out to him.

"Excuse me, miss. Could we please have this heart charm, and one with the letter 'L', attached to my girlfriend's bracelet?" The salesclerk takes a moment to admire the wonder that is Xander, before giving me a snide glance and acquiescing to his request. I remove my bracelet and hand it over with a smug grin. When my pretty new charms are in place, we head out to see some more of the sights. Next stop, the London Eye.

The view from the top is incredible. You can see the whole city sprawling out before your eyes in all its majesty. Xander pulls me close, his lips finding mine, connected by an invisible force. I'm on top of the world right now, literally and figuratively.

"There is one last place I'd like to take you, but it's outside of the main city. We need to take a train. You up for it?" His eyes smolder with love, and the butterflies are running rampant in my stomach.

"Yes. I'd go anywhere with you."

His scruff tickles me as I kiss him with everything I have. I don't even notice that the Eye has come to a stop and the doors are open for us to disembark. The attendant clears his throat to get our attention and the people waiting to get in give us a clap as we step out of the pod. I'm so embarrassed!

I don't ask where we're going when we get on the train. I'm happy just to be with him and trust whatever it is, I'll like it. And boy do I like it.

The journey is relatively short, and I enjoy cuddling into Xander as we listen to the quiet clickety-clack of the train on the tracks. Our car is pretty empty until the next stop when a crowd gets on and shoves their way down the aisle to find seats. I immediately stiffen. The man coming toward me looks scarily like Ron Peterson on first glance. Every muscle in my body tightens.

"Are you okay?"

I glance up, relieved to see the man in front of me doesn't look so much like the monster that haunts my dreams. My mind must be playing tricks on me. I'm starting to get a little anxious at the thought of going home tomorrow. I still haven't heard any news from my mom.

I shake off my funk and assure him I'm fine. He knows I'm lying but he senses that it's not the time to talk and simply pulls me closer, calming me, assuaging my fears. Shortly after, we arrive in a town called Teddington and he drags me excitedly from the train.

"I figured since you're big on literature, and history, and London, we couldn't leave without visiting Hampton Court."

My face lights up, splitting into a massive grin. "Seriously. As in Henry VIII and Anne Boleyn, Hampton Court?"

He chuckles. "Is there another Hampton Court I don't know about? You are *too* cute." I punch him in the arm for laughing at me.

"Was that your attempt at hurting me? That was just pitiful. Let's go check this place out."

"I've always wanted to come here."

"I noticed *The Tudors* Blu-rays in your room and took an educated guess that you might enjoy it." I don't know why I'm surprised that he would notice such a small detail, but I am. It's heartwarming that he puts so much thought into making me happy.

We spend a few hours exploring Hampton Court and it doesn't disappoint. The walls are steeped in history, transporting you back, allowing you to reach through time and space... and touch something remarkable.

After an amazing day, we head back to the hotel and freshen up before having a fabulous dinner in one of the hotel restaurants.

"I can't thank you enough for this trip. I've had the most amazing time. I'll never forget it." He holds my hands across the table.

"This is just the beginning for us. We have so many adventures ahead of us." He lifts my hands to his lips, placing a chaste kiss on each palm.

"Where do you want to go next? Paris, Rome, Budapest?"

"I'll settle for being with you back in New York. You're everything I want."

WE'RE UP EARLY FOR OUR FLIGHT. I'M SAD OUR TRIP IS OVER, BUT I'M really excited about what's next for us.

"You ready to go home?"

"Yeah. This has been amazing, but we'll be together back in New York, and that means everything is going to be great."

When we touch down in New York, I'm looking forward to seeing Addi and telling her all about London. She'll go crazy when I tell her we finally said the 'L' word to each other.

David is here, ready to drive us home and it's comforting to see his stoic face waiting for us. Xander gets us settled in the back of the SUV. He lifts me into his lap and wraps the seatbelt around us both. "Would you mind if I stay with you tonight, sweets? I'm not ready to leave you yet."

I take a moment to scent him, breathing him deep into my lungs. "I'm not ready to *let* you leave." We spend the car ride kissing and whispering sweet nothings to each other like lovesick teenagers. It's disgusting really... and I love every moment of it.

When we pull up outside my apartment, I relish the idea of spending the night in my own bed with the man I love. He grabs our bags and tells David to pick him up in the morning.

As I open the door, I notice that Addi isn't here. Xander obviously has the same realization as he drops the bags on the floor and backs me down onto the sofa.

"I love you so fucking much." It's all I need to give myself over to him completely. He quickly strips both of us before sitting me on his lap. I can feel his rock-hard cock pressing against my clit.

"I can't get over how stunningly beautiful you are. You take my breath away." I thread my fingers into his hair, tugging his lips to meet mine in a toe-tingling, mind-melting, earth-shattering kiss. Deep and sensual, loving and hungry. I lift my hips in invitation and he wastes no time impaling me on his throbbing erection. We are two pieces of a puzzle, destined to fit together.

He guides my hips up and down the length of him, kissing my breasts while his strong hands press into my thighs. With every stroke, he hits my sweet spot and caresses my clit, the myriad of sensations almost too much to bear. I slide my hands down onto his shoulders as I ride him faster and faster, chasing the release that only he can give me.

"Yes! Right there... fucking hell... yes... yes... I love you." As soon as the words fall from my lips, Xander finds his own release, joining me in the all-consuming ecstasy our bodies create together.

We take a moment to enjoy being skin to skin before we grab our clothes from the floor and get ready just in case Addi makes an entrance!

Xander takes our bags into my room while I put on a pot of coffee before checking through my mail. I discover a note from Addi on the fridge telling me that she's gone away with Carter for a few days and will be back late Monday night. There is also a Post-it telling me to call my mom. I'll call her before bed to see if she has some good news.

I grab my mail from the table by the door, lazily sifting through it. Bills, bills and… a large brown envelope. I set the unexciting stuff down on the table and open the large envelope with my name on it. When I pull out the contents, a chill runs through my body. This can't be… he wouldn't. There's a handwritten note attached.

To Miss Lily Tate,

I thought he owed you your little trip to London before you found out what he's been doing behind your back. Don't feel bad. He's always been in love with me. We're meant to be.

Woman to woman, I figured it was about time you knew. He shouldn't string you along when his heart's not in it. He's mine, and he will always BE MINE.

Natalie Mason

I run to the bathroom, knowing what's coming. I make it to the bowl just before I lose the contents of my stomach. Xander comes rushing into the bathroom behind me.

"What's wrong?" He kneels beside me and starts to rub my back. I can feel the tears, but I don't want to give him the satisfaction.

"Don't fucking touch me. Just get the hell out of my apartment." I realize I'm still clutching the photos in a death grip.

"What the fuck, Lily? What's going on? I'm not going anywhere, you're sick. I'm going to look after you." He moves to run his hand down my cheek, but I can't stand it. I feel like I'm about to break.

"I said don't fucking touch me." I want to cry at the look of hurt and confusion in his eyes, but then I glance at the photos in my hand.

"Here." I say shoving them into his hand. "Take these and get the fuck out of my apartment and my life." He looks down at the photographs, horror, and anger flashing across his face.

"Fucking Natalie." He runs his fingers through his hair, dropping his gaze to the floor.

"This is *not* what it looks like. I can explain." I'm furious now. He's broken my heart and I fucking let him. I suspected as much when I met him, and I ignored it because I wanted to believe I'd found my knight in shining armor.

"I don't want to hear your pathetic excuses as to why I'm looking at photos of you kissing your ex. And I'm pretty fucking sure these were taken the night before we went to London. That's what you were wearing when you disappeared for hours with no explanation, in the middle of the night." He tries to grab my arm as I move to leave the bathroom. I glare at him with venom in my eyes.

"Can we talk about this? I promise you I can explain."

"I don't want to hear it. You were with her and then you came back, showered her disgusting smell off, and crawled into bed with me. And I let you fuck me. I knew the shower was odd, but I just ignored it because I didn't want to see what was staring me in the face. I gave you everything, Xander. Fucking everything. I stupidly thought it meant something to you."

"It did mean something to me. It *does*. It means everything to me. *You* mean *everything*." I can't listen to this. I need to protect myself, and if I let him stay and tell me his bullshit lies, I'll let myself believe him because I *want* to believe him more than I've ever wanted anything.

"If you care for me at all. Please, leave." I start sobbing, shirking his attempts to comfort me. "Please, Xander… just go."

"I'll go for now, but we need to talk about this. I haven't been cheating on you. You owe me a chance to explain." I want to say no, but every fiber of my being is telling me that I'm going to have to talk to him at some point. I can't bear the thought of us ending this way.

"Fine, but I need some time. I have to be ready to start my new job on Monday and I can't deal with this as well. We'll talk when I'm ready."

All light has faded from his beautiful blue eyes as he lifts his bag and heads for the door. I feel like my world is crashing down around me as I watch him leave. He turns to face me as he steps into the elevator.

"You're it for me, Lily. You're a part of me. I'd be fucking lost without you. Please remember that I love you, more than anything." As the doors close and he disappears from my life, it's more than I can handle. I collapse to my knees, distraught and heartbroken.

I can't sleep. I can't get the image of Xander and Natalie out of my head. My body becomes sore from the wrenching sobs that have consumed me for hours. I eventually pass out through sheer exhaustion, my heart ripped from my chest. All intentions to call my mom and Addi are completely forgotten.

I don't know if I'll be able to see him again, the thought of it, too painful to contemplate. How could my day turn out so differently from the way I thought it would? I thought I was coming home from the trip of a lifetime, to start the next exciting chapter with the man I love.

It's amazing how five minutes can change the course of your life forever. I know that better than most, but I guess I let myself believe for a brief moment that I could have a happily ever after.

CHAPTER 20

LILY

I'D LIKE TO SAY I WOKE UP TODAY AND REALIZED LAST NIGHT WAS JUST A bad dream, but unfortunately that's not my reality. I want to pick myself up, dust myself off and prepare to start my new job on Monday, but instead I lie in bed most of the day, sobbing, missing Xander even though I don't want to.

I can't bring myself to eat anything. I feel sick to my stomach every time I think about what he did. When I finally drag myself out of bed and into the kitchen to get a glass of water and some painkillers for the hammering in my head, I notice an envelope has been slipped under the front door.

I'm loathe to open it, worried at what I might see, but when I bend down to pick it up, I know instantly it's *his* handwriting and a massive lump forms in my throat. I sit down on the sofa, gingerly opening the envelope that smells of Xander. I run my fingers over his writing, breathing in the scent that gave me such comfort twenty-four hours ago. I wipe the tears from my eyes so that I'm able focus on the words in front of me.

Dearest Lily,

I want to give you the time you asked for before we talk face to face, but I can't stand the idea of you thinking badly of me for another second. I thought it might be easier on you if I explain myself on paper.

Firstly, I am so unbelievably in love with you, Lily, I have been since the moment I met you. I've made mistakes, but I have never been unfaithful to you. I haven't even looked at another woman since I held you in my arms on campus.

Natalie contacted me the weekend of our first date. You were so insecure. I didn't want to ruin a perfect weekend by dragging you into it. She called me to ask for my help.

I didn't want anything to do with her, but I felt I had to help her. She contacted me several times, then she started showing up at my work. I was starting to question her story and I confronted her when she showed up at Cube on the night of your graduation.

I told her in no uncertain terms that she had to leave me, and you, alone. The day before we left for London she called again, upset and asking if I could meet her. I stupidly believed her and when I got there, she tried to rekindle things between us. I realize now that it was a setup to get those pictures.

As soon as she kissed me, I pushed her away and told her I'm in love with you. I told her that there would never be anything between us and I gave her hell for lying to me and using my good nature against me. She knew I would help her if she were in trouble. She knew it was the only way I would even consider seeing her.

My mistakes were to believe a single word that came out of her vindictive mouth and keeping it from you. I could have avoided putting you through all of this if I had just trusted our relationship and told you what was going on.

For that I am eternally sorry.

I would never do anything to intentionally hurt you or cause you even a moment of pain. I hope you can believe that and give me a chance to make it up to you.

Please don't let Natalie and my idiocy ruin what we have. I love you so much, I feel like my heart has been ripped out of my chest and there is just a gaping hole where you're supposed to be.

You're a part of me. No matter what happens between us, you will always be a part of me, and all of me will forever belong to you. What you choose to do with it is a choice that only you can make.

Please give me a chance to prove how sorry I am and how much I love you, sweets.

Always yours,

Xander x

Bruno Mars—Long Distance

I can't control the tears streaming down my face. I don't want to be gullible, but deep down I believe him. He should have been honest with me, but I know how protective he is.

I'm tired out by the emotional rollercoaster I've been on over the past twenty-four hours, and my eyes are practically swollen shut. I make the decision to call Xander tomorrow once I've had a good night's sleep, so we can talk things through rationally and hopefully get things back on track somehow.

I'm startled awake by a call from the doorman—there's a flower delivery for me. I know they will be from Xander, and a flutter of hope swells in my stomach at his willingness to put his heart on the line for me.

When I hear knocking, I pull my tired body up off the couch, opening the door to a beautiful bouquet of flowers. My first thought is that they're not from Xander. He always sends me roses, and these are calla lilies. As I lift them into my arms, I get a glimpse of the deliveryman…

My entire body begins to shake in terror. The face before me has haunted my dreams for the past eight years. I would know that scarred face anywhere… Ron Peterson. The flowers drop to the floor in front of me. I'm frozen—my head screaming at me to run, shout, or do anything… but I can't move.

"Hello, Lily. I've been waiting a very long time to see your pretty little face again. Have you missed me?" He runs his fingers down my face as he speaks, spurring me into action. I try to push him out and slam the door but he's too strong. He bursts into the room knocking me onto the floor. I crash into our wrought-iron coat stand, my head hitting the jagged hook as the force sends it flying into the wall.

My head hits the hardwood floor with enough force to elicit an almighty thud, and warm blood begins to matt the hair at the back of my head. I scramble backwards on my hands and feet, trying to find anything I can use as a weapon.

"Your daddy isn't here to save you this time, *Lily*." Even the way he says my name is repugnant. I try to reach for my phone, but he's one step ahead, grabbing it before me and throwing it to the floor, smashing it underfoot. He slaps me full force across the face before kicking me in the ribs, breaking at least one. Pain shoots through my chest as his boot makes contact.

"Don't fucking try anything, you little bitch. Do you have any idea what I've been through in the past eight years because of you? You were fucking begging for it that night and I gladly obliged, only to be fucking beat up by your prick of a father. It was his own fault he ended up dead."

Just the mention of what he did to my dad causes bile to rise in my throat. I retch as he bends down, the stink of him invading my senses.

"Bit of a gag reflex there, sweetheart. Don't worry, I'll sort that out for you." My head is pounding and my ribs ache as he pulls me to my feet.

"You're coming with me." I try to struggle free, but he just shoves me down, straight into the coffee table, smashing it to pieces below me. A stabbing pain sears through my back, but I'm on my feet again before I have a chance to comprehend my injuries.

"I'm not fucking around here. Unless you want me to gut your little roommate and that fancy boyfriend of yours like pigs, you better come quietly." My eyes widen in shock.

"Yes, Lily. I did my research. I know all about your pathetic little life. It's amazing what you can find out these days. I've been staking this place out all week. Saw your pretty little friend going in and out with some guy. She looks like a bit of a slut, that one. I'm sure I could have fun with her before I slit her throat."

"Don't you fucking touch her." I manage a kick to his shin before the next punch connects with my face. My lip and nose are bleeding, but I don't really feel the pain. I'm numb.

"And that boyfriend of yours. He didn't look too happy last night. You frigid for him, too? I'll enjoy carving him up." Rage boils inside me, unlike anything else I have ever experienced. Even worse than the night my dad died.

"I swear to God, if you go near him, I will fucking kill you." He pulls a roll of duct tape from his jacket.

"And how are you going to do that, you stupid… little… cunt?"

I'm not going to get out of this alive, but maybe if I do as he asks, he'll leave Addi and Xander alone. I don't say a word, racking my brain for a plan to get away from him.

"Good girl. I think you've done enough talking."

He grips my arms with one hand while pulling a length of tape free with the other. He breaks it with his disgusting rotten teeth and secures it around my wrists. Once he's sure I can't break free, he puts a piece of tape over my mouth, before pulling me out of the apartment and down the stairwell.

When we emerge at the back of my building, he has a car waiting —a blue Ford Mustang. He opens the passenger door, pushing me in headfirst. Why wouldn't he put me in the trunk? What the hell is back there?

"Time to go for a ride."

I kick at the door against his arm as he tries to lock me in. He stumbles to the ground but manages to slam the door on my leg as I struggle to break free. My head is spinning, my body overcome with pain.

As the engine roars to life, his fist smashes into my cheek, my mouth instantly filled with the metallic taste of blood. "Don't piss me off, little girl. I love watching you squirm in fear, but the moment I stop being amused by your pathetic attempts to fight me, you're worthless. Try that again and you'll wish you were dead already."

He reaches past me into the backseat, his vulgar stench invading my nostrils. The last thing I see is a gun just before the cold metal presses against my temple. My blood is pumping so hard I can hear it whooshing in my ears, the rapid thud drowning out everything else around me.

As the darkness descends the chilling realization sets in—Addi won't be back until Monday, and I told Xander not to contact me. No one is going to know I'm missing. I'll never get the opportunity to tell Xander that I believe him. To gaze into his exquisite blue eyes again and tell him how much I love him.

CHAPTER 21

XANDER

IT'S BEEN TWO AND A HALF DAYS SINCE I LAST SAW LILY AND I'M GOING out of my fucking mind here. I cannot believe that little bitch Natalie got the best of me, again. I had a nagging feeling when she first contacted me that I shouldn't trust her, but she knew exactly what buttons to press. I couldn't refuse an abused woman, even Natalie.

I thought *she* ripped my heart out when she left me, but that was a fucking scratch compared to how I feel right now. I've sent Lily letters every day, hoping she would get in touch and let me explain myself face to face. I'm trying to give her space, but if I don't hear from her by tomorrow, I need to go and see her before I fucking implode.

I feel like I can't fucking breathe without her. I poured my heart out in those letters like a fucking pussy-whipped loser, but I don't give a fuck. If it's her pussy-whipping me, I'll take it any day of the week… for the rest of my life. I can't believe the hole in my chest after three days of not hearing her voice, her laugh, or seeing her sexy little smile.

She slays me every time I look at her. She is everything I never realized I was missing. I just shut down after what Natalie did to me, and I thought I was fine until that day at Columbia when we crashed into each other's lives. The minute I touched her, my body came to life, and when I looked into those enchanting emerald green eyes it was like a defibrillator to my heart. I knew she was it for me in that moment. I felt like she was looking straight into the very depths of my soul.

I couldn't believe it in London when she whispered in my ear that she loved me. It took everything in me to pretend I was sleeping. I had been planning the way I wanted tell her for a week, but all I wanted to do in that moment was conquer her body and her heart, claiming them as mine.

On the flight home, all I could think about was our future together, the life we would build together. I still can't believe how quickly it was shattered. If I could go back, I never would have taken that phone call in the Hamptons.

I answer the phone to David knowing that something is wrong at the penthouse or the office. He isn't just my driver, he's my right-hand man. If I need something he makes it happen. I knew he wouldn't call unless it was important.

"Sorry to bother you, Mr. Rhodes, but Miss Mason has turned up at the penthouse and is causing quite a scene. She's insisting that she speak with you. Lobby security called me, and I came straight over and explained to her that you aren't in the city this weekend." I can't believe it. The first time I go out of town since she tore my fucking heart out and she manages to fuck it up. I listen as David relays his conversations with the building security guard and Natalie in great detail, until I can't bear to hear another word.

"What the fuck is she playing at? Find out what she wants, David." This shit was done and dusted eighteen months ago.

"I'm doing my best, sir, but she's not very forthcoming."

"I get that." She's a colossal bitch.

"She's insisting that she speak with you."

"I don't care... fuck... just ask her what it will take to get rid of her and make it happen. I'll be back tonight. We'll talk then."

That was my first mistake. When I got back to the city I spoke with David and then contacted Natalie. That's when she spun her web of deceit.

After a phenomenal weekend with Lily, I can't believe I'm ending my weekend with Natalie sitting crying on my sofa.

*"You're the only one who can help me, Xander. Please. Tim has been...
he's been hitting me for months."* I hate Natalie, but the thought of any man,
even the man she left me for, hitting a woman, makes my blood fucking boil.

*"I've tried to leave him, but he won't let me. I'm trapped and scared, and I
don't know what to do. Will you help me?"*

"What do you want me to do, Natalie?" I can hear the resignation in my
voice. I'm going to help her, even though I don't want anything to do with her.
I don't even want to be in the same room as her. She makes my skin crawl.

*"Can you get your investigator to try and dig up something on Tim?
Maybe there's something I can use as leverage to get him to let me go."* I can
do that.

*"Okay. I'll help you this one time, but this doesn't make us friends. I still
want nothing to do with you after this."*

*"Thank you so much. I knew I could count on you. I know I hurt you. You
trusted me. I know what a big mistake I made."*

*"I don't want to hear it, Natalie. I'll contact you when I have any
information."*

I got rid of her as quickly as possible that night, but I still felt dirty,
like I'd cheated on Lily somehow. Looking back now, I can't believe I
was so fucking gullible.

She contacted me a few times over the next couple of weeks to
give me information that she thought might help the investigator dig
up some dirt on Tim. That was fine, until she started showing up at
my office, then I started bumping into her when I was at the gym or
out getting a coffee with Carter. I tried to ignore it, hoping she would
get the message, but when she turned up at Cube, I knew I had to set
her straight.

*"Xander. Man, we have a problem. Put it back in your pants and get out
here."* What the fuck, man? I'm going to give him no end of shit for this. I
make sure that Lily is presentable and pick up her torn panties as I head to
the door. I don't need to look at her to know she'll be mortified. She's so
fucking lovely.

"This better be fucking important, Carter." I guide him away from Lily,
letting her exit without having to face him.

"Natalie is here. She knows you're here, man. I told her to wait down-

stairs, but you better go deal with her before she ruins your girl's night."
What the fuck is she playing at?

"Thanks, man. I'll deal with it." He comes downstairs with me. I think
he's worried I'm going to cause a scene in here, but when he realizes I'm not
going to explode, he leaves me to get rid of her.

"What are you doing here, Natalie?" She's looking at me as if she's
surprised I'm not happy to see her. This girl is fucking delusional.

"I wanted to see you." If she doesn't stop running her hands up and down
my arms I'm going to turn into the fucking Hulk in a minute. I've had
enough of this.

"Natalie. I said I'd help you with Tim. That does NOT mean I want to
spend any time with you, or that I remotely like you, or forgiven you for
fucking me over." Her face drops. "You need to stay the fuck away from me,
do you understand? I'll stop helping you if you start interfering in my life.
I've moved on, and I'm happy. I'm fucking ecstatic, so do yourself a favor and
go... NOW!" She turns on her heels, making a quick exit with her tail
between her legs, and her pitchfork up her ass.

When I went back to find Lily that night she had disappeared into
the toilets, and we had a massive fight. I still didn't fess up.

The day before London I took a call from Natalie in hysterics
while I was at my parents' house with Lily. She told me Tim had been
violent and she had evidence to prove it. I agreed to meet her later
that night hoping to put an end to my dealings with her for good. Of
course, it was a setup.

"Thank God you're here, Xander." Tears are streaming down her cheeks.

"I was so frightened. I thought he was going to kill me." We're standing
outside of her building and she's shaking in my arms.

"It's okay, Nat, I'm here. I won't let him hurt you anymore. That son of a
bitch is going to jail."

She calms in my arms as I attempt to soothe her with words of comfort.
When she stops crying, I pull her from my body to look at her and see if she
needs medical attention. Who hits a fucking woman? What a dick.

I look her up and down but see no visible evidence of injury, and while
I'm distracted, she makes her move. Her lips are on mine, her hands fisting in
my hair. "I've missed you so much. I knew you still loved me."

I instantly push her away. All the pieces falling into place as I realize just what a fool I've been. "You fucking bitch. It's all lies, isn't it? Tim never fucking touched you, did he?" Chilling rage sends vibrations coursing through my entire body. I'm trying to calm myself, but it's fucking difficult. "This was all just another one of your sick fucked up games. I almost lost Lily because of you. Don't ever contact me again, Natalie, or I will make you regret it. Do you understand?" She just stands there in silence.

"Do you fucking understand me?"

She nods, but the look on her face is spiteful, evil, and just fucking twisted. I can't believe I ever had feelings for her.

That was the end of it. I stormed off and went to my offices for a couple of hours to get my anger under control. I didn't want to go home to Lily with all that shit going on in my brain. I needed some time to clear my head and calm down before I went back to her. I felt fucking dirty after Natalie's lips were on me.

When I finally got home, Lily was awake. I *had* to take a shower before I could touch her. I didn't want to taint her with anything of Natalie. I felt guilty as fuck when I got into bed and she asked me to kiss her, but I couldn't help myself. I made love to her with an intensity and passion that consumed me.

Now, because of all that shit, I might never see her again. I *can't* let that happen. I *won't* let it happen.

I'M SO FUCKING MISERABLE SITTING AROUND THIS PLACE ON MY OWN. Everything reminds me of Lily. I can still smell her on my bedding, and I'm on the verge of insanity when my phone rings. It's too late for a work call so I spring to my feet to grab the phone from the nightstand hoping that it's her calling. Surely my letters are getting through to her by now.

It's Addi.

"Hi. What's up?"

There's an uncomfortable pause before she speaks. "Is Lily with you?" What?

"No. I haven't seen her since Friday night when I dropped her off. She won't talk to me."

"Shit…" A chill runs through my body at the panic in her voice.

"What's wrong, Addi? Tell me now."

"The apartment is a mess. There's blood on the floor, tables are broken… knocked over… and there's no sign of Lily." I can't fucking breathe right now.

"I called her mom, and she hasn't heard from her since before you went to London. Xander… did she tell you about Ron Peterson?"

"No. What the hell is going on? Who the fuck is Ron Peterson?"

"He's the man who attacked her and killed her dad." Her words are frantic, filled with terror as she continues. "He escaped from prison the day before you guys left for London. They haven't caught him yet. Oh God, what if he's done something bad… what if he's… I'm so scared. I don't know what to do. Please, help me… we need to help her… we have to find her before…" She breaks down, her words lost among the grief-stricken sobs tearing from her chest, ripping her heart out as she contemplates what might have happened to her best friend.

"Holy Fuck! I've been feeling sorry for myself thinking she was ignoring me for three days, and all this time she's needed my help. I'm going to make it right, Addi. I'm going to find her and bring her home." She's inconsolable. I can't believe this is happening. Why didn't she tell me? I would have had security posted at her building. "I need to get off the phone. I'll be in touch. Did she take her phone?" Please God, let her have it. I can track her easily if it's with her.

"It's here, shattered in pieces on the floor. How are we going to find her?"

"Stay there in case he calls wanting money or something. Call the police and let them know what's going on. I'm going to call my investigator and I *will* find her. It's going to be okay. Just try to stay calm so you can give the police as much information as possible. I'll call as soon as I know anything." I need for this to be okay. I need Lily to be safe. I can't contemplate any other outcome.

I immediately call my P.I, Scott, to gather every shred of information on Ron Peterson, in hopes of finding something… anything that the police could have missed in their attempts to find him. David is by my side, organizing for us to hit the road as soon as we have a lead. I'm pacing my office like a fucking caged animal. I feel like my guts have been ripped out, like my heart is being destroyed with every moment that passes. I need for the fucking phone to ring. I need to be doing something to get her back.

It's three hours before Scott calls back. The longest three hours of my life.

"Please, tell me you've got something. Anything."

"Yes, sir, I believe I do. Mr. Peterson was in frequent contact with an ex-cellmate in the week leading up to his escape. I believe he helped him to escape the prison and flee undetected."

"Okay. What else do we know?" Please, something that will lead me to her.

"The cellmate, Adam Walters, bought a blue Ford Mustang on the black market three days before Peterson escaped and the vehicle in question is no longer in his possession. I called in some favors and a friend of mine paid a visit to Mr. Walters. After applying… pressure, he admitted that he gave the vehicle to Peterson. They got the license plates and I've managed to trace its whereabouts. Dumb fuck didn't know it had a tracker installed. He made my job too easy. I have a location for you, sir." Thank fuck.

"Excellent, Scott. Give me the address."

"It's off I-90. Secluded spot. Doesn't seem to be close to any commercial buildings. I can give you exact coordinates. Do you have a pen?"

"Yes." I take down the details and hang up as quickly as possible to punch the coordinates into my phone.

"Come on, David. I know where she is." I'm praying I'm not too late.

As we make our way down to the car, I call Addi and tell her where I'm heading. I'm taking the Ferrari, it will get me to her quicker and I need to be driving. I can't sit back any longer without actively doing something to help her. David is coming with me. We're both armed—ready for whatever we're about to walk into.

I speed through the city, running lights, weaving in and out of traffic trying to get off this damn island. Minutes feel like days, my mind racing, terrified of what I might find. I'm going to fucking kill him when I get my hands on him.

As we weave in and out of traffic on the interstate, my heart is hammering in my chest, adrenaline coursing through my veins like molten lava, preparing me, to take back what's mine.

As the highway fades from sight and the street lamps become sparse, David tells me what roads to take, edging closer to Lily by the mile.

"It should be up here on the right, Mr. Rhodes."

There is no evidence of life on this road. No homes, barns, outhouses, or even street signs. It's so dark, I'm scared I'll miss something that could lead me to her.

As I take a sharp corner, my high beams flash into the trees…

My heart jumps out of my chest. Dread seeping into every fiber of my being. I swerve to the side of the road, positioning my headlights to better see what's in front of me. I hope I'm wrong.

"The license plate is a match, sir. I'll call 911 immediately."

A blue Ford Mustang lays crumpled on the forest floor. The front end completely unrecognizable, the doors crushed in on themselves. The trunk of the car is open—a shovel, saw, and plastic sheeting spilling out onto the ground. The car sits on its roof… there's no sign of movement. No screams for help. No chance of survival.

I throw open the door and scramble from my car, my limbs fighting against me, terrified of what I'll find. "Lily!"

David comes running behind me, grabbing my arm. "Sir, I don't think you want to see this. Let me do it."

I struggle out of his vice-like grip. "I have to, David. She's… my life."

As I get closer to the carnage, my mouth fills with the salty taste that inevitably precedes vomit. The passenger's side comes into view and there, broken and bloodstained, is the love of my life—lifeless.

I drop to the mud, reaching tentatively through the broken window, sweeping her red-soaked golden hair aside to check for a pulse.

It's weak… but it's there. "Lily, baby. Can you hear me? It's Xander. I'm going to get you out of here."

I turn to David, screaming at him. "Get me a knife. I need to cut her out of the seatbelt. She's alive!"

"We need to wait for the ambulance. You don't want to risk paralysis if we move her." He sounds so calm and cold.

"Fuck that. I need to get her out… now."

I hear a groan from within the car, but it doesn't come from Lily. She's still unconscious. "Stupid cunt deserves it."

I see red—bloody, murderous, all-consuming rage. "I will fucking kill you!"

"David, stay with Lily."

I jump up, wading through the dirt to the other side of the car, his evil gaze coming into view. "What are you going to do, pretty boy? Kill me?" He cackles. "You don't have it in you. Besides, it won't change anything. She's as good as dead."

I reach inside and punch him as hard as I can, his screams of pain echoing out into the dark of night. "Don't you fucking mention her."

He laughs, blood audibly gurgling in his throat. His legs are crushed under the steering wheel. He has one arm that's still moving, but he can't reach me, and more importantly, he can't touch Lily.

"Sir, the ambulance will be here in five minutes. Come and be by Miss Tate's side. She needs you." David's right. I shouldn't be wasting my breath on this guy when Lily is struggling for every breath she takes. I rush to her side, my concern growing with the smell of gasoline permeating the ground around us.

"We need to get her out… now. There's a gas leak. Help me."

David runs over, grabbing a knife from a holder on his ankle. I hold Lily as still as I possibly can while he cuts through the tough material of her seatbelt. Her wrists are bound with tape, bloody and bruised. When he manages to slice through the final threads, her entire body slumps down into my arms. I can't breathe. She's lifeless.

As I carefully move to lift her from the car, I see Ron moving in my peripheral vision, but I'm focused on getting Lily to safety. He reaches inside his jacket, groaning in agony as he pulls out a gun, aiming it at Lily's back.

"You think I'm going to let you take your whore? She has to pay for what she took from me."

I spin to shield Lily from his aim. "David, take her!"

As her limp frame is lifted from my arms, the gun is turned on me. "Well, if I can't have her, neither can you."

David's voice pierces through the darkness. "Xander... your foot." My eyes dart down to see a lighter. He must have left it there when he took Lily from me.

The next few moments move as if in slow motion. I sweep the lighter from the grass, my gaze fixed on Ron Peterson. "Say goodbye, pretty boy." It takes less than the beat of a heart to pull the trigger, but my heart beats only for Lily, and I won't leave her alone.

I flick the lighter and throw it into the car before running for cover. Within seconds the car explodes, bursting into flames as it takes the man who killed Lily's dad to hell on a one-way ticket.

Sirens ring out in the distance—the only hope I have of saving my girl before it's too late.

CHAPTER 22

LILY

I DON'T KNOW HOW LONG I'VE BEEN HERE... IN THIS LIVING HELL. EVERY bone in my body aches, and every inch of my flesh is agony to the touch. I'm pretty sure my right arm is broken and several of my ribs. The last thing I remember was swerving the car off the road.

I blacked out when Peterson hit me with the butt of his gun outside my building, then the next thing I know, I'm waking up on a dark road in the middle of nowhere. I pretended to still be out for another hour, trying to find the courage to take him down—and in doing so—myself. He was so focused on whatever redneck song was on the radio, he didn't see me coming. With every fiber of my being screaming for relief, I lunged over and spun the wheel, sending us into a tailspin. When we collided with the barrier at the side of the road, the car flipped. The sound was deafening, the world around us seeming to defy gravity. As we crashed to the ground, a shudder of agony rippled through my body, as if I were being flattened by the force surrounding me.

After that, everything became hazy—short pockets of lucidity, followed by a dreamlike state and a deep sleep. It took Peterson at least twelve hours to wake up. That's when the real torture began. He replayed in detail, over and over, the satisfaction he derived from thrusting that blade into my dad's stomach—evil words—vile and disgusting thoughts. He enjoyed every minute of it. I used to think that maybe, just maybe, he made the wrong choice in desperation, and that he was paying for it in prison—maybe he still had a shred of humanity. But he doesn't. He's sick and twisted, and I'm going to take my last breath trapped in this car wreck with him. As I drift back into the darkness, I take comfort in the knowledge that I've saved Xander and Addi from this monster. I only wish I could let them know—that I could let Xander know it's okay—that I died content, knowing I got to experienced real, honest, uninhibited love.

~

"WHEN IS SHE GOING TO WAKE UP?" I'M ALIVE...

"Will there be any permanent damage? Is she paralyzed?" Xander...

"I'm here with you. Come back to me, sweets." I'm here...

"Addi is bringing you some home comforts for when you wake up. Knowing her she'll bring a pair of Jimmy Choos, a ridiculously inappropriate outfit, and a manicure set." Addi...

"You need to wake up, baby. Addi is driving me nuts. She loves you so much, I can't help but have a soft spot for her." Why can't I open my eyes?

"I'm so in love with you, Lily. I'm lost without you. I need you to wake up. I need you to *save* me."

He sounds so desolate, so alone. All I want to do is reach out and touch his face, soothe his worries, but my body won't listen to my commands. I can feel the warmth of his hand in mine, but I can't seem to give him a sign that I'm here and I'm listening. A twitch, anything, I'll take it.

"Shouldn't she have woken up by now? Surely there is something you can do." How long have I been out?

I hear the doctors coming in and out, my mom and sisters, and Addi—but the constant is Xander. He's always here, next to me, telling me he loves me, reading from my favorite books, and playing music from his iPod.

I hear Maroon 5, *Won't Go Home Without You*. All I can do is focus on the lyrics, pulling at my heart making me even more desperate to wake up, not just for me—for him. He's hurting and I can't stand it.

I need to open my eyes, dammit. I need to get back to him. Move, dammit!

"Oh my God. She just squeezed my hand. Lily... can you hear me?" I just squeezed his hand! I can do this. It takes all my strength just to open my eyes—blurry at first, a haze of colors and lights in an unfamiliar room. Xander's hands are in my hair, his soft lips pressing against my forehead. Everything slowly comes into focus, every stunning line of his face. He looks weary, his eyes glazed with tears, but he is still the most beautiful sight in the world to me.

"Xander." My voice is a husky whisper.

"I'm here, sweets." The love in his eyes is overwhelming. He quickly moves to pour me a glass of water. Cradling my head with his hand, he brings the glass to my lips letting it wet my lips before I manage a sip.

"I love you. I'm so sorry." I break down, tears spilling from my eyes. If only I'd listened to him that night, we might have avoided this.

"Don't ever apologize. You did nothing wrong. This was *not* your fault." He runs his thumb over my bottom lip before tentatively touching his lips to mine. "I've missed you so much. I'm never going to let you go."

"Sounds good to me."

A light, relieved chuckle escapes him, his breath caressing my face, a sweet smell of mint and Xander tickling my senses. "I better go call your family and Addi to let them know you're awake." Panic rises in my chest. I grab his arm in desperation, every muscle screaming in agony.

"Please, don't leave me."

A tortured look crosses his face. "I'm not going anywhere. I'll press the call button for the nurse, and I can let everyone else know from here." I let out a shaky breath, scared by my reaction to being on my own.

When the nurse comes in to check on me, I notice her frequent glances in Xander's direction.

"Welcome back, Lily. You gave us quite the scare. You have a wonderful man here. He hasn't left your side since you came in. We've had to bring him food from the cafeteria so he wouldn't waste away." I thought I couldn't love him more, but the swell in my chest at her words and the shy look on his face, tells me I was wrong.

"How long was I out?" It must have been a day or two. Xander seemed relieved when I woke up.

"It's been ten days." TEN DAYS! What the hell happened?

"You had some major injuries, Miss Tate. You are very lucky that Xander found you when he did. Any longer and you wouldn't be here talking to us now."

"You saved my life." His face is pained as he looks up into my eyes. The nurse leaves us, reminding me I need to rest on her way out the door.

"What's wrong? You saved me."

His head drops into his hands, his body slumped in despair. "I should have gotten to you sooner. Fuck... I should have known you wouldn't just ignore me. I should never have lied to you. If I had just been honest from the start, I would have been with you. I would have been able to protect you. I was almost too late."

I reach for his hand. "He waited for you to leave. He told me he had been watching the apartment, waiting until you and Addi were gone. He would have gotten to me no matter what. The important thing is that you *did* find me, and you saved my life. I can never repay you for that." He rests his forehead on our tangled hands.

"I have never been so terrified. I thought I was too late. You were so broken... my heart stopped beating. *I thought I was too late.* I thought you were..." He can't even say the words, anguish and turmoil evident in his voice. I can't imagine what the past ten days have been like for him.

"I'm back now, and nothing is going to come between us again."

"Lily, I killed him. I took his life. He was going to shoot you. He was going to shoot me. But it doesn't change the fact that I knowingly caused his death. I threw a lighter into the car, and walked away as it burst into flames, taking him with it. How can you ever look at me the same way?"

I can see how much he's been struggling with this, his heart heaving with the decision he was forced to make. "You saved my life, and your own. I will never look at you with anything but reverence and respect. You stood up and fought for me, for us. You did exactly what my dad did except this time, the right person prevailed. I love you, and I can never thank you enough for giving me a chance to live, and to come back to you. To tell you how much I love you."

I suddenly feel exhausted, my eyes heavy—too heavy to keep open. The darkness takes me, but I don't feel scared, Xander is here...

WHEN I WAKE UP, I'M SURROUNDED BY FAMILY AND FRIENDS. MY MOM and sisters are here, so is Addi and I can see Jason in the corner. Where is Xander? Addi immediately registers the panic on my face. "He's just gone to grab a shower and some fresh clothes. He'll be back any minute." She moves to sit in the chair next to my bed. "Lilliput. You scared the shit out of me. I'm so happy to see you, friend." She leans in to give me a tentative hug, careful not to hurt me.

"I'm glad to see you, too, Addi. I love you." She can't hold back her tears any longer, burying her head in my neck.

"I love you, too. You're my family. I don't know what I would do without you." We spend long minutes wrapped in each other's arms, crying like idiots by the time my mom interjects.

"Right, you two. This is supposed to be a happy moment. Don't start me off, too." Addi makes space for her.

"Hi, Mom." That's all it takes for the floodgates to open and the sobs to flow, rolling in waves, racking my mom's chest.

"Baby girl. I love you so much, darling. I was scared I would never see you again. Your strength and will to survive is awe-inspiring, Lily. I'm so glad I've got a second chance to be a better mom for you. You are everything to me, and I promise to show you every day just how precious you are." She kisses my cheek, crushing me a little too tight, but I don't complain. The pain is worth it to feel so completely cherished.

My sisters are a mess of snot and tears as they welcome me back to the land of the living—gushing about making time to visit me more often. I doubt it will happen, but I love that they want to try.

Jason gives me a soft cuddle, telling me how glad he is that I'm okay and how worried they all were. I lose track of what he's saying when I sense *him* in the doorway. My eyes are instantly drawn to where I can *feel* his presence. It's magnetic.

Xander is leaning against the doorframe, his corded arms crossed over his chest, his long lithe legs crossed at the ankle. He is the picture of heaven. A dazzling grin spreads across his handsome, chiseled features, and we just stare at each other, relishing our intense connection. Everyone else in the room fades into the background, their words a dull hum in the distance.

He strides toward me, never taking his eyes off me. The emotion welling in my chest is a palpable knot of love and adoration. His proximity makes my head spin. As he touches his lips to mine, something ignites inside me. It's not lust, my body is too sore for that—it's something much stronger—a melding of two souls. Xander becomes a part of me in this moment. The last piece of the puzzle I need to feel complete. A piece I know I could never live without.

I don't notice everyone else slip out of the room, leaving us in our own little bubble, caressing our lips and tongues together in a dance that belongs only to us. It could be minutes, it could be hours, all I know for sure is that it isn't long enough.

"Hi... my sweet Lily." God, I love his voice. It envelops me in a warm hug, soothing me with its low sexy rasp.

We spend the next few hours wrapped up in each other. Relishing every touch, every kiss, and every word spoken between us. He had them bring in a cot while I was asleep so he could stay with me at all times. Now that I'm awake, he insists he's still going to stay, unwilling to let me out of his sight. I don't put up a fight. I want him here with me.

I spend another week in the hospital before the doctors even consider letting me go home. Xander has been by my side the entire time, drawing funny little doodles on my arm cast. It's covered in little love hearts and his version of the London sights. I've found something he doesn't excel at! A dog could draw a better picture than him and I find it completely adorable.

I'm slowly but surely getting back on my feet, my bruises are fading, and my aches and pains are getting less every day. I have four broken ribs, so they are going to take longer to heal, but I'm lucky they didn't puncture my lung. I won't be getting my cast off for at least three weeks, maybe four, but I'm hoping to get home long before then.

Addi contacted T Magazine and let them know I'm out of commission for a while. They offered to keep my job for a while at least, which is more than I could have hoped for.

The doctor comes in to see me and it appears that he and Xander have become like old friends!

"Well, Miss Tate. If you promise to take it easy, and you have someone to take care of you, I think we can let you go home today. You'll need to come back to get the cast removed, but other than that, lots of bed rest, no heavy lifting, and no sex until your ribs heal."

The look on Xander's face makes me laugh which is not a good thing when you have four broken ribs. He turns to the doctor with a serious look on his face.

"You're killing me here, doc." He winks in my direction. "Can I take my girl home now?"

"As soon as the discharge papers are signed, yes. Make sure you look after her."

Xander glances at me with a gentle smile.

"I plan to, doc… I plan to."

He leaves us to get organized, and after Xander helps me dress I need to rest for a minute. Who knew it could be so tiring putting on yoga pants and a hoodie? He sits on the bed beside me, a nervous look on his face.

"Lily. I need to talk to you about something before we leave." That sounds ominous.

"I want to take care of you, and I can't bear the thought of being away from you. I was hoping you would consider moving into my apartment. I can help you recover, and then, when you feel better, you can redecorate the whole place. I just want to be with you. I love you. You are a part of me. The part I can't be without. Please, say yes."

I'm shocked by his declaration. We've not been together that long, and I would really miss living with Addi, but everything inside me is desperate to say yes. I don't want to spend another night of my life *not* being in his arms, cocooned in the warmth of his love and affection.

Without any further thought, the words trip off my tongue. "Yes, Xander. Of course, I'll move in with you." His eyes are ablaze with fire and desire, but he controls his touch as he claims my mouth, his tongue dipping in to gently caress and explore, conquer and worship.

With the discharge papers signed, Xander wheels me out to the front of the hospital, the fresh air filling my lungs, cleansing my soul. David is waiting on the sidewalk with the door to the SUV open wide and a grin on his face. I think that's the first time I've seen him smile. He's quite handsome.

"It's a pleasure to see you up and about, Miss Tate." My gratitude takes over and I pull him into a firm hug.

"Thank you for what you did, David." He gives me an embarrassed half-grin before handing me back to Xander.

"All part of the job, Miss Tate." Xander lifts me carefully into the car.

"I can't wait to get you home. To *our* home."

I remember the mess at my apartment that day. "What about my apartment? Addi?"

"She stayed with her parents for a few days while I got extra security measures fitted at your apartment, and had the place cleaned and restored to its former glory. She's fine, and eager to come visit you in your new home. I asked her permission to steal you away. I told her to let you rest. The journey home will be enough excitement for one day. She's going to come by tomorrow to check up on you."

Knowing that everyone is safe and sound, I drift off, tucked into Xander's lap as we make our way back to *our* house.

He's my home now.

CHAPTER 23

LILY

I'M SO EXHAUSTED FROM THE JOURNEY HOME THAT I ONLY WAKE LONG enough for Xander to lift me into his arms. I don't remember anything after the ping of the elevator doors opening in the lobby.

I wake up in Xander's bed. I guess it's my bed now, too. I'm happy to be surrounded by his intoxicating scent. It's ingrained in his sheets and gives me so much comfort snuggling further into the covers, cuddling his pillow to my chest. I take a deep, painful breath before settling back down to sleep for another hour or so.

When I finally come around properly, he's lying next to me on his side, staring at me.

"Hey, sweets. How are you feeling?" The adoration in his eyes melts my heart.

"Much better now that I'm home with you." He gently runs the back of his hand down my cheek with a smile of true contentment.

"I can see that. Sleeping in our bed must be a good thing, you've been asleep since yesterday afternoon." I can believe it—I feel so much better than I did in the hospital. "It's given me the opportunity to look at your beautiful face, back where you're supposed to be. With me." A smile tugs at the corners of my mouth at his sweet words. He leans forward, pressing a gentle kiss on my lips. "Lily..." He chokes up, choosing his words carefully. "I thought we might never have this again. I've never been so scared in all my life." I cup his scruff covered cheek in my good hand.

"I know. I thought the same thing. I was so scared I wouldn't get the chance to tell you, I believe you about everything that happened with Natalie." It's the first time she's been mentioned since we came back from London.

While I was in the hospital, I didn't care about what happened. I just wanted to be with Xander. Happy to be alive and happy to have the chance to tell him how much I love him. She seems so insignificant now. He came for me, he saved my life, he stayed by my side and gave me the *will* to wake up. When I look into his eyes, I see sadness at the mention of her name.

"I am so sorry for everything with Natalie. Can I tell you what happened? I don't want there to be anymore secrets between us…" I nod, feeling slightly anxious about what he's going to say.

He explains the whole upsetting situation, from his first contact with Natalie in the Hamptons to the point when we were standing in my apartment with the photos she sent. I thought I would be annoyed or upset knowing he lied to me, but what I feel for him in this moment is… pride. She broke his heart and his trust less than a year ago, and yet he managed to find compassion in his heart for her. He's a good man, with a beautiful heart and he couldn't stand to see *any* woman being abused by a man. I can't be upset that he fell for her lies. If he hadn't tried to help her, he wouldn't be the Xander I know and love with all my heart.

He mistakes my silence for anger.

"I'm so sorry, baby. Can you forgive me?" I lean in, giving him a tender kiss, filled with all the love I feel for him. His hand moves into my hair, holding me in place as his tongue performs an enchanting waltz with mine. Our souls entwined in a single kiss. I pull back just far enough to gaze at him as I speak.

"I forgive you for lying to me. As for what happened, it makes me love you even more, if that's possible." He looks puzzled. "You are such an amazing man. Strong, confident, and commanding, but at the same time you have an unparalleled capacity for love and compassion, and a tenderness that soothes my soul." A whisper of a smile creeps onto the corners of his mouth. "The fact that you were able to put aside the hurt she caused you and help her because you thought she was in trouble is... admirable. Not many people would do that. You're special, and I'm so thankful we've got another chance together."

He cuddles me down onto his chest as he moves onto his back, our limbs tangling into what seems to have become our 'position.' I've missed this so much.

"You're the amazing one. I love you so much. I'm in awe of your strength, sweets."

I don't know why I want to know, but I ask the question anyway. "Have you spoken to her since the photo incident?"

He hugs me a little closer. "No." His voice is cold, angry. "I couldn't stand the thought of it. I was focused on getting you back, because you're the only thing that matters, Lily. Now that you're home, trust me, I'll be dealing with her for what she did to us."

I attempt to soothe his agitation, rubbing my hand over his toned chest. Not easy with my arm in a cast, but oh my God, he feels good.

"I don't want you to do anything. You're better than that. *We're* better than that. We're together and happy and she will never have that because she's obviously incapable of real love. Enough of our time has been wasted by other people. I'm sure she'll get what's coming to her. Karma's a bitch, especially when you are one."

He lets out a shaky breath. "I'll leave it, only because you're asking me to. You've been through enough. But if she so much as breathes in our direction again, I'll make her pay for it. Understood?"

"One more breath, and she's toast." I manage a smile out of him. We lie in each other's arms for a while before Xander brings up the other elephant in the room.

"You know you can talk to me about what happened with Peterson don't you?" A chill runs through me at the mere mention of his name.

"I know. I'm just not ready to talk about it yet. I hope that's okay." He kisses my forehead as he brushes the hair back from my face.

"I understand. I just want you to know I'm here when you're ready.

You're not alone." Those last words are more of a comfort to me than he could ever know—*I'm not alone.*

Xander gives me permission to come downstairs for brunch before I'm confined back to my bed. He's taking doctor's orders very seriously! It's great to be out of bed for an hour, but I'm tired out by the time he lifts me back to our room. I need to sleep for a couple of hours before Addi arrives.

I wake up to the sound of Addi and Xander talking, their voices getting closer to our room. I can hear her concern as she grills him about how I'm doing, and if I'm coping. He reassures her that he's taking good care of me, as they appear in the doorway.

He helps me to sit up, positioning my pillows so my ribs aren't too sore, my broken arm is propped on yet more cushions. He kisses my forehead before leaving us to catch up.

"I'll be in my study if you need anything. Just shout or call me." I can't help watching his sexy gait as he leaves the room.

Addi sniggers at my obvious ogling! "I see your injuries haven't calmed your new raging libido, Lilliput." I laugh but immediately hold my ribs. No more laughing for me.

"Don't make me laugh, Addi. It hurts." She looks apologetic but continues to snort, so I'm thinking she's not that sorry! She envelops me in a tight but gentle cuddle, careful not to hurt me.

"Don't ever scare me like that again, okay? I think I've aged about ten years in the last two weeks." I see the toll it's taken on her as she sits next to me. She's lost weight. She was already the thinnest woman I know, but now she looks unwell. I feel bad that I've put her through so much.

"I promise." I decide to change the subject. "So, what's happening with you? Last I knew, you were away for a few days with Carter. What's going on there?"

She chuckles as she pulls her knees up to her chest. "I can't believe that after everything you've been through, you're thinking about my love life."

"I love you and I care about what happens to you. You're my family. Besides, there has been enough heavy stuff, let's talk about something more exciting. Spill your guts, Warner." She rolls her eyes in defeat before filling me in on what's been going on.

"Well. I took your advice and gave him a chance. We went to the Hamptons for a few days, and it was amazing. I mean *really amazing*. I've never felt like this before, and it scares the shit out of me. Things have been on the back burner since you went missing and the subsequent hospital recovery."

"Please tell me things aren't over between you two because of me?" I couldn't stand it if that was the case.

"It's not over. I spoke to him and told him I had to focus on you. He was really understanding. Now that you're getting better and you're out of the hospital I'm going to see him this weekend and we'll see where things stand." I'm so relieved.

"I hope everything works out between you guys. You seem good together. Maybe we can go out together sometime? The boys are best friends after all."

"How weird is that? We're dating best friends. Problem is you'll go off and marry Xander and when Carter and I don't work out, it'll be weird at parties and stuff." I slap her shoulder with my good hand, sending a searing pain down my ribs.

"Don't be so negative. There is no reason to think it won't work out between you and Carter. You are an amazing woman, Addi, and he's lucky to have a chance with you."

"Thanks, friend." She dips into her bag. "Anyway, enough of all this messy emotional stuff. I brought chocolate and one of your favorite movies." She holds up the *Dirty Dancing* DVD, which elicits a squeal. I love that movie.

Xander has a great flat-screen TV hidden in a stunning oversized cabinet in the bedroom. Once it's set up, she snuggles up next to me on the bed and we enjoy a normal, fun night together, watching

Patrick Swayze and eating the massive bar of chocolate she brought with her.

I must have fallen asleep because I'm roused by Xander sliding into bed beside me.

"Addi?" I murmur.

"I had David drop her home a while ago. Go back to sleep, sweets. I love you." I take a deep breath, enjoying his amazing smell as he kisses me good night.

"I love you, too."

⁓

XANDER HAS BEEN THE MOST ATTENTIVE BOYFRIEND I COULD EVER ASK for over the last few weeks, attending to my every need. He goes out of his way to make my days special in some small way. He and Addi have been taking turns spoiling me. I've seen her almost as much as when we lived together which makes the whole transition a little easier on both of us.

Within three weeks, my cast is off, and all my home comforts have been brought to the penthouse. He even brings me letters he wrote to me when he thought I had ended our relationship. He's been working from home most of the time, so I wait until he goes to his office for a few hours to sit and read the first letter.

Sunday
Sweets,
I was hoping that my letter yesterday would have given you reason enough to hear me out.
I'm struggling to give you the space you need. Every minute of the day I want to come and see you, look at your beautiful face and listen to your sweet voice to soothe the ache in my chest.
I understand that you entrusted me with so much

and I let you down. I will never forgive myself for that.

I can only ask that you find it in your heart to forgive me and allow me to spend the rest of my life making it up to you.

Every song I hear, every room in my apartment, reminds me of you. Your face, your scent, the way your body feels when it comes apart beneath me, and most importantly your heart. The way you make me a better man just by being in your orbit.

I meant what I said in London, Lily. I want to give you the world if you'll let me. I miss you.

Forever Yours,

Xander x

Coldplay—The Scientist

Tears stream down my cheeks as I realize the torment he must have felt, believing I didn't want to be with him, and all the while I was desperate for him to come for me. I thought I would never see him again.

I can't control the sobs that rack my body as I remember what that monster did to me. He might be dead now, but he still haunts my dreams with a new nightmare. I wake up screaming most nights, drenched in a cold sweat, the terror causing my body to shake.

Every night, Xander rocks me back to sleep, holding me in his arms, assuring me I'm safe and that Ron Peterson will never hurt me again. He never complains, even though I can see the toll it's taking on him. He has dark circles under his ice-blue eyes, his beautiful face marred with worry.

I hear his hurried footsteps rushing down the hall at the sound of my cries. I feel awful knowing that I'm causing him further stress, but I can't stop the torrent of emotion, spilling out of me. Through my tear-filled eyes, I can only see a blurred vision of him, as he comes bursting through the door and into our bedroom.

"Lily... baby... what's wrong? Are you okay? Are you sore?" He scoops my crumpled form up off the bed and holds me tight as I give in to the enormity of my ordeal.

"Do you want to talk about it?" I nod, knowing I have to get it off my chest.

Between sobs I tell him the full sordid story. I see so many emotions in his eyes as I speak—love, anger, grief, rage, and more love. It's difficult for a man like Xander who is normally so dominant and in control, to hear how Peterson tormented me in those final moments.

When there are no tears left to cry, and no more story to be told, he lifts me effortlessly from the bed and carries me into the bathroom, setting me down gently on the counter while he runs a bath for us.

He gently undresses me before undressing himself and lifting me into the tub. He tucks me close and relaxes back into the water. Every time he touches me it's as if I'm going to break. I appreciate his tenderness, but my ribs are much better now, and I miss his *not* so gentle touch. I ache to feel him inside me, his body looming over mine as he drives us to the edge of ecstasy and pushes us over into a freefall of sensation.

I've asked him to make love to me, but he's been so self-controlled, wanting to make sure I'm fully healed so he doesn't hurt me. I know it must be killing him because my own frustration is at breaking point. Every innocent touch of his hand ignites a burning desire. As soothing as this bath is, lying against his taut, naked body is driving me crazy. I need him—now.

"Xander?" He squeezes me a little closer.

"Yes, sweets?" Here goes nothing.

"I *need* you to make love to me. I need that physical connection to you. Please, honey. My ribs feel better. Xander... please... touch me." I take his hand and press it to my breast, my nipple instantly hardening at the touch of his strong, warm hand. He nibbles my ear, his breathy voice fighting for control.

"I don't want to hurt you, baby. You've been through so much." He can't help trailing kisses down my neck, his argument dying on his lips as they stoke the fire between us.

"I'm good. Please… it hurts *not* to be with you." The last of his willpower evaporates.

He's up, lifting me out the tub and into our room within seconds, our lips locked in an urgent kiss.

"Fuck… I've missed your body so much. I want to bury my cock in you and stay there forever."

"Sounds perfect to me."

He lays me gently on the bed before grabbing a towel. My gaze is locked on his body as he sweeps it over his washboard abs, and down the hallowed V, before dropping it to the floor. Holy. Fuck.

There is no mischief in his eyes tonight. He stands in front of me, dominating, and sexy as hell. A thrill of anticipation courses through me, my body desperate for his expert touch. My nipples pucker as his red-hot gaze roams every curve of my body.

"Show me how ready you are for me, sweets." I part my legs wide, my entrance warm and slick. A groan escapes his chest. "So fucking beautiful."

He crawls up the bed settling between my legs, licking his sinful lips as his gaze drops to my pussy. He darts his tongue out, running from my wet entrance up to my throbbing clit. My body convulses under his expert touch.

"Mmm. Even sweeter than I remember, Miss Tate." His firm hands press my thighs wide as he sets to work, driving me toward a quick and powerful climax.

"That's number one." A sly grin creeps over his lips, my juices glistening in the moonlight shining through the window. "Now I'm going to take my time."

He moves down my leg, starting at the instep of my foot, trailing soft kisses up my calf, to the back of my knee. It's a heady feeling and ignites a trail of desire as he places open-mouthed kisses up my thigh, stopping just before he reaches the apex. Then he starts the process all over again on my other leg.

By the time he shifts his attention to my stomach I'm writhing beneath him, threading my hands through his hair. His hands skim my flesh, his mouth following their path, nibbling, licking, and suckling. When his tongue reaches my breasts I arch off the bed in response to the pleasure shooting to my core.

"Careful, baby. Tell me if I hurt you."

"I'm not sore anymore. Touch me… hard."

His hand reaches up to cradle my breast, pinching the nipple until it's a tight little bud, awaiting his expert tongue. I'm panting and moaning underneath him, desperate to taste his full lips and his lascivious tongue. He licks from my nipple, up and along the length of my collarbone before nibbling his way up my neck. His tongue dips into my ear and it's beyond erotic. I snap my head round to capture his mouth with my own.

"I love the way you kiss me."

He groans into my mouth, driving me wild. "Fuck… I'm not going to last at this rate. It's been too long since I've been nestled in your tight little pussy. Just kissing you is pushing me to the brink."

"I want you inside me… now."

He slips his hand between our naked bodies, gripping his hard length, running the tip over my entrance, covering himself in my juices before slowly pushing every hard inch of himself inside me.

"Holy Fuck, Lily. You feel amazing."

I've missed this feeling more than I can express. He starts to move inside me. The sensation is explosive as I writhe beneath him.

"Slow down, sweets, I need to pace myself… it's been a while." I continue to grind my hips, coaxing him to move. "Don't make me restrain you, Miss Tate. You know I will… happily."

If he was trying to calm me down, that did *not* work. I'm so turned on. I wrap my legs around his waist. He captures my lips with his, sucking my bottom lip into his mouth before giving it a little nip. He interlaces our hands and extends them above my head before catching both of my wrists in one hand. I love the feel of his strong hands pinning me down. He holds his weight with his other arm propped at the side of my head, giving me a perfect view of his corded forearms and toned biceps.

He slows his movements, forcing me to comply with hard, long, thrusts. His lips descend on my neck just below my ear and it's like a trigger. I struggle beneath him, wanting… needing more of him.

"I've got you, sweets, don't worry." He pushes my wrists down into the pillow as he takes his other hand and slides it between our hot, naked flesh. As soon as his fingertips connect with my pulsing clit, I detonate around him.

"Oh my God, Xander… fuck… Xander!" I'm overwhelmed, riding out the aftershocks of my orgasm, tightening around his throbbing cock. It feels so fucking good.

I fist my hands in his hair, pulling him down onto my breasts. He's ravenous, his hunger for me evident in every groan and satisfied hum that escapes his throat as he sucks me into his mouth, flicking his tongue in circles around my nipple while gradually building towards his own release. He sets an increasingly punishing pace, rocking his hips against me, pumping his cock in and out of my soaking wet pussy, his balls slapping against my ass with the force of each breath-taking, earth-shattering thrust.

"Lily… I'm going to come, baby… you feel too fucking perfect. Come with me…" His sensual, rasping demand is my undoing.

"Come… now, baby!" He explodes, his come spilling inside me, ripping another mind-altering orgasm from my body.

He lets go of my hands, allowing me to rake my nails down his back as we buck frantically, wringing every sweet drop of ecstasy from each other's bodies. I'm lost in the moment. Nothing else exists. Our bodies are joined in the most intimate of ways, our hearts beating in sync, and our lives forever changed as we become one.

His head slumps onto my chest, panting in the aftermath of our vigorous lovemaking. We lie in a tangle of limbs and sheets, letting our heartbeats slow to a steady rhythm.

"I'm so fucking in love with you, Lily Tate. I can barely breathe."

CHAPTER 24

LILY

WE HAVE SPENT ALMOST EVERY WAKING MOMENT TOGETHER RECENTLY and the realization that I am finally ready to start my new job is daunting on many levels. I've not been on my own for any length of time since I was kidnapped, so I'm a bit apprehensive about being out by myself amongst a crowd of strangers.

Xander said I should focus on my novel and let him look after me, but as tempting as it sounds, I'm just not built that way. I do acquiesce to his incessant requests to buy me some new clothes for work. I could use some more work appropriate clothing! We spend the Saturday before I start in Saks with a personal shopper. The woman has great taste and is aware of Xander's deep pockets. She chooses perfectly for me, and I'm thrilled when it's all packaged and ready to be delivered to the apartment. He spoils me all weekend, which makes it even more difficult to leave him for the day, come Monday morning.

I'm dressed in a classic black dress and jacket. Xander steps out of his walk-in closet dressed in a very sexy grey suit. It's been a while since I've seen him in a suit. I'd forgotten just how good he makes them look. GQ—eat your heart out.

"Do we have to go to work, sweets? You look too edible to share with the rest of the world." He strides toward me with hunger in his eyes. "I can work from home ninety percent of the time, and you should be writing your novel full-time." I can see the merit in his idea. Having him all to myself and naked for most of the day would be fantastic, but I'd never get any work done! He cradles my face, his mouth finding mine, his tongue licking at my bottom lip igniting a familiar fire in my belly.

"We need to go before you distract me too much. I can't be late on my first day." He gives me the most adorable puppy-dog eyes and pout before planting a quick kiss on my lips and dragging me from the bedroom.

David is ready and waiting to take us to our respective offices and I'm a little nervous as we sit in the back of the town car. When we pull up outside my new office on West 38th Street, my stomach is churning. He pulls my chin round so I'm staring into the depths of his ice-blue eyes before he speaks.

"You are going to be great. You're perfect for this job and remember the reason you wanted to do it in the first place. This is about making contacts for your own novel when it's written. Eyes on the prize. You are an amazing person and everyone here is lucky to get the chance to work with you."

He kisses the tip of my nose.

"You can call me anytime and I'll be back to pick you up at 5.30 p.m., okay?" I snuggle in to take one last long sniff of his addictive scent before getting out of the car and heading into the building.

I needn't have worried. Everyone has been so warm and welcoming. No one has probed me about why I was starting work seven weeks later than scheduled. I've had a great first day, sitting in on meetings, getting a feel for the place, introducing myself to new colleagues, and getting my first assignment.

I've been given a paranormal thriller trilogy to read and review. The third in the trilogy has just been released and it's taking the book world by storm. I've downloaded them onto my kindle and have already carried out some initial research on the author.

Xander will be happy to hear that I don't even need to be in the office most of the time. I'm required to attend the Monday morning meeting to get my assignment and find out what's happening with the rest of the magazine, and on Fridays to upload and submit my work. During the week I can work from the apartment, reading books and emailing the editor proofs of my review.

Throughout the day Xander sends me little texts of encouragement.

10:30 a.m.

> Mr. P: Love you, sweets. The next chapter starts today. X

2:00 p.m.

> Mr. P: How's my favorite blogger/author getting on? X

> Me: Great! Can't wait to tell you all about it. Love you X

5:00 p.m.

> Mr. P: I'm coming to get you, Miss Tate. I hope you're ready for me. X

That last one has me squirming in my seat. I make a start on packing up everything I need for the week and shutting my desktop computer down before he arrives. A few of my new colleagues come over to my desk before leaving for the night to ask how my day has been. It's great to be part of something again, but at the same time the flexibility to work from home.

I step out of the elevator at exactly 5:30 p.m. to see him standing in the lobby, the top button of his shirt undone, showing a smattering of deliciously dark chest hair just below his collar. I feel like I haven't seen him in days.

On the ride home I tell him all about my new job. He is more than a little excited at the prospect of me working from home three days a week.

"Oh baby, I love your new job. I hope you know we have naked Tuesday, Wednesday, and Thursday here at the penthouse." He wiggles his eyebrows at me with a devious grin.

"I'm never going to get anything done around you, am I?"

"You are going to get plenty *done... to... you.*"

MY DAYS AT HOME THIS WEEK HAVE BEEN AMAZING. XANDER HAS BEEN working from home, too, and made space in his rather large study for me so that we can work together. He wasn't wrong when he said it was a requirement to work naked in the penthouse. I think we spent about fifty percent of our time working each other into a naked frenzy!

The rest of my time was spent immersed in books—laughing, crying, shouting at the characters, and loving every second of it. It's so exciting discovering new authors. I still can't believe this is my job.

Xander spends his time working and laughing at my plethora of emotions as I read. His phone rings non-stop throughout the day. I don't know how he stays sane. Everyone wants a piece of him... every minute of every day. I guess it comes with the territory when you're as successful as he is.

When I'm finished and ready for the office on Friday, I decide to take some time to myself and go for a walk in Central Park. Xander offers to come, but I know he has a million things to do because he's been choosing to spend time with me when he should be working. I convince him I'll be fine if he wants to go into the office for a few hours. He finally agrees and grabs some papers he'll need while I run to the bedroom for something and slip it in my pocket. He walks me down to the lobby before we part ways, with a plan to meet at his offices and go for dinner at eight.

It's a beautiful day, and as I wander round the park, I breathe in the sights and sounds, letting them wash over me. There was a time not too long ago, when I didn't think I would be here. It changed my perspective on life and love, in a profound and meaningful way.

I don't take my time with Xander for granted. I never really grasped that when my father died. I was so focused on my own grief, I didn't see that he gave up his life to let me have a chance to *live* mine. I owe it to him to make something of myself. It really hit home for me when I thought I wouldn't have the chance to make him proud.

I find a quiet spot in the park and make myself comfortable on the grass before reaching into my pocket for Xander's final letter to me when I was missing.

The last time I read one of these, it destroyed me to think of what we were both going through at the time. Maybe being out in public will help me hold it together. Or… maybe I'll be a blubbering mess in front of everyone in the park.

I take a few deep breaths before reading the eloquent penmanship of the man I love.

Monday

To my sweet Lily,

I was really hoping to have heard from you by now. You need to let me explain what happened and make it right. I've given you all the time I can. If I don't hear from you today, I'm coming to see you tomorrow. I can't wait any longer.

I know you're upset, but I can't let you throw away what we have. I WON'T let you. You are the best thing that has ever happened to me.

As my words don't seem to be getting through to you, I thought I would borrow some inspiration from the literature that you love. I decided Charlotte Brontë says it best in Jane Eyre. I'm paraphrasing but bear with me.

I'm asking you to be by my side, to be the better

half of me. I want you to be mine, and only mine, baby. You're my equal and I offer you my heart. I want to share my life with you, Lily.

I know if you look beyond the hurt you're feeling right now, you will know in your heart how much I love you.

I'm going to deal with Natalie's lies and deceit, but not until I have you back. You are the only person who matters to me.

You are my heart, and I will always put you first. Please, Lily... call me. I need to hear your voice.

Yours always,

Xander x

Gary Go—Black and White Days

I'm struggling to contain the lump in my throat. Xander is every-thing I need and want. He can be so incredibly sweet and emotional, and yet he is also the strong, confident Xander that I love. He seems to sense when these sides of his personality are required and gives me exactly what I need.

It's six o'clock, and he's probably still working, but I must go to him. I type out a quick text.

> Me: Can I come to your office for a minute? X

Two seconds later my phone beeps.

> Mr. P: Sure. Everything okay? X

> Me: Everything is fine. See you in 5. X

As soon as I reach his building a sense of calm washes over me. The security guards have been informed that I'm coming, so I'm ushered straight through and make my way to the elevators. When the doors open, he's standing in the reception area waiting for me.

"Are you okay?"

I take his hand in mine and whisper in his ear. "Take me to your office." He searches my face for any signs of upset, but I smile back at him, so touched by his beautiful letter.

I'm glad Xander's office is private with large wooden doors and frosted glass so that the open-plan office outside of his can't see in. As soon as the door closes behind us, I throw myself into his arms, capturing his face in my hands, his scruff tickling my palms as I draw his mouth to mine. He doesn't stop to ask questions, simply pouring everything he has into this kiss. Locking the door, he lifts me off my feet, crushing me to his chest.

"Wrap your legs around me." I do as he asks, digging my heels into his perfectly toned ass as he walks us over to his desk.

He sets me down before pulling at my t-shirt, our lips parting only long enough for him to rip it over my head and throw it on the floor. His fingers make short work of my bra, pulling my hands from his hair to slide my straps off.

"Fuck, you're beautiful." I lean back on my elbows, his papers underneath me as his lips move down to my breasts. A moan of sheer bliss escapes me. "You need to be quiet, Miss Tate. I really don't want my employees to hear how fucking sexy you sound when you're screaming my name." His eyes lift to meet mine. "Can you be a good girl and stay quiet for me?" I nod, biting my lip as a wave of pleasure ripples through my body. "Good, then let's get rid of these jeans, shall we?" He runs his fingertips down my chest, over my stomach and stops at my waist. He quickly removes my shoes.

"Hold onto the desk, Miss Tate."

I grip the edge as he savagely tugs my jeans down my legs and off, discarding them alongside my t-shirt. It's a thrill to be almost naked in Xander's office, hundreds of people on the other side of the door, oblivious to what we're doing. He hooks his fingers under my panties on either side before dipping his nose down to nuzzle my pussy. "You are so fucking wet. Something turning you on?" A fire ignites inside me at his brazen behavior.

"You, Mr. Rhodes... you're turning me on." With a sly grin he bites his bottom lip and it's so unbelievably sexy, I can feel myself getting wetter.

"Fuck... Lily. The heat coming off your tight little pussy right now is intoxicating. Shall I show you what that does to me?"

"Yes."

"Yes, who?" Holy shit this is hot.

"Yes... Mr. Rhodes."

He slowly removes my panties, tucking them in his pocket before loosening his belt, and unzipping his pants. I can barely breathe with the anticipation of seeing his beautiful cock, hard and ready for me.

His hand disappears under the waistband of his boxer shorts before lowering them just enough for his raging erection to spring free. I want so badly to drop to my knees in front of him and take him into my mouth. His cock is so big, steel encased in velvet soft skin, tight, long, thick, and rock-hard just for me. "I want to fuck you with my mouth." He strokes himself, his eyes locked on mine, molten blue on emerald green.

"You want this in that pretty little mouth of yours, Miss Tate?"

I'm so turned on, my reply is nothing more than a breathy whisper. "Yes."

He pushes my legs apart as far as they will go before kneeling in front of me.

"You'll have to wait. Right now, I'm going to eat this delicious pussy of yours and make you writhe on my face until you can't stand it anymore."

He sucks my clit into his warm mouth, the scruff of his chin scraping against my folds, creating a myriad of sensations that blow my mind. I don't even realize I'm panting Xander's name until he stops dead.

"Now, Miss Tate. I told you to be quiet. I'm not sharing the sound of your orgasm with anyone." He licks the length of my folds. "Understood?"

"Mmm." I sink my teeth into my arm to stop myself from screaming his name.

His hands hold firm at the apex of my thighs, his fingers spreading my folds, his tongue delving deeper. He's fucking my pussy with his mouth, thrusting in and out, driving me higher and higher towards my release.

"You taste so good, baby. I can't get enough of your perfect pussy." His tongue descends on my clit, circling and flicking, lavishing it with open-mouthed kisses as he slips his fingers inside me. Holy fuck!

My hips writhe as I push tighter against his face. I'm biting my arm so hard it's almost painful, but the pleasure is too intense for me to care. I grab my heavy breast in my hand as he continues to lick, suck, and kiss me. I see his eyes widen as he takes in the sight of me touching myself, kneading my soft flesh, teasing my tightly budded nipples.

"Lick it, Miss Tate. Take that tight nipple of yours into your mouth while I make you come." I didn't know that was possible. "Don't make me wait. Do it... now."

I lift myself up onto my elbows before pulling my breast with my hand. I dip my head down, taking the tight, puckered flesh into my mouth. My gaze fixed on him as a fire explodes behind his eyes.

The feel of my own breast against my tongue is wildly arousing, made even more so by his obvious delight. Xander is relentless, his fingers fucking me, keeping time with his wicked mouth—making love to me—worshipping my body.

"Bite your nipple."

I do as he asks, the intense pleasure of his mouth and mine on my body at the same time sending me into a tailspin. My orgasm rips through me. I throw my head back as I convulse on the desk, my legs shaking uncontrollably.

I bite down on my lip to stop myself from crying out, so hard I taste blood. Xander places his strong hand on my stomach, holding me in place, letting me ride out my orgasm against his face. When I'm completely spent, he stands up, my juices dripping from his chin, his erection even harder than before.

"Up you get, Miss Tate. Time to get on your knees for me."

A thrill runs through me at his demand. I suddenly have a new surge of energy and desire as I lift myself from his desk. He's still completely dressed, which I quickly set to work on remedying.

"May I take off your shirt, Mr. Rhodes?" I look up at him from under my hooded lids.

"Yes."

He doesn't touch me as I stand naked before him, unbuttoning his shirt, pushing it off his shoulders to the ground. I run my hands over his toned, tanned flesh, before dropping to my knees, my gaze never leaving his. I grab his ass in one hand, steadying myself as I wrap my fingers around the base of his cock and start pumping my fist up and down, flicking my tongue out onto the head with every upward stroke.

"Jesus, Lily." I'm hungry, desperate to give him the release he needs. I take his tip into my mouth before sliding down as far as I can. His cock twitches. "Fucking hell."

His words are a whisper as he struggles for control, knowing that he can't be loud in here. I lick him from root to tip, lapping up the pre-come beading on the head of his engorged cock. He lets me set the pace, thrusting up and down the length of him, until he can't take it anymore. He grabs handfuls of my hair at the back of my head and holds me in place as he starts frantically pumping in and out of me, hitting the back of my throat with each thrust of his hips.

"Fuck... I'm going to come."

One more thrust and he stills, his cock pulsing as his orgasm rips through him, releasing his hot come down my throat. I gently move my lips over him as he rides it out, his eyes squeezed shut trying to contain the groans I know are fighting to escape. He pulls me to my feet, crushing his mouth to mine. Nothing else matters—just the two of us... in this moment... together.

"I'm not done with you, Miss Tate." His dick grows hard again. "Turn around and lean over the desk. Spread your legs wide for me."

A jolt of electricity shoots to my core in anticipation of impending ecstasy. When I do as he asks, he moves between my legs, positioning himself at my slick entrance.

"Always so wet, sweets."

In one hard thrust he fills me to the hilt. A moan escapes me before I have to bite down on my lip again to stifle my reaction. He starts pounding into me, forcing me to grip the desk for purchase. He's animalistic, so primal and domineering in this moment. I can't get enough of him. I'm quickly on the verge of another mind-blowing orgasm when Xander reaches down and presses his thumb against my clit. I'm lost to the explosion that obliterates my awareness of everything around me. I start to scream his name, but his hand covers my mouth almost instantly.

"Quiet, baby. Oh... fuck."

He keeps his hand over my mouth as he loses himself to his own orgasm. He bites down on my shoulder to contain his own cries of pleasure as we buck wildly against each other until we are completely sated. Xander slumps against my back, kissing down my spine.

"Oh my God. That was... intense."

We stay this way for a moment, catching our breath, savoring our skin-to-skin contact, his come dripping down my thighs, before the reality of where we are kicks in. Xander gets some tissues from his desk to clean between my legs. I grab my clothes and quickly dress while he puts on his shirt and zips his fly.

"Fuck, I love watching my come spilling out of you."

He walks up behind me and grabs me round the waist, lifting me over to the sofa. He positions me in his lap, cuddling me close to his chest.

"As *amazing* as that was, do you want to tell me what's going on? Why did you want to see me?" I nuzzle into his chest, trying to find the right words.

"I read the last letter you sent me while I was missing." His arms tighten around me.

"I was sitting in the park reading your beautiful words and I was just completely overwhelmed by the intensity of the love I feel for you. You're my world, my better half. I love you with all my heart, with all that I am. I need you to know that." He lifts my chin with his fingers, pressing a tender kiss to my lips.

"I love you, too, sweets. It's you and me now... okay?"

"That's all I want."

"Then that's what you shall have."

I suck his bottom lip into my mouth before he devours me—not with a wild, desperate kiss, but one so sensual and heartfelt, it resonates in my bones.

Xander grabs some work he still needs to finish due to my... interruption. We decide to forego dinner in a restaurant and get takeout on the way back to the penthouse.

We have a great night eating Thai food, laughing, and watching old movies. It's great to just be together and enjoy each other. We've been through so much already and have learned to appreciate the little things.

CHAPTER 25

LILY

F RIDAY IN THE OFFICE IS EXCELLENT. I KNOW THIS SOUNDS NERDY, BUT I really enjoy the morning meeting. I'm fascinated to hear what everyone else has been working on this week, sharing my own work, and getting to know everyone a little better. By lunchtime I've uploaded my blog for the online magazine and sent my article to the editor for the published version. I can't wait to buy a copy with my first ever article in it.

I send a quick text to Xander before heading out to lunch.

> Me: Just submitted my first article for publishing. Yay me. Love you. X

Almost immediately I hear back from him.

> Mr. P: So proud of you. I love it when you SUBMIT. Can't wait to see you. 5:30 p.m. sharp! Love you, too. X

It amazes me how he always makes time to respond. I know he must be extremely busy with work, and it warms my heart. I have a nice lunch and head back to the office to get a jump on my assignment for next week.

The afternoon goes by in a blur of downloads and research. When the clock hits 5:30 p.m. I'm out the door and on my way to Xander, the butterflies taking flight at the thought of being back in his arms.

I'm not disappointed when I see him leaning against the SUV, his tie loosened, his top button undone. I can feel his magnetism drawing me to him. He grabs me and kisses me, pushing me against the car, his body pressing into mine.

"Hi, baby." He has such a carefree smile it's contagious.

"Hello, yourself. I missed you." He nibbles on my neck.

"Then you won't mind coming for a walk with me, and we'll get some dinner? The one we were going to have yesterday." That sounds like a perfect way to start the weekend. He puts my bag in the trunk before ushering me into the car.

"I thought you might want to change into something more comfortable, so I brought you some clothes to choose from." Nothing I own. It's all brand new. He's unbelievable.

I take advantage of the blacked-out windows, changing into a cute lemon sundress and ballet pumps before fixing my hair and makeup. I open the door for Xander.

"I'm surprised you didn't come in for the show." I smirk at him.

"I would have, but we're on a schedule and we definitely would *not* make it to dinner if I got into the car with you half-naked." He bites his lip and I know he's wiggling his eyebrows behind his aviators. I put on my sunglasses and leave David behind to go for a walk in the evening sunshine.

Xander pulls me to his side, his fresh scent and cologne assaulting my senses, sending tingles down my spine. As we walk and talk, laughing and planning our weekend, neither of us notices the person standing directly in front of us until she speaks.

"Oh, honey. You took him back after what he did? That's just sad. What lies did he tell you this time?" Natalie. The smug, bitchy grin on her face makes me want to slap her. Xander's body tenses as he moves to put himself between me and *her*.

"Natalie…" I stop him, pressing my hand to his chest, his heart beating wildly beneath my fingertips. I slowly lift my mouth to his, placing a featherlight kiss on his lips, his cheek cradled in my palm.

"I've got this. Let me deal with it." He looks wary but nods his agreement. I whip round to see her staring daggers in my direction.

"Nice to finally meet you, Natalie." My voice is calm and controlled. It ruffles her. "I've heard so much about you. None of it good, of course."

She opens her mouth to speak but I cut her off.

"No, Natalie. I think you've said and done enough. It's my turn now." Xander's hand moves to the base of my spine. "I should really be thanking you for sending me those photos."

She sneers. "And why is that?" Venom drips from her every word.

"Well… it made me realize just what a colossal *bitch* you are. I now understand just what Xander had to put up with, and what you put him through. After all of that, you managed to show just how amazing he really is, that he would even help the likes of you if you were in trouble." Her jaw almost drops to the sidewalk as I continue. "You see. I actually love Xander, and he loves me. Nothing you could *ever* do will change that. It's pathetic really, that you had to resort to lying and scheming just to be in the same room as him. I can understand your desperation. It must sting to realize you threw away the best thing that will ever happen to you in your sad little life, and for what? To get your tits out on a magazine cover?"

I've got her now. There's anger bubbling in her eyes.

"You don't know anything about me, you little whore. He'll get bored of you soon enough and come crawling back to me." Wow. This girl is delusional. Xander makes a move, rage emanating from him in waves, but I speak up before he wades in. He doesn't need to stoop to her level.

I throw my head back and laugh. "Wow. You really are a crazy fucking bitch, aren't you, *Nat*? I'm only going to say this once, so listen up… You are nothing to us. You are *less than nothing* to Xander. He *hates* you. I *hate* you. I'm pretty sure most people who meet you… *hate you.* Now, here's the important part." She looks scared now. Let's dial up the crazy. "The next time you see us in the street, you better cross to the other side. If we walk into a shop or a restaurant that you happen to be in, you better make yourself scarce... because... Natalie... if I *ever* see your evil little face, or hear another word coming from that forked tongue of yours, I *will...* rip your fucking head off. I will ruin your pathetic excuse for a money-maker. Do we understand each other? So much as breathe in Xander's direction and I will *end* you. Got it?"

She knows better than to answer. One more word from her and I won't be able to hold Xander back. She turns on her heels and crosses the street. My entire body is shaking, vibrating as Xander spins me in his arms.

"That was... amazing. I didn't think you had it in you. You're so... sweet, and so... badass! That was *such* a turn on. No one has ever done anything like that for me before." He cradles my face, his mouth capturing mine in a passionate kiss.

"God, I love you so much." I wrap my legs around his waist, not caring that we're in the middle of a busy street.

"I love you, too." We remain entangled for a few minutes before he lowers me back to the sidewalk and we continue our walk to the restaurant. We hold hands, exchanging loving smiles and longing glances as we go.

We arrive outside a great looking Indian restaurant, and the smell coming from inside is positively mouthwatering.

"Come on. You're going to love it in here." He excitedly pulls me through the door, and there, at a table in the far corner, are Addi and Carter. I turn to Xander.

"Happy? I thought you might be missing your friend."

I throw my arms around his neck. "This is fantastic. Thank you."

We're quickly seated with our friends to enjoy an evening of laughs, good food, and great company. It's lovely seeing Xander and Carter together. They're so... boyish. Xander relays the events on the street with Natalie to whoops and hollers from Addi and Carter high-fiving me for my bravery. We all have a giggle at my out of character tirade.

They seem to be getting along well. I recognize the way he looks at her. I see it in Xander's eyes every time he looks at me. I'm so happy Addi has found someone who appreciates her. I'm not going to mention it because I'm worried she'll freak out again, and mess things up with a really great guy.

After a fun evening we agree to make a plan to go to the Hamptons at some point before the summer is over.

Xander and I enjoy a leisurely stroll back to the penthouse, the buzz of the city surrounding us as we revel in our own little bubble—our real-life fairytale.

XANDER SEEMS A LITTLE OFF THIS WEEK. I CAN'T QUITE PUT MY FINGER on it, but he's been a bit on edge. I've asked him about it, but he just blows it off and changes the subject. He's also been pretty cagey on the phone which is odd. Usually, I would offer to give him privacy for his calls and he's the one who pulls me into his lap while he talks. This week he's been closing the door behind him.

Saturday morning arrives, and the weirdness continues. Xander says he has to go to the office for a few hours, leaving abruptly. I get a sinking feeling in my gut, his behavior reminiscent of when he was lying to me about Natalie. I try to shrug it off, spending the morning lazing around the apartment, curling my hair, giving myself a feel-good makeover. When I've done all the girly primping I can justify for a day to be spent in the house, I receive a text.

> Mr. P: Miss Tate. Could you come and meet me in South Field? X

That's odd. We hadn't planned on going out anywhere. Oh, maybe we're going to have a nice picnic. It's a perfect day for it. I quickly text him back.

> Me: I'll be there in 15. X

I grab my purse and sunglasses before heading out to meet him.

~

WHEN I ARRIVE AT SOUTH FIELD, IT DOESN'T LOOK THE WAY I remember it. A pathway has been carved out amongst a sea of roses as far as the eye can see, in every color imaginable. It's breathtaking. As I follow the path, I see an opening to a pond filled with water lilies. It's more beautiful than any Monet. As I continue on my way, I realize I'm the only person here. My phone beeps in my pocket.

> Mr. P: Keep following the path, sweets. X

It never ceases to amaze me when he reads my mind at the exact moment I'm think something! I keep going, taking in the beauty that surrounds me. Every ten meters or so there are plaques with some of my favorite quotations from classic literature including the one Xander had engraved on the notebook he gave me.

As I get closer to the library I come to an archway of flowers and foliage with Xander's trademark pearls and crystals interwoven throughout. It's a stunning sight. I notice charms, just like the ones on my bracelet, hanging from the top of the archway. It's magical. I don't think I've taken a breath since I set foot on campus.

On the ground in front of me is a phone that looks exactly like mine. I lean down and pick it up. The lock screen shows one of the funny selfies we took when we were in London. When I slide my finger across the screen, I notice there is a text on the phone. I open it, tears misting my eyes at the effort he has gone to for me today.

> Mr. P: This is where it all began, Miss Tate.
> Look up. X

I lift my eyes as I step forward into what feels like secret garden. Xander is standing in front of me, looking like a vision sent from heaven. His hair is mussed, as if he's been wringing his hands through it. His chiseled features are beyond beautiful as a panty-dropping smile splits his face. I can't take my eyes off the perfection walking toward me.

I am lost for words when he stops mere inches away from me, his smell intoxicating my senses—clean laundry and cologne. He cups my face in his hands, searching for something. Our lips meet in a passionate kiss, our tongues caressing, my hands sliding up and down the length of his muscular back.

Before I get a chance to speak, Xander drops to one knee at my feet, reaching into his pocket and removing a black velvet box. My heart is hammering in my chest as I stare down into his beautiful ice-blue eyes, the love I feel reflected back to me in his unwavering gaze.

"Lily Tate. We've only known each other for three months, but I feel like I've known you my whole life. The day our worlds collided here in South Field changed my life in every way imaginable. You've given me hope for a future I never thought I would have."

Tears stream down my face as I listen to his words, my emotions overflowing.

"Every day, you show me a love I never thought I would find. Every hour I spend with you, you bring me joy, every minute I get to call you mine, I cherish, and will never take it for granted."

He is more eloquent, more beautiful, than anything I've ever read. I'm overwhelmed.

"Lily… I love you with all my heart. I have since the moment I looked into those stunning green eyes. I felt like I was looking into the other half of my soul. If you'll let me, I will love you, cherish you, protect you, and do everything in my power to fulfill every one of your dreams in this life and the next."

He opens the small, elegant box, holding up the most breathtaking ring. A large solitaire brilliant cut diamond in a high four claw setting with diamonds running down either side of the band. It's more perfect than I ever could've imagined. *He* is more than I could ever imagine. I am overcome with pure, unadulterated joy as he continues.

"Will you do me the great honor of becoming my wife? Marry me, Lily."

My hand flies up to my mouth, holding in the sob I know is trapped in my throat. I watch as he lifts the ring from the box, taking my left hand, holding the ring at the tip of my finger.

"May I? You're killing me here, sweets. Please, say something." There is unease in his eyes as he awaits my answer.

"Yes, Xander. Of course, I'll marry you."

I sob tears of joy as he places the ring on my finger and stands up, pulling me into the most intense kiss. Every fiber of my being reacts to him, to his touch, his scent, and his heart, that beats in time with mine.

"I love you so much, Lily." He continues to shower my face and neck with kisses as I melt into his body, holding tight to stop my knees from giving way underneath me.

"I love you, too. More than I could ever express. You're my... everything."

Standing in the spot that changed my life on an average Monday afternoon in May, I knew I'd finally found the missing piece of myself, my better half, and the love of my life.

Wherever life takes us, I know that every chapter will be amazing with Xander by my side, writing our story together, hand in hand, hearts entwined. We are two halves of the same soul—forever and always.

EPILOGUE

XANDER

Four Months Later

Why do I feel so fucking nervous? I've been waiting for this day since the moment I met her. I'm almost as nervous as the day I proposed, but it was worth a week of feeling sick to my stomach to hear Lily say "Yes."

Lucky for me she did say yes because I'd arranged a party afterwards at Jason's restaurant with help from Addi. Both of our families were there, Addi's family and some of our close friends. My mom was a crying mess as soon as we walked in the door to a roar of applause!

It was lovely to see Lily enjoying herself as everyone fussed over her, ogling her ring, giving me the thumbs up. Her face is so fucking beautiful when she's happy. I want to put that smile on her face, every day for the rest of our lives.

It's been a full on four months getting ready for this wedding. There has been so much going on, but most importantly, Lily and I are deliriously happy together. She also started her novel, which is amazing and I'm so fucking proud of her. She decided to use her experiences with Peterson and try her hand at a crime thriller. I think she surprised herself with that decision, but she's the happiest I've ever seen her when she's sitting writing on her laptop.

I think it's been somewhat cathartic for her.

Since she started putting it all down in print, her nightmares have become less frequent. It's been so hard watching her relive those horrors night after night. I just want to take it away for her. I'm in awe of her strength. She's the strongest woman I've ever met. She's been through so much, and yet, she has such a gentle and loving spirit that just calls to me to protect her.

THE DECISION OF WHERE TO HAVE THE WEDDING WAS A NO BRAINER FOR me, and when I suggested it to Lily, she absolutely loved the idea. So here I am, four months later, standing in the center of L'Arena in Verona, Italy, waiting for the love of my life to arrive.

Carter is my best man and from what I understand of the role, he should be calming me down right now. Is he? Fuck no. I think he's more nervous than I am. I've given up trying to work out what he and Addi have going on. One minute I think things are getting serious between them, and the next, I have to listen to Carter piss and moan about her blowing him off.

I love her, she's Lily's best friend and she would do anything for her, but I'm not convinced she's what's best for *my* best friend. He puts on a good front, but I know it's taking its toll on him.

A few months back we managed to make some time to go up to Carter's place in the Hamptons for the weekend with them. We had a great time. Well... Lily and I had a fantastic time. I managed to whisk her away for a few hours to the secluded cove where we shared our first kiss. I can remember how fucking perfect she looked writhing underneath me, the sunset as a backdrop, and the last vestiges of sunlight kissing every curve and line of her amazing body. If there is such a thing as heaven, that was it. I'm hard just at the memory.

I need to adjust myself without drawing attention. How the fuck do you do that while standing at the altar with your family and friends staring at you? I'm just going to have to think about something else! One glance at Carter and it does the trick. He looks like he's going to vomit

"Fuck, Carter, you look worse than me. What's up?" He laughs.

"Ignore me, man, I'm just being a dick. Addi fucking freaked out this morning. What a surprise! Don't sweat it. This is your day, and I'm all over the best man thing." I think he's trying to convince himself more than me. I need to have a chat with her when Lily and I get back from our honeymoon.

Lily has tried to talk some sense into her, but I think she needs to realize what she's doing to Carter every time she does this kind of thing. He needs to man up a little. It's easy for me to say that, but I would do anything Lily asked of me, and I don't fucking care who knows it. I'm the poster boy for pussy-whipped! She's just so damn amazing.

I thought sitting down to plan the wedding would be a nightmare, but as usual Lily astounded me with how easy going she was. It probably helped that she'd started writing her book, so a lot of her free time has been spent tapping away on her laptop.

Once we had agreed on Verona as the venue, our mom's went batshit crazy, warp speed, hyperdrive over the wedding plans. We just decided what we wanted and let them get on with it. That worked out great for me, because it gave me so much more time to get her naked and sweaty, screaming my name. Fuck. If I could go and get her from her suite at the hotel right now, without being decapitated by my mother, I would do just that. I'd calm my nerves by pinning her down and fucking her so hard she forgets her own name.

I really need to stop thinking like this right now. I'm surrounded by family and friends in the most amazing amphitheater in the world. They still perform open-air operas here at night after the sun goes down. I'm going to bring Lily back here for our first anniversary so we can enjoy L'Arena the way it was meant to be experienced. She'll fucking love it. She loves everything about this city.

We arrived three days ago and the first thing I did was take her to Juliet's balcony. I managed to get a photo of her leaning out over it, staring down at me with the most beautiful smile on her face. She's the picture of perfection, every bard's muse, and she's mine! That was the only time we got to explore the city just the two of us, but it was magical. I can see why Shakespeare was inspired. It's steeped in history, culture and most of all, romance.

Addi and the rest of the women insisted that Lily and I slept apart last night, which is why I think I'm so fucking antsy. I haven't seen her today. As much as I resent them taking my wife-to-be, I have to give credit where it's due. My mom and Jocelyn have done a phenomenal job with the décor. The amphitheater has been sectioned into three separate, stunning areas.

There's the dining area—tables draped in crisp white linens with lanterns set on top of mirrors in the center. Lily picked out a deep purple for the color scheme and our moms didn't disappoint. From the menus to the place cards, to the petals scattered on the tables, everything matches, and it all looks breathtakingly elegant. A perfect reflection of my bride.

The second area is for dancing—twinkling lights cover every surface, marking out an expansive dance floor and stage for the band. I can't wait to have Lily in my arms, with her tight body pressed hard against mine, teasing me with what's to come. Making love to her for the first time as Mrs. Rhodes. Just the thought of it makes me rock-fucking-hard.

Saving the best for last, area number three is where I'm standing right now—the place where I'm going to make Lily my wife. There are two hundred white chairs set out in rows with a white silk aisle running down the center. The chairs are all tied with purple organza, finished off with a crystal brooch.

Everyone is seated and staring in my direction as I stand like a fucking idiot, pacing up and down, and turning my hair into a mess running my hands through it. I keep checking with Carter to make sure he has the rings. The priest keeps trying to give me a reassuring smile, but every time I look at him it makes me think about getting through the vows I wrote for Lily without breaking down like a pussy in front of two hundred friends and family members!

The altar is a replica of the archway I commissioned for proposing in South Field. She loved it so much, she insisted that we have the exact same one to get married under. I love how sentimental she can be. It just makes me love her even more.

The tiered steps surrounding the ancient amphitheater, are covered in thousands of lanterns, creating an otherworldly atmosphere, romantic, somehow intimate, and beyond captivating.

Logan is standing at the other end of the aisle where screens of Monet's water lily paintings create a partition so that Lily can stay hidden until the music starts. The water lilies were my contribution to the day. Every time I look at a water lily it makes me think of her, how stunningly beautiful she is, and how I am the luckiest bastard on the face of the planet that she let me in—let me see what's beneath the surface. Behind her obvious beauty is something infinitely more special, the most attractive heart and soul that will ever exist.

After asking for the hundredth time if Carter has the rings, I get him to check me over. Is my tie straight, is my waistcoat sitting properly, is my fly down? I know it's ridiculous, I've been dressing myself for the past twenty-seven years at least, but I just want everything to be perfect for Lily. I don't want to disappoint her.

I'm wearing a dark grey three-piece suit. She insisted. Apparently, I do, and I quote, *'very good, should be illegal, things to a three-piece suit.'* I think she's crazy but I'm happy she likes it. I'm wearing a fitted white shirt and a silver silk tie. The groomsmen are wearing something similar but with a purple tie to match the bridesmaids—Addi and the twins.

Carter pulls me to his side and gestures his head toward the back. Fuck, my heart is really hammering as I look to Logan who confirms in a single nod that I am about to see Lily. A shiver runs through my body, a thrill of excitement and anticipation, ready to see my girl walking toward me… fucking… ME.

A string quartet starts playing *Back to You* by John Mayer, and everyone falls silent, turning to catch a glimpse of my gorgeous bride.

The bridesmaids make their way down first. The look on Carter's face as he watches Addi walk toward us tells me everything I need to know. He is head over heels in love with her. She gives me a smile and a wink before taking her place and locking eyes with Carter. I'm glad to see the feeling is mutual. I take a deep breath, trying to calm my nerves as I shift my gaze to the top of the aisle.

She appears in the distance, ethereal in her transcendent beauty—breathtaking, angelic, and utterly stunning. Her gown is ivory lace, delicate and intricate, just like the woman inside.

The bodice is fitted, tight to her ample breasts and cinched in at her tiny waist before flowing out endlessly. She looks like a princess. Her flowing golden curls cascade down her back, some of her hair swept up in effortless elegance. She's holding a small bouquet of white roses with crystals and pearls woven through the foliage. She calls that my 'signature' when I send her flowers.

As she walks toward me with Addi's dad by her side, our eyes lock and my nerves become a distant memory as I take in the vision of my bride. My heart stops beating in anticipation of her reaching my side. She is so fucking beautiful.

It feels like an eternity by the time she's finally standing next to me, with a smile that melts my heart. I take her hand in mine as Mr. Warner takes his seat, a jolt of electricity sparking between us as our skin comes into contact.

Standing here, taking in the sight of her close up, she is fucking flawless, and even more beautiful, if that's possible. Her makeup is soft and natural, highlighting her features, her eyes sparkling like emeralds.

I notice an intricate tiara, and a few crystals holding her loose tendrils in place. She looks like a goddess. She decided not to wear a veil, which suits me, I don't want anything covering her face.

Before the ceremony begins, I place a feather light kiss on her cheek before whispering so only she can hear. "You are a vision. I love you so much… Miss Tate." Her sly grin tells me she knows this is the last time I'll ever call her that.

I don't hear most of what is being said during the ceremony, my attention locked on Lily. Luckily, I do hear the priest announce that it's time for us to share the vows we've written for each other. I thought I would be nervous, everyone waiting for me to pour my heart out, but I'm not. She is the only person in L'Arena with me as I begin to put into words what today means to me.

"Lily. As I stand here before you today, enchanted by your beauty, inside and out, I vow to love you with all that I am, with everything that I have. I will strive to be the husband you deserve. Since the moment you came crashing into my life, I've wanted to be a better man. In you I've found the other half of my soul. You're the better half of me. I will support you in every endeavor and help make your dreams a reality. I will always be by your side, to celebrate the good, to comfort you through the bad, and to hold your hand as we write the chapters of our life together. I've loved you from the moment I first looked into your eyes, and I will continue to love you through this life and the next. You will forever be my best friend, my lover, my wife, and my one true love. My beginning, my end, and everything in between. Forever yours."

I struggle to get the words past the massive lump in my throat. As I look into the eyes of my reason for breathing, tears streaming down her face. I place the ring on her shaking finger, my name engraved on the inside for only her to see.

I cradle her face in my palms, wiping her tears away with before kissing her forehead. I exhale a long shaky breath, preparing myself to hear her sweet voice reciting the vows she has written for me.

"Alexander. I was lost before I met you, walking through life, but not really living it until you found me. Every moment with you is a gift, every look, every touch, every word that comes from your lips, I cherish. My notions of love and romance only ever came from the pages of a book, an ideal that no man can live up to. Except you do live up to it. You surpass it in every way imaginable on a daily basis. You are the missing piece of my heart, the reason it beats in my chest. With every breath I will love you, honor you and strive to be worthy of your love, through the good times and the bad. When you are happy, I will share your joy, when you are sad, I will share your pain. I give every part of myself freely and willingly to you because I

know that you will always protect me. I love you with everything that I am, today, tomorrow, and for the rest of time. Forever yours."

She slays me with her eloquence and her ability to speak to something deep in my soul. As she slides the ring onto my finger, my entire body vibrates, her touch eliciting such love that it radiates from every fiber of my being.

I don't wait for permission to kiss my bride. I couldn't stop myself if I tried. We're like magnets, drawn to each other, our desperate desire to connect driving us closer until our lips meet and everything else becomes white noise in the background.

I run my tongue along the perfectly pouty seam of her luscious lips —tasting her, begging her to open up for me. Her sweet little tongue darts out to meet mine, tangling together in an outpouring of love and devotion. I vaguely hear the priest announce that we are now man and wife, registering the roar of applause from our friends and family, but I can't bring myself to stop kissing her… my wife.

My hands fist in her soft hair, pulling her closer as her body melts into mine. I feel like my chest is going to explode. I pull back to catch my breath, my teeth nipping her lip before I gaze into her eyes.

"You're mine now, Lily. Only mine. Always." Her shy smile is so fucking beautiful.

"Always yours… Mr. Rhodes." Her tone, so seductive.

"That's right… Mrs. Rhodes."

I like the way that sounds and feels on my tongue—almost as good as she's going to feel on my tongue when I taste her for the first time as my wife… so sweet… and all mine.

Until the end of time, I will be enchanted by her… my Lily… forever flawless.

THE END
Buy RELENTLESS now
Sign up for NEWSLETTER
Buy THE CONTRACT now
FOLLOW ON:

INSTAGRAM
FACEBOOK
TIKTOK
AMAZON
BOOKBUB
GOODREADS

ALSO BY EVA HAINING

Manhattan Knights Series
Flawless
Relentless
Endless
Complete Manhattan Knights Series Box Set

Club V Series
The Contract

Mustang Ranch Series
Mustang Daddy
Mustang Buck
Mustang Hollywood
Mustang Ranch Books 1-3 Box Set
Mustang Christmas
Mustang Belle
Mustang Player

Hall of Fame Series
Fumble

A Very Fumbling Merry Christmas
Interception
Screwball
Strike Zone

<u>*Standalones*</u>
Wild Rugged Daddy
A Christmas To Remember

ABOUT THE AUTHOR

I'm happiest when wandering through the uncharted territory of my imagination. You'll find me curled up with my laptop, browsing the books at the local library, or enjoying the smell of a new book, taking great delight in cracking the spine and writing in the margins!

Eva is a native Scot, but lives in Texas with her husband, two kids, and a whizzy little fur baby with the most ridiculous ears. She first fell in love with British Literature while majoring in Linguistics, 17th Century Poetry, and Shakespeare at University. She is an avid reader and lifelong notebook hoarder. In 2014, she finally put her extensive collection to good use and started writing her first novel. Previously published with Prism Heart Press under a pen name, Eva decided to branch out on her own and lend her name to her full back catalogue! She is currently working on some exciting new projects.

ACKNOWLEDGMENTS

First and foremost, I need to say a massive thank you to my amazing husband. You've shown me what true love and romance is. You have supported me through the good, the bad, and the downright awful, and championed every endeavor I've embarked on, no questions asked. Without your constant love and encouragement, I never would have had the confidence to make my dream a reality. I love you more than words could ever express. Maybe one day I'll be able to get you that Ferrari 458 Italia and make *your* dream a reality!

I need to give a big thank you to my betas, and proof-readers. You took a chance on me and gave your free time willingly. You helped sculpt the raw material into the polished article. Thank you Lauren and Leslie. Without you, I never would have had the courage to let anyone read my work. You've been a constant source of friendship and support and I love you both dearly. Leslie—Your red pen still haunts me to this day!

Ria Alexander—You and I have taken quite the journey together with Xander. We may live thousands of miles away from each other, but you have become part of my family, and for that I will always love this book. I love you more, my dear friend.

Sharron—Thank you for being so supportive from the very beginning. You saved me from myself more times than I can count. I feel blessed to call you family. Love you.

I need to say a huge thank you to my editor Jaye Hart—Not only are you a kickass editor, you're an even better friend. Your unwavering belief in my writing is the reason Flawless found a home with Prism Heart Press. I am eternally grateful! Thank you for putting up with the crazy mind of this writer—the doubts, the fears, the last-minute tweaks (complete rewrite of book one). I couldn't have turned this book into something I can be proud of without your total commitment and support of my process. I look forward to our next adventure! I love you, friend.

And last but by no means least, thanks to you, the reader—for taking a chance on a new author and supporting this fabulous genre. I hope you enjoyed reading about Xander and Lily's journey as much as I enjoyed writing it.

The next book in the series is Addi and Carter's story—Relentless. There is more of Xander and Lily in there, too! There's still a lot for them to do together. Thank you for your support. Please feel free to contact me via social media.

SOCIAL MEDIA

www.instagram.com/evahainingauthor

www.facebook.com/evahainingauthor

www.twitter.com/evahaining

www.tiktok.com/@evahainingauthor

www.amazon.com/author/evahaining

www.bookbub.com/profile/eva-haining

https://www.goodreads.com/author/show/20271110.Eva_Haining

www.evahaining.com

www.evahaining.com/newsletter